BANTAM BOOKS | NEW YORK

In Wilderness

a novel

Diane Thomas

Copyright © 2015 by Diane Thomas

Published in the United States by Bantam Books, an imprint of Random House, a division of Random House LLC, a Penguin Random House Company, New York.

BANTAM BOOKS and the HOUSE colophon are registered trademarks of Random House LLC.

Grateful acknowledgment is made to Counterpoint Press for permission to reprint a poem from *Axe Handles: Poems* by Gary Snyder, copyright © 2005 by Gary Snyder. Reprinted by permission of Counterpoint Press.

LIBRARY OF CONGRESS CATALOGING-IN-PUBLICATION DATA
Thomas, Diane C. (Diane Coulter)
In wilderness: a novel / Diane Thomas.
pages cm
ISBN 978-0-8041-7695-8
eBook ISBN 978-0-8041-7696-5
1. Terminally ill—Fiction. 2. Solitude—Fiction. 3. Vietnam War, 1961–1975—Veterans—Fiction. 4. Squatters—Fiction. I. Title.
PS3620.H627I5 2015 813'.6—dc23 2014025351

Printed in the United States of America on acid-free paper

www.bantamdell.com

246897531

First Edition

Book design by Susan Turner

For Christopher. And for Bill, always.

In the midst of life's journey
I found myself in a dark wood,
for the right path was lost.

—Dante Alighieri, *Inferno*

• • •

As the crickets' soft autumn hum
is to us
so are we to the trees
as are they
to the rocks and the hills

—Gary Snyder

In Wilderness

February 1962

Prologue

She will remember this moment all her life, she is sure of it.

She will remember the seven men seated with her around the oval table in the agency conference room, even the four clients, whom she does not know. Will remember how the men sit in an assortment of relaxed postures, each with his paper cup of coffee in its blue plastic holder within easy reach and a wadded or refolded paper napkin and a color-matched paper plate nearby with crumbs or some larger portion of a Danish in it, and how most of the small glass ashtrays scattered on the table now contain at least one cigarette butt; will remember how the room still holds the scents of the coffee and the pastries in its smoky haze.

She will remember, too, the exact way her husband, Tim, stands at the far end of the room beside three easels, each of which displays a logo designed for the company the clients represent; will remember how Tim holds the pointer loosely in his right hand, angles it toward the farthest of the drawings, and she knows that he is proud of all of them—because each one is good, because he can see in the clients' faces that they know this, and because all three of the designs are hers. She will remember noting that this pride, and the necessity of hiding it before the clients, makes him nervous, which he shows in ways that only she can recognize: how he slides the toe of his brown loafer rhythmically back and forth on the plush beige carpet, sniffs at intervals.

"Any one of these will afford an exceedingly effective visual anchor to a powerful corporate campaign for 1963. . . ." His words, directed to the clients, soothe her and wash over her.

She will remember that this is the first day she has worn her glen plaid suit, an extravagance she felt guilty for when she bought it on sale in the fall, and that she likes the suit even more than she imagined liking it, feels pretty in it and regrets somewhat that soon she'll have to give up wearing it for several months, despite the reason. She will remember, too, how she notices for the first time that the room's familiar floral drapes are slightly worn and thinks perhaps she should say something to Tim about this; after all, this is his advertising agency, and as his wife it might be her responsibility to do so.

She notes all these details unconsciously, recalls them solely because they form a frame around this moment, a kind of shrine for this occurrence that has just become the intense focus of all her attention: For the first time, she has felt the baby move.

In this instant, her pregnancy has transformed itself from something she accepted from her gynecologist on faith to something real. The evidence is there: the smallest flutter in her belly. Like one strong beat from a single pair of tiny wings. Or the littlest tropical fish whipping around to swim back to the other side of its aquarium. A movement that might easily have gone unnoticed, except that it so definitely was not a thing that came from her.

Please, baby, please, please do it more. Strong little butterfly, dear little fish. She folds her hands across her belly just below the table, her belly that at four months hardly protrudes at all, belly that lets her wear her glen plaid meeting suit. Oh, please do it again.

She leans back, smiles a quiet half smile that might be interpreted as rapt attention to the meeting going on around her but is not that at all. Yes, oh, yes, it's moved again, as if the tiny fetus has become so intimate with her it can discern her thoughts. The room around her—all she noticed of it, even the men's voices—has receded now. She and this small being are together all alone in a vast, empty space. It's what she wants, for all of it to go away except her and the little swimming fish inside her. So she can cry from happiness.

But it's too late. Already, tears well in her eyes; she can feel the first one trembling on her lower lashes. She turns her head away from the men seated at the table, rises. "Gentlemen, excuse me for a moment." Walks quickly from the conference room, the office, past the bank of elevators. To the ladies' room, empty as usual. There she sits inside one of the stalls and lets the tears run down her face to slide over her widening smile.

By the time she returns to the conference room, the meeting has ended and Tim has left for an off-site presentation across town. She stays to put away the papers, scraps of drawing board, bottles of colored inks strewn about her modest office. Back home, she hardly has time to take off her jacket, pour two glasses of Chablis, before he bursts through the door, his face pale with worry.

"Kate, are you all right? You missed the last part of the meeting."

She nods, still smiling; she has smiled all the remainder of the day. "The baby moved. This little flutter. I cried and had to leave the room."

"Oh, Kate, my wonderful Kate."

He crosses their still-unfurnished living room, wraps his arms awkwardly around her, stands there holding her. It is, she thinks, like Russian nesting dolls, the whole thing. The air and sky enfold the earth, the countryside, that itself enfolds this city she has lived in all her life, which in turn embraces their neighborhood of spreading oaks and budding daffodils; the neighborhood, its trees and flowers, holds their home—old, rambling, bought just last year because it seemed designed and built to furnish echoes for the sounds of children—and this home holds her and Tim, here in this room with all its narrow strips of wooden lath exposed for plasterers who come next week; inside this room Tim folds her in his arms, her a warm and living bunting for their baby, the tiny, determined entity that is the solid center all the dolls enclose, the heart of everything.

The baby flutters once again and she takes Tim's broad hand, places it against her belly, looks into his face that's nothing but a blur through her fierce, joyous tears. And her whole body trembles from the sum of it, that sum's enormity: That she should be here. In this universe. With everything.

And, yes, she will remember every piece of this. Forever.

Early Winter, 1966

1

The Woman

IN ADVERTISING, SHE HAS LEARNED, YOU LIVE AND DIE BY THE RULE of Three: "Less tar, less nicotine, same great taste."

It's the same in life: "Third time's the charm." The gray–haired gastroenterologist seated across from her behind his cluttered mahogany desk is Dr. Third Opinion, her last hope, who was supposed to sally forth and save the day.

But Dr. Third Opinion has not sallied forth, has chosen instead to betray her, to align himself with doctors one and two in his assessment that her pain and suffering come from her body's failure to assimilate her food. Not to put too fine a point on it, she's starving; soon her organs will start shutting down; she's got at most six months.

And there you have it: "Three strikes, you're out."

Assimilate. Good word, that. Significantly more abstract and intellectual than *digest*, which might far too easily lead to overcontemplation of actual physical functions. She nods to indicate she knows the word's import, knows the import of all his words. Which she does, her mind's eye picturing each in a contrasting typeface—Garamond, Bodoni Bold, Helvetica—as if they are a dummy print ad sent her for critiquing. Dying. D. Y. I. N. G. She can get no closer to the thing than metaphor: exiting early from an unproductive meeting in some new office high-rise, into an empty hallway with harsh lighting, where she will wait alone for an elevator that never comes. This is not particularly satisfactory.

"What's its name, this thing that's killing me?"

Names matter. For a while they were her specialty, extracting from thin air the perfect single-word descriptor for a suburban subdivision, line of carpeting, or processed sandwich spread. Before names she specialized in graphic design—logos, illustrations—and married her boss. After names she got promoted to creative director. This doctor, like the other two, tells her he does not know the name of what is killing her. Among all the colleagues, laboratories, scientists, and sorcerers her physicians have consulted, not one has come up with an answer. She is dying of a lack of information.

If she opens her mouth to scream now, she will never stop.

By her count she'll make it through Christmas into 1967. Maybe see the trees leaf out, but that's less certain. Thirty-eight seems young to die. But maybe if you're ninety-six so does ninety-seven. She has disciplined herself these past four years to give no outward sign. Of anything. Except she can't quiet her trembling hands.

"I see." She doesn't, it's just what one says. Or maybe not; she's got no idea what one says, she's never died before.

The doctor frowns, delicately clears his throat. "If you'll forgive me, there's one question I try to ask all my patients. For my own edification, really, so if you'd rather not . . ."

"Oh, no, it's fine."

Truly, it is. He looks so earnest, the doctor. He seems a kindly man, in his white coat; she hopes his gray hair is premature and that he can look forward to a long career.

"Can you recall for me the last day that you felt completely well?" The doctor pauses. "There's no hurry. Take all the time you need."

All the time she needs would be six decades, although right now she'd be quite satisfied with five. Or four. Yet answering his question needs no time at all. The last day she felt completely well was May 24, 1962, a day she still remembers for an incident of such transcendent beauty she mistook it for a foretaste of all her life to come.

With her belly gloriously swollen, she was seated on a red step-stool in the baby's room, or what would be the baby's room in two more months, drawing pictures on its robin's-egg-blue walls. A kite, eyes closed in rapture, rode the blowing wind; a rabbit in a frock coat and monocle had just popped out of his rabbit hole; a library table frowned beneath its load of books. *Alice in Wonderland, Tom Sawyer, Little Women,* she was lettering their titles when there came a loud commotion from the peaceful residential street—brakes grinding, men shouting, and a strange hissing sound. She flung her brush onto the canvas drop cloth, can still see it there in a faint spatter of black paint, and ran down the hall into their bedroom, hers and Tim's, to see what was the matter.

Outside the open window, a city truck was spraying the runtiest of the ginkgoes in the grassy strip beyond the sidewalk, the tree with all its fan-shaped leaves eaten to filigree. The window framed a tracery of leaves and branches in a pearly mist shot through with rainbows. She remembers thinking she did not deserve to come upon such beauty, that she already had her child inside her, which was far and away beauty enough. Nonetheless, she stayed there, nose pressed against the rigid metal screen, for ten, maybe fifteen minutes, filled with too much gratitude to move. Stayed until the spraying was completed and the truck lumbered off down the street. A small collection of leftover rainbows lingered as drops of consolation on the screen—along with an oily film inside the draperies that, Tim said the next morning, stank like a cheap Florida motel and gave him tropical dreams.

When she is finished speaking, the doctor gazes past her with so great a sadness she experiences a moment of confusion, unsure if she has also told him how, only a day or so later, the headaches started and her energetic child quit moving. She never spoke of it, but even that unyielding denial did not save him. Tim couldn't face it, made believe it never happened, left her to grieve alone. Became first a shadow and then slipped away, under the door or something. Left her controlling interest in the agency, an unwanted guilt offering, began another someplace far away—Milwaukee? Minneapolis?—she never can recall exactly where. Sometime in there her illness got its start and grew without her knowing, like gossip you don't hear until too late.

Dr. Third Opinion sighs. He leans back in his creaky chair, stares past her into some middle distance to her left. "A hundred, hundred-twenty years ago, we used to tell patients like you, patients we had no hope of curing, to go west, move to the country, take the Grand Tour of Europe. Anything. A change of scene. After all this time, we can't do any better."

"Were they healed? The ones who went away?" Hates her voice's horrid, hopeful whine.

He shrugs. "Who knows? I doubt most of their physicians ever heard from them again."

He writes in his prescription pad, tears out the page. "This is for Valium. Refillable as long as you need it."

She squints at it, can't read his writing, bets it cuts off in six months.

"And don't hesitate to call me if you need to."

"Thank you, Doctor, that's most kind." What good would calling do?

After he leaves, she checks her reflection in the mirror by the door. Dull dark hair, hollow eyes, drawn mouth; the glen plaid suit hangs so loose on her now. She regrets not keeping her religion after high school. As things stand, she's got no idea of what's wanted, no chips to bargain with, nothing to trade. If she believes in anything, she believes in Sartre: Death is nothingness, silence under a bleak sky.

Absence of pain, one hopes. Not much help otherwise.

She touches the pearl earrings she put on earlier that morning, her gold watch. She wants to cry and doesn't dare, for the same reason that she didn't scream. The sure knowledge she will die descends upon her then, not unlike that earlier mist, and cloaks her in its shimmering protection. From that moment, she becomes a different person, never certain anymore what she will do.

* * *

WHAT SHE DOES FIRST is unremarkable. Drives straight home, gathers all the Valium bottles from her medicine cabinet and dumps their contents out onto her bedside table. She's not sure why, except they're pretty there against the dark, polished wood. She pushes them around with an index finger, the five-milligram yellow tablets toward the center, the two-milligram whites into radiating petal-lines around them, the ten-milligram blues stretched out to make a single leaf and stem. Doctors always prescribe Valium for you when they don't know what else to do. She always dutifully filled her prescriptions, as if each new bottle might include some fresh, heretofore undiscovered healing charm. The pills always only made her feel peculiar, so she never took more than one or two from any of the bottles. Her finished flower is quite large.

A daisy. Have a happy day.

Slowly, deliberately, she licks the tip end of her finger, picks up a white petal-pill, brings it to her tongue like a communion wafer.

"He loves me."

Licks her finger, brings up another petal-pill.

"He loves me not."

"He loves me," from the bright yellow center.

From the blue stem, "He loves me not."

"Who loves me? God?"

Blue pill. "He loves me not."

Rakes the remaining flower into her left hand, gulps it down with water from a glass on the night table, and—mildly surprised, one rarely knows at the outset where any choice might lead—stretches out on her brass bed to die.

Considers pulling up the covers should her feet get cold, decides it won't be necessary.

She has always loved this bed, one of the few items of furniture in the house that she herself picked out and paid for. The rest Tim brought home, leftovers from his redo of the agency. Bauhaus in agencies was trendy not so long ago; now it's dated. Poor Tim. Some things about him can still make her sad.

She raises her head, looks around the familiar room. How long has she been lying here? Shouldn't she at least be feeling drowsy? Except for a slight swelling, a slight itchy swelling, in the roof of her mouth, nothing has changed. Children are playing in the street, riding in those little pedal cars. Pleasant sound, children's voices. Girl and boy from two houses down, she's seen them often. Her own child, had he lived, would be about the boy's age.

What if these children are who find her body?

How awful that would be.

The itchy swelling in her mouth has spread into her throat, begun to gag her. She runs for the bathroom, heaves up colorful Valium sequins into her bright white toilet.

Stands up, rinses her mouth—should have known pills wouldn't work, she vomits everything—then goes into the kitchen and puts on a pot of coffee, brings in the morning paper off the porch. It's Friday, the paper comes rolled in its want-ad section. She pours her coffee, sits on a stool at the kitchen counter, stares down vacantly at the lines of tiny type. Reads them because they're what's in front of her.

1961 Corvair, excellent condition, 8,000 miles. She has no use for a second car.

Free kittens, 10 weeks old, guaranteed cute and sweet. There's a phone number. Maybe she should have a kitten; sweet, fuzzy kitten to take her mind off dying.

Don't be stupid. Poor little thing'll starve beside your corpse.

She shakes her head to clear the image.

For sale: Splendid forest isolation. Rustic mountain cabin adjacent to national forest and sizable private wilderness preserve. Outbuilding; acreage with meadow, garden spot and pond. Three-hour drive. Nicer to think of than a starving kitten.

She sighs, drains the last of her coffee, gets up and takes the otherwise unread paper to the den, drops it atop a stack of newspapers in a copper bin near the fireplace. She needs to get to the office before people start to wonder where she is. Bright, creative people with their whole lives ahead of them—people who, if they knew what she was facing, could not comprehend it.

* * *

DURING THE TWO WEEKS she's been dying, which is how she's come to think of them, she's turned into a master at delegating. It's what she does best. Doles out pieces of responsibility—one here, one there—until they're all gone and she can stare out over her uncluttered desk to her office door that's always closed these days and try to think of nothing. It's all she has stamina for anymore. She's begun to feel much weaker, and her everything's-just-fine charade has grown harder to maintain. She gets to the agency later in the mornings, leaves by early afternoon. Has said she's "working on a project." No one asks her what it is. No one asks her anything; the agency evidently runs quite well without her. Amazing how one can attain a status so high he (or she) is of no use at all.

At home, as in the office, she mostly spends her waking hours sitting in the den and staring straight ahead. Nights, she's learned sufficient sleeping pills and Valium will, by God, take her where she wants to go: into oblivion. It's late November, turning cold. The heat that blows through the floor registers is never enough this year to keep her warm, no matter where she sets the thermostat. Probably something to do with her dying—the next phase of the process has to start somewhere. She's taken to building evening fires in the den's stone fireplace. Then she lies on the sofa and tries, or at least pretends to try, to read—that age-old prescription that's supposed to take one's mind off things. Thrillers. The only books fast-paced enough to stand a chance at holding her attention. Books filled with characters who die, often violently, which for some perverse reason she finds comforting.

Tonight's a good night; she actually kept down a little food. She twists up several pages from her stack of newspapers to get a good fire going. Used to gather pinecones for this purpose; there are always lots of pinecones in the backyard. Front yard, too—one more thing she and Tim had loved about this house was all the trees. She doesn't gather pinecones anymore. So much easier to just use newspapers, watch them catch the fatwood, watch the logs begin to burn. Her stack is dwindling. The pages in her hands are weeks old.

For sale: Splendid forest isolation. Rustic mountain cabin adjacent to national forest . . .

A ring-shaped coffee stain puckers the page. She remembers how it got there and the first time she read the ad. Reads it again. The words, the picture they create, leave something peaceful in her mind. Later, for a while at least, she will think how easily she might have missed seeing the ad, and will feel then, for an instant, as if she is free-falling from some great height.

What she does the next day in her office—behind her closed door, at her uncluttered desk—astounds her: She phones the listing agent and asks if the property is still available.

She's buying it as an investment, won't need to look at it, she tells him. At her insistence the closing comes immediately, the week before Christmas. If she's lucky, she still has five months—or what portion of that time she can endure.

SHE HAD NOT EXPECTED dying at such a relatively young age to be awkward, unseemly, cause for embarrassment and shame. Or that it carries with it a perceived self-centeredness, a seeming lack of concern for those one leaves behind. How to tell them at the agency, all those bright and lively people, most younger than she, that, yes, dear innocents, death is about to come for me, as it will come someday for even you?

She puts it off well into January. Then comes the meeting at Pantheon Scientific. Client's office: vertical blinds, thick gray carpet, no color anywhere, and everything smelling oppressively new. Dry heat whooshes from one ceiling vent, faint music from another. Slivers of three o'clock sun slant straight at her from between the sharp-edged blinds. She moves her chair to dodge them. Other shards come at her from a different angle. The storyboards shake in her hands.

It's finally happening. All the wild terrors she has held at bay in darkness for so long are bounding free into the daylight. Now. She is watching the workings of her body slow, like dancers on a run-down music box, watching the walls cant toward her and the solid floor ripple beneath her feet. The heat, the piped-in music, something, steals her breath. In a moment she'll be retching up on the client's new gray carpet and/or lose the memory of her name.

"I'm sorry. I feel unwell."

She hands the storyboards to the most senior of the junior partners, rises, cracks her shins on some part of the table, runs out of the room.

KATHERINE SELLS HER CONTROLLING interest in the agency to that most senior junior partner, tells them all she's lighting out for California—it seems a fitting euphemism—and that she'll be in touch. Then, because she fears her poor lie won't stand up to scrutiny, she sneaks in on a Saturday, when the whole building is deserted, to collect her things. She really only wants the wall hanging she bought after Tim left, an abstract, hairy thing that, like a fireplace, warmed her for a while; but she can see now it's too large to take where she is going. She stands in front of it and traces with a fingertip a vibrant hunk of scarlet wool that meanders over and under silk strands the color of spiders' webs—then yanks the weaving off the wall, sinks with it to the floor. She buries her face in its coarse fibers for what must be a long time. When she gets up, her eyelids are sticky and swollen. She brushes off her clothes, smooths out the weaving, hangs it back up on the wall. Has said good-bye.

On her way out, she runs her fingers across familiar names lettered in stainless steel on doors she passes, names of people she will never see again. Outside, the light has changed. The rain has stopped; an unforgiving wind whips cloud remnants across a cold blue sky. A piece of newspaper sails low, past iridescent puddles rippling in the street. Unaccountably, she smiles.

THEY GAVE HER SEVEN Polaroids at the closing: a small stone cabin (photos of all four sides); a privy with an attached woodshed (the "outbuilding"); a small meadow, backed by brooding evergreens, that might once have held a garden still encircled by a rusty fence; and a pretty, cattail-bordered pond. She takes these photos out of their manila envelope several times a day and touches them—delicately, as one might touch a talisman. At least as often, she reads the description on her deed, stares at the plat as if by some obscure magic such staring might allow her to project herself into that place that she has not yet seen. She grew up in a downtown Atlanta apartment seven stories off the street, spent summers in Chicago with her grandparents, has never in her life come closer to a forest than the dark splotches she's seen from airplanes. This tract of land she's purchased is the most exotic place she might have strength to get to, and then only once.

If she can wind up her affairs and be there by mid-February, she'll have at most four months. On her good days she haunts bookstores, libraries, hardware stores, comes armed with lists, specifications, questions written on lined paper. Reads with interest the few books she finds on wild foods, healing herbs, survival in the wilderness, buys four small, useful paperbacks. Each choice brings her departure closer, makes it seem more real.

She buys a sleeping bag, commissions a clerk in the Army Surplus Store, a tanned young man who looks like he spends time outdoors, to reinforce its underside with leather (his suggestion) and to make a harness for it she can slip her arms into. Then she can pack it full of her belongings, drag it the two miles the agent warned she'd have to hike in from the road. The young man is proud of his work. When she comes to pick it up, he helps her fit her arms into the harness and strap it on. The process soothes her: his firm, competent hands. Except for medical examinations and procedures, she has not felt the touch of anybody's hand for a long time. Some things one must not think about. Known things, like someone's touch. Unknown things: nursing a baby at one's breast.

At home she tramps around wearing her harness, dragging her new sleeping bag behind her to get used to it; she buys a dozen bricks to gradually increase its weight. Her days are filled with preparation. Nights, she sometimes forgets her pills: Her sleep's improved from sheer exhaustion. No time for tears, or fears, or anything but what she has to do.

* * *

SHE BUYS THE GUN last, asks for the smallest one that's powerful enough to kill a human being. The gun store clerk, somebody's too-blond grandmother in too much lipstick, assumes she wants it for protection. She does, but not the way most people think. A Smith & Wesson with a four-inch barrel is what the grandmother recommends. The name conjures Saturday cowboy movie matinees. The gun itself looks more like it belongs in old black-and-white gangster films.

The grandmother leads Katherine through a padded door into an indoor shooting range in the back of the store. There Katherine takes one shot at a man's black silhouette on a large piece of paper that's hung on a wire some twenty yards away. The grandmother has to press Katherine's finger where it curls around the trigger so that she can bear to pull it, bear the proof that she holds in her hands an object with the power to kill, intentionally or by accident, a human being like herself. Even then she doesn't hit the silhouette, hardly hits the paper target. Knocks off a small piece of the upper right-hand corner and that's all.

Stands there jangled, terrified.

"You'd best aim low," the woman says. "Ready to go again?"

Katherine shakes her head. "I know it works."

Because the woman won't sell them to her individually, she buys a tiny, very heavy box packed tight with bullets. In the parking lot, Katherine opens the box, takes out six of the bullets, can't justify more considering their weight, drops them in her coat pocket. That's one for each chamber in the gun, a reasonable number. In case she misses. Or has second thoughts and has to try again. She leaves the box with the remaining bullets at the back door to the gun store, gets into her car and drives away.

THE HOUSE SELLS QUICKLY, to a young couple who plan to paint it Restoration blue and then have children. From what Katherine sees of them, she envies them in a desultory sort of way and also likes them, is pleased on her house's behalf that they are moving into it. Hopes they will take care of the hollies and nandinas, something Tim never bothered with and that she'd lacked the energy to do. Goodwill picks up her furniture, clothing, household items, even her brass bed, the day before she has to leave. At the last minute she takes off her pearl earrings and her gold watch, tosses them in one of the bags of clothing; where she's going she will not be needing them. Alone in the empty house, she calls out "Hallooo," the way a child might, just to hear the sound of it. Thinks how she should have stayed, died in a hospital like everybody else.

Too late now.

Before dark she gathers together everything left in the house, all the items she plans on taking with her, lines them up on her bedroom floor in the order she will pack them: a thin blanket, wrapped around the gun; five-pound bags of beans and rice; tin plate, cup, knife, fork, spoon; two small, lightweight cooking pots with lids, nested with a screwdriver and nails; hammer, hatchet, axe; two heads of cabbage, two winter squash; a picnic-size pasteboard salt shaker. And in her small backpack an extra flannel shirt, jeans, sweater if there's room, if not she'll wear it; socks and underwear to last three days; one pair of sturdy shoes, or perhaps these would be better in the sleeping bag; one nightgown; one large bar of soap for washing everything (dishes, clothes, herself), dishcloth, washcloth, towel, toothbrush, a small tube of toothpaste; three rolls of toilet paper.

These are the things one needs in order to survive.

If surviving is the thing one means to do.

One could say that depends.

One supposes.

She will also pack her four paperback guidebooks: *Weeds and Wildflowers of the Southern Mountains, Eastern Trees, Surviving in the Wilderness, A Child's Book of Forest Animals*—had wanted a *Complete Shakespeare* or something similar to read, but feared there wasn't room; and a steno notebook to write in, plus three cheap ballpoint pens. Finally, she will carry matches in one pocket to make sure they stay dry; and in the other pocket, her six bullets—if left to bounce inside the sleeping bag, or maybe even in her backpack, they might perhaps explode. Odd the things one doesn't think to ask about.

Scattered through the house it had all seemed a great lot, perhaps too much to fit inside the sleeping bag and backpack. But here in front of her it makes a small, vulnerable pile. Outside, the sun has not yet set—in these last weeks she's grown acutely conscious of the lengthening of days. A car screeches to a halt at the end of the street, with a sound like fingers skidding on glass. She picks up the hatchet, its wooden handle the color of dark honey, its steel head as smooth and cold as jewelry. The guidebooks are already thumbed and softened from use; the tinware gleams dully. A few good things. With which she will live out the remainder of her days.

She curls up in the sleeping bag, then lies there rigid—what if she wakes too ill to go? Hours before dawn, she rises, packs the sleeping bag and backpack, loads them in the back seat of her yellow Mustang, a car for a bright future, bought last spring in an excess of hope. Her breath smokes in the cold air. The driver's-side door's familiar squeak prompts—what?—not actual memories involving the car but memories she wishes she'd had, and she cries a little going past the quiet houses one last time. Driving up the freeway ramp she experiences an optical illusion: For a moment her windshield frames only the still-dark sky, as if she is barreling straight into the stars.

BY THE TIME SHE turns off the state highway at the tiny clapboard grocery she remembers very little of the drive she has just made, which is not unusual. But seeing the turnoff road is asphalt, she panics. What if it's nothing but a scam—the Polaroids, the deed, the whole thing? Or what if there really is a cabin, but it's surrounded by other cabins in some sort of fish camp place or something? What will she do? She might truly have to go to California, God forbid.

But soon the asphalt turns to gravel, then to dirt, and finally to ruts, and she can feel herself relax, quits holding on to some part of her breath. Dry canes of underbrush claw at her car from both sides, and bare, black tree branches meet overhead. In summer this would be like driving in a cave. The ruts continue for some time, then after a long curve the Mustang slams into a laurel thicket.

End of the road.

Katherine wrestles her canvas sleeping bag from the back seat, slips her arms through its harness, then straps on her backpack, locks her car, and heads for the bright orange surveyor's tape the agent tied around a maple tree to mark the trail. Once she unties the tape and drops it in her pocket it's as if the trail has disappeared, and for a moment she fears she is already lost. Even though she's just a few feet from the little bank where it begins, she has some trouble finding it and, when she does, walks forward tentatively, conscious of her heavy burdens and the uphill climb.

The bright mackerel sky she remembers vaguely from the highway has given way to a pewter overcast that turns the woods ominous. She should not have come. Brambles catch her long wool coat as if to hold her there. How far is two miles? How many steps? How rough is the trail? How steep? Can she get to where she's going before nightfall? She doesn't know. Not any of it. She jerks hard at her sleeping bag and labors up the narrow path. She got herself this far. There's nothing for it now but to go forward. To whatever's there.

The clouds part for a moment, but it isn't reassuring. The bare trees cast deep shadows. She has lost some time somewhere. Hours. And she's got no memory of them, none at all. Not by any means the first time such a thing has happened, but disturbing nonetheless. She left Atlanta in the predawn darkness, she remembers that. By her calculations it should be noon now, perhaps a little earlier. The light looks like maybe four p.m. Worrisome. To lose four hours. Five. To get only this far so late. A bear, a boar, a wildcat, they're all there, if you look for them, as shapes among the late-day shadows. She is truly alone.

Which is what she bought and paid for, what the agent promised, but how could she know that this was what was meant? Always before, alone meant being in her house or at the agency with no one else around, but still able to hear noises in the street, muffled voices from an adjacent office, music from a neighbor's radio. She had—has—no concept of this new alone, where there's no one but herself for miles.

And the forest is not silent as she had expected. The wind in the tall pines sounds so much like traffic on a distant freeway that she imagines once again the agent lied, that she will come upon a busy highway around the next bend. Wishes for it, even. Winter tree branches creak against themselves like haunted doors, blue jays shriek above her, and a squirrel thrashes in the dead leaves not three feet away, as noisy as a man. Off and on, she's certain something's following her. A shadow large enough to be a deer or bear, slides between the trees up on the ridge. Once, a tan dog glares at her from a hillside then trots off. Other dogs bay in a distant valley. She shudders, and for a while walks hunched into herself, turtle-like and looking down.

But the raw dirt on the new-cut trail shows no one's footprints but her own, and gradually she lets the forest's beauty stun her, even slow her progress. The wilderness beyond the trail appears to separate itself into an endless string of rooms that beckon like a fever dream, rooms for gnomes and forest nymphs who live in them with their own mysteries. On the ground: crisscrosses of pine straw, fallen twigs, overlays of rotting leaves; she views them without depth perception, as one might modernist paintings in a gallery. For a while she carries in one hand a rotting branch ruffled with lichen soft as pale green broadcloth. Long after she drops it, the woodsy perfume of its bark stays on her palms; she inhales it greedily, repeatedly. Once, when she sits to rest, she rakes dry leaves aside with her gloved hand and peers at dirt the color of dulled copper, knows that for the first time she has truly seen the ground.

She stops often. It's almost twilight when she at last gets to the cabin. At the end she runs—it's downhill—both from relief and from fear of what might stalk her in the coming dark. After a hurried visit to the privy, and too exhausted even to light a candle, she dumps the contents of her sleeping bag onto the floor and crawls inside it still wearing her coat.

But sleep won't come despite all her exertions. She lies there wide awake as winter night slides in around her. None of her nature books talked about nighttime as a preview of the grave, an oversight that's inexcusable. They should have warned their readers how stone cabins left a long time vacant give off fireplace drafts that call to mind interiors of tombs. Clouds hide the moon, or maybe there isn't one. The darkness in this place is nothing like a city darkness, always filled with city lights. It's black and thick, something to dodge, or else reach out and grab on to, like a weighty velvet stage curtain. It turns her hearing keen: A small wind whirls dry leaves and an owl hoots somewhere back in the forest; closer, something steps lightly on the ground. Fright lifts the fine hairs on her arms.

At the agency she once conceived a campaign for an airline bringing day flights to a town formerly served only by a red-eye. Cartoon businessman trying to sleep, feet sprawled in the aisle, versus that self-same businessman accepting a lunch tray from a smiling stewardess. "The difference between night and day." She'd thought then she knew what that meant. She'd been an arrogant little fool.

The floor's cold under her sleeping bag. How strange to think that in Atlanta it's another Friday night and everybody from the agency is drinking at Wallbangers with everyone from every other agency. No one will say her name and someone else sits in her chair.

The owl is gone. As long as there was an owl, there likely were no larger animals around to frighten it. She scrunches farther down inside her sleeping bag, maneuvers it so deep into a corner that her head nearly touches the cold stone wall. Perhaps sheltered in this manner she can sleep. And she must sleep; if she can't sleep she will almost certainly die even sooner than she fears. She tries to relax. Tries to think about each part of her body, tense it and then release the tension, like one of her doctors showed her. Toes, feet, ankles; she lies very still. Knees, hips, belly. In this stillness she hears a new sound. Hears it unmistakably, almost feels it. A faint, rhythmic rustling, as of something breathing very near.

An echo of her own breath bounced back to her off the wall. That's all it is, that's what it has to be. She can prove it, hold her breath and make the phantom breathing stop.

Only, it doesn't stop. Something that isn't her keeps breathing right beside her, separated only by a wall.

She lies frozen, listens to the sighing of her pulsing blood, afraid to move even her eyes. Tries to align her breathing perfectly to this faint second breath, this breath that is not her breath. Breath that is the least whistle of air passing through a chink between two stones.

She tries to make her own breath disappear inside it, so that her suddenly too-solid body disappears as well.

In. Out. In. Out. Soothing. Terrifying. She places her palm against the wall's rough stones. Feels on her skin a spot of moist, illusive warmth, a vibration so slight it must be her imagination.

Jerks her hand away, cries out.

"Please, God, please. Oh, please don't let me die."

The breath that is not her breath stops.

And then begins again. Longer. Slower. Deeper.

Relentless.

Inside this new breath, her breath—exhausted, hopeless—finds a resting place.

And, finally, she sleeps.

2

The Watcher

THE WHOLE THING STARTS WITH A MISTAKE, A REDBIRD IN THE WIN-
ter woods and he's stoned on it already. Acknowledging, of course, he's
so wasted to begin with he's screwed up the day marks on his wall and
set out thinking it's his birthday, Sunday, and it's cool to raid the
dumpster at the grocery store out by the highway, bring back something to celebrate. Stale Slim Jims, package of smashed cupcakes.
Smashed cupcakes with icing. Only, turns out he can't because it's
Friday, Monday, Saturday, who the hell knows, and there's people
there.

Dog knew. Hightailed it down the back side of the mountain to
sniff her own kind, get a little doggie hump. Won't do her any good.
Dog, somebody somewhere loved you so much they spayed you. Live
with it.

So here he is. Alone up on this ridge, whacked out of his gourd
under a heavy sky and the air tasting like snow's coming before night-

fall. And here's this red dot bobbing so close he can reach out and grab it. Except dope fucks with your depth perception and it's not a redbird after all. It's some city bitch trudging along the trail way down below. In what Memaw used to call a "Sunday coat" and prissy little fur-topped boots, and dragging what looks like a giant turd behind her. What's she doing here, so far back in his woods she's like a fairy tale, poetic-vision acid-trip, phantasmagoria-of-the-month?

Phantasmagoria. Yeah, old Professor Beckman would be proud.

Danny pinches out the joint he's held cupped against the wind, drops it in the pocket of his torn fatigue jacket, moves soundlessly to keep her in his sight. Looking back, he will recognize this moment as his first act of commitment.

For now, the reality of her blows his mind. Her substance, her sheer suddenness. Like the first time you get sent out, how it hits you that you're really there and you're so scared you see, hear, taste, smell everything at once. All of it, not just what your eyes are trained on. The wind and where it's coming from, the bugs, the snakes, the shit-stink gook-jungle muck under your feet. From then on you're always keeping track. Watching, listening, sniffing the air. Shaking it all up together like some bar drink in your head to figure what of it might kill you.

You get good at it so you won't die. That's when it starts to feel good, that danger standing all your nerves on end. Feel good in ways you never say. Like Pawpaw with the squirrels and deer, you move in close enough to hear them breathe, then closer. So close you see the small muscles in their faces twitch, smell what they ate for dinner or if they got lucky in the middle of the night. Given time, people lay out their whole lives in front of you without a clue you're even there. You watch, always, with a degree of awe.

And if you're Danny you don't quit watching. Not even when they send you home. You stalk everything that's human, till you think you're better off with the wild animals so you set up house with them. Then one day here comes this red *thing,* and there's this cosmic *coincidence* of you thinking you've turned twenty, only you're a few days off. And there she is, and here's you watching her—and it's like you got a birthday present straight from God and Jesus.

Who fucked the date up same as you.

He kneels behind a fallen tree, raises his left arm, stiffens it into an imaginary rifle, braces it with his right hand. Takes aim at the woman struggling up the trail. *Pow.* His imaginary rifle kicks from his imaginary shot. Feels good, that old familiar push against his trigger finger.

Even if it's nothing but thin air.

Pow.

He frowns hard at the implications of what he's just done, jams his rifle hand deep in his pocket, creeps closer to the trail below.

Well, goddamn. Army-issue sleeping bag, that's what she's dragging. Stuffed it to the gills and sewed a harness on it. Resourceful bitch. Plods right along.

And he knows where she's headed. He's been expecting her, or someone like her, ever since some asshole with a chainsaw came cutting a path back to the Old Man's cabin. Danny had an hour, tops. Packed up his hatchet and his little handsaw, the hospital scissors he'd swiped to trim his beard, his tin cup, cook pot, bent spoon, broken piece of mirror, extra shirt. Hauled away the ashes from the fireplace and the stove, balled up a fistful of weeds and wiped the floor clean of his footprints, covered his yard prints with dead leaves. Made it like he never once existed in that place. Like he was nothing but a ghost. Then he took his duffle and himself on up the mountain, in the fearful lightning and the coming rain, to the burnt-out house he sleeps in now. Ever since, he's been trying to wrap his mind around the idea of someone that's not him living at the Old Man's place.

Can't do it.

Its location, the deserted cabin Jimbo used to hole up in when he went hunting, was the one piece of information Danny brought back from the war that turned out okay. Shit, better than okay. Before Pawpaw died he taught Danny some carpentry, enough to find work at it after he got grown, more than enough to know what he was looking at. Enough to know whoever built that cabin didn't use a single nail below the rafters, put so much of himself in it his spirit must have seeped into its walls. The more Danny studied on that house, thought about some old man—it was always an old man, white hair, kind eyes—pouring his whole soul into planing a board or some such, the

more he loved that old man like he was his father. No fucking whore
dragging a sleeping bag behind her can know shit like that. And she is
a whore—and other names he will not think or say.

She won't know either that's why Danny built the table, to honor
the Old Man. Used the few good boards from the caved-in smokehouse like the Old Man would have done. Told each board out loud
before he took it, "Board, I'm making you a better piece of wood than
you can ever dream of." When he was done making the table he made
a bench for it, and then another. Two benches, as if he thought he
might have company. Took awhile to see how fucking weird that was,
him making that other bench.

In the Old Man's cabin Danny slept a sleep too deep for dreams.
He aims his "rifle" at the woman's red coat. *Pow*.

Moves in closer. So close his mind flips out all the way to San
Francisco. The park, the girl's blond hair—so like Janelle's, so like his
mother's—coiled tight in his clenched hands so he could keep her by
him. Later, her lying there so still he didn't stick around. But this isn't
San Francisco. And he's only watching. Be here now—isn't that what
all the hippies say?

Yeah, be here now. Crouched close to another human being because it feels so good. Maybe that's the reason no one ever speaks of it,
this watching aspect of the art of war. Because it's not supposed to feel
this good. Supposed to feel like shuffling papers at a desk in Saigon—
thin, pale, dry. This woman here is all those things, yet if he wanted he
could take five steps, maybe four long ones, and jam his tongue deep
in that ear that peeks out from her dull-dark, pulled-back hair. Lick
till her moans curl deep into whatever ghost he has become.

But Danny shall not want to, shall not want. The Lord is his shep-
herd, for whatever shit that's worth. All Danny has to do is keep his
own number one commandment: Do not touch another woman. Not
ever again.

But he can watch. Yeah, watch till his heart and all the rest of
him's content. The hard part isn't learning how to move so they don't
see you, it's learning how to keep your heart from pounding so hard,
your breath from coming so fast, that they hear. There's a trick. Imagine yourself someplace quiet, safe. Danny is always with his Memaw

on a particular late-summer day in the shade of the huge water oak beside their cabin. Her bulk weighing down the rusty metal yard chair, her lap filled with dark red cherries. His mouth is stained with them, his body ringed with pits there on the dusty ground close by her swollen feet in their stretched-out cotton hose. Nothing can startle him, wound him, kill him, so long as they two sit together in that clean-swept yard.

This close, the woman's older than he thought. Maybe older even than his mother would have been. He's never stuck his tongue inside a woman's ear. They're supposed to like it, he's been told. Not old Janelle. She only liked straight kissing. On the mouth. And no hands below the waist, no finger fucking. Ever. Not even way back when he thought they'd got engaged. He wonders what this woman likes. From the look of her, not much of anything. Danny aims his "rifle" one more time. *Pow.*

The woman trudges up the new-cut trail some longer. Then she sits on a rock to rest and he can see she's nothing but sharp points—shoulders, elbows, knees. And shaking with a tremor that looks like it never lets her be. He smells the sickness on her before he gets his first good look. The acrid stink of medicine mixed in with puke and a third odor, a cloying sweetness he's smelled twice before, both times on men dying.

Her face bears this out. Blue-veined skin stretched tight across her skull, drawn up mouth, cavernous eyeholes. The eyes themselves stare dully. She pants, sweats in the February air, but doesn't make a move to unbutton her coat. Instead, she raises a gloved hand to wipe her damp forehead, lets it drift down to her pocket. Pulls something out—a Mars bar. A goddamn Mars bar. She shoves half the candy in her mouth, chews like she hasn't eaten in a week. Nibbles the remaining half, the last bite with both hands covering her mouth. Swallows, lowers her hands, clasps them primly in her lap and sits perfectly still, her jaw clamped shut. Then suddenly—oh, shit—she doubles over, spews the whole mess out onto the ground.

"Damn it all to hell." Says it quietly, like a single word. Like she's not much given to cussing. Spits once, then again.

Then she takes off her right glove, wipes her mouth with the back of her hand, wipes her hand in a clot of leaves, all of it so matter-of-fact, resigned, familiar, Danny knows whatever's killing her has shown its face. She rubs a dangling run of snot off her nose, chafes her arms. Then glances up to where a pair of buzzards circle high as angels in the pure, white sky.

What happens next drives the last reefer haze out of his brain. The woman straightens her spine. Her breath now coming quiet as his own, she turns her face up to the birds as if she's basking in the sun.

"Hi, babies," she says. "I'll leave a window open. You can pick my bones."

You don't feel for them. You're there to figure out what's going on and take appropriate measures, that's all. At first he thinks she's crazy, one of those dumb bitches that quit eating for meanness or no reason till they waste away to bones. But then he sees whatever's wrong pisses her off too much to be a thing she chose. She moves so slowly, looks so annoyed by it, he pities her and knows it for a weakness he must overcome. When she stops to rest again, so shrunken, scared, and hopeless in the fading light—just a few feet from where you see the Old Man's cabin, his meadow and his pond—Danny has to fight the urge to run out, grab her shoulders, shake her till her teeth fall out, the urge to holler, "Get up, lady, look down there."

Even though he's got no personal stake whatever in her getting there. Even though, truth be told, that outcome runs counter to all his interests—especially his interest in continuing to fish the Old Man's pond.

At last she stands up, takes the few steps. Then it's like some fit comes over her. She goes rigid as a plank and starts in trembling. Gives the sleeping bag a mighty tug, starts running down the hill with it bouncing behind her, nipping at her heels. And all the while she's letting out these eerie little wild-bird cries as if she can't believe she really made it.

You must not let yourself feel anything.

She jerks the sleeping bag onto the porch, takes a key out of her Mars bar pocket, turns it in the new brass lock. The front door sticks.

Always does after a rain. She shoves her brittle shoulder into it. Once. Twice. It gives, and Danny is surprised to feel relief where he is not supposed to.

That's why he doesn't come close as he might when she goes in, doesn't want to know what she is doing in those rooms he ought still to be living in. Yet he's not so far away he doesn't hear the kitchen faucet cry out like a red-tail hawk. Or hear the stupid bitch let drop one of the cast-iron stove eyes with a clang so sudden and so loud he has to clap his hands over his mouth to keep from screaming.

Later, in twilight, he moves behind her down the privy path. When she doesn't shut the door, he turns his back—there are some things he doesn't need to see. Yet he can't help but hear the clear, pure chiming of her urine in the slop jar the Old Man for some weird reason set inside the privy hole. The same dark-night sound as Memaw on her piss pot when he was a little boy.

His familiar tears come then. Silent, constant, they slide down gullies chapped raw by their predecessors running to his beard. She's come here to die; he's known it since he stared into her face back on the trail. For a little while he fooled himself into a kind of future. Someone to watch, someplace to be. Tomorrow, maybe the next day, next week even. Now it's gone.

He should leave before the snow starts. Should not scuttle toward the cabin, pick a corner she can't see from any window. Should not crouch there, sit and straddle it, should not slide in close enough to touch the walls, then closer, nor stretch out his arms, embrace the two sides of the house, nor lay his cheek against its smooth, cold stones.

Should not imagine her a foot away, sleeping where he used to sleep.

There's a chink in the mortar, level with his face, where he can hear her breathe. He wishes he could suck it in, her breath so close like that, presses his ear hard against the crumbling mortar. Hey, whore, Dead Lady, you want a lullaby? I'll sing you one inside my mind. Here goes. *Hushabye, don't you cry, go to sleep my little baby. Bees and butterflies are picking out your eyes; oh, you poor, poor little baby.*

Those are all the words he can recall of what his Memaw used to sing. He loops them round and round inside his head, while his fingers and his thighs grow numb gripping the stones and a barred owl hoots from somewhere way back in the pines. *Hushabye, hushabye.* He hears the wind and his own breathing and the Dead Lady's, stays there a long time.

Then something happens.

"Please, God, please. Oh, please don't let me die."

Danny presses the side of his face hard against the wall, hangs on till her sobs die back, even their echoes. Clings with his aching body long after she is through, as if that in itself might keep the thing from happening.

Not till the first frail snowflakes drift into his hair does he unbend himself from his stony embrace and move soundlessly back up the mountain in the dark.

3

Gatsby's House

SLIMY, SNOWY MUCK. TWO FREEZING FINGERS POKING FROM YOUR gloves. You could fall, you know, roll down the fucking mountain, knock yourself out on the Old Man's porch, wake up and find that skinny bitch dead in the cabin. Who would find you innocent? No one, that's who. You are not an innocent-type life form, and that's the truth.

But Danny won't fall. A moon's just slid out of the clouds. Sky, snow, it's all turned pure, pearly white. Plenty of bright light to guide old Danny home. *"There's a moon out to-ni-ight. Let's go strolling through the paaaaarrrk."*

He knows better than to sing a song like that. Even in his mind. Anything to do with parks can set him thinking about *that* park.

Or maybe it's the woman did it. So scrawny she put him in mind of hippie girls. And hippie girls put him in mind of *that* hippie girl in *that* park. Put him also in mind of old Janelle, who was different from hippie girls in every way there is, except that she's a girl. And who he has not thought about all day not even once. Till now. Which is some kind of record probably.

Thinking about Janelle—how in high school, with her cheerleader captain and him quarterback, they'd been king and queen of everything—leads him to thinking about other shit that makes you want to drink and drug till you pass out and die. Or maybe only blow your brains out, since it's quicker. Shit like that day he ran the ball, a day he every minute goes out of his way to never think about. Won't think about now either. Can't think about. Because the weather's different. Night. Cold. Snowing.

On that other day the sky was a clear, high blue. October weather. For the Homecoming game.

Her bus from Athens—she'd gone to the University and he'd gone to little Larramore, halfway across the goddamn state from her, because he'd got a football scholarship—came in at 12:09 p.m. He still remembers. Him standing at that scummy grocery near the campus, in the driveway circle where the buses stopped to let off passengers. Him staring down the road and actually praying, "Please, God, don't let her be late." The game started at two and he had to be there by one-thirty, suited out and everything. Remembers how her bus was seventeen whole minutes late when it pulled in, should have been there at 11:52. Him waiting with the rigid florist's box, a white orchid with a golden throat to match her hair. Not purple like what other guys had bought. Different, special just for her.

She looked so pretty getting off the bus, pausing for a second on its single step in her sky-colored suit and high-heel shoes. Carrying her little train case, shading her eyes to search for him. His fingers shook when he pinned the corsage on her left shoulder. The too-short pins that came with the flower in the box were tipped with tiny pearls.

"It's for all day," he told her. "For the game and then for dinner and tonight," his voice gruff because he had just pinned a flower on his girl, the same thing all the guys were doing, but so far from anything he'd ever dreamed could be a thing that he might also do. That boy who'd spent so many days out in the woods with Pawpaw, hunting squirrels so there'd be meat for dinner.

He left Janelle with Jimbo's girlfriend at the stadium and so knew where she was sitting. Tried to keep his eyes from even looking toward her that whole afternoon, while him and all the other freshmen players warmed the bench. Watched the score, their score, spiral up so high that late in the fourth quarter he and one other freshman got sent in "just to get the feel of it."

Then there was the ball high in the air above him, some boy in an opposing jersey jumping, reaching for it, Danny jumping higher, reaching too. Cradling it hard and running. Thirty yards. So many yards people applauded, even though it didn't matter, the score so lopsided they had already won.

That night she wore her corsage on a dress that looked like dresses goddesses in statues wore. They danced awkwardly on the crowded floor of the gymnasium to music from some singing group he'd heard once on the radio. At intermission he led her outside into the cool air, to the practice field. There they sat in the bleachers, the only couple who had thought to walk that far. He put his arm around her, lowered her head down to his shoulder.

"If I was in a fraternity and had a pin I'd give it to you," he said as he stroked her hair.

"I know," she said. "I don't need one."

He can't remember if he wanted her right then, thinks maybe he did not. Not that way anyway. No, he wanted her right then for all his life. Wanted to hold up in front of her a certificate that said he knew the things you need to know to be a lawyer and provide for her. Wanted to stand up in Memaw's little church and promise he would spend his whole life with her in that silly house she'd cut out from a magazine, with its wide porch and all that stupid woodwork. Wanted to make babies with her, babies that would be like both of them.

After a few minutes sitting out there in the autumn night with the dry leaves rustling and drifting down, he did want her that other way. Wanted her so bad he stood up abruptly, said, "We need to go back now." For her own good, to protect her from himself, from what he so desperately wanted before it was time. Because that was what you did. Because she was the kind of girl you'd do that for.

They walked back slowly, both of them reluctant. He removed his coat, draped it around her shoulders, took her hand. Far away, they heard the singers starting up after the intermission. Their music floated through the building's open doors. *"The evening breeze caressed the trees tenderly."* They stopped, stood listening. In that moment Danny felt his life as he had always thought it was supposed to be, the way he had imagined it from books and his own yearnings. That this realization came to him in this way, as a fullness inside himself that would render him able to accept such a life, seemed so remarkable he allowed himself to believe in it, standing with this perfect girl across the practice field from that small-college gymnasium where a quartet of somewhat famous, not-so-young men sang their second set. Allowed himself to believe his world had at last become exactly as it should be, every part of it, and that this was the way it would remain for him through all his future. Like the Bible said: "Now and forevermore."

Yeah, well. Wish in one boot, piss in the other, see which one fills up first.

It's near morning. He's got no watch, but he can tell the hour. Time's in his blood and bones and he can sense its passing. So he knows it takes just shy of ninety minutes to make the hard climb from the Old Man's cabin up to Danny's mountaintop home. Up to the iron gate, where he unwinds the heavy chain he wraps around its bars to keep bears out.

First time he touched that chain, back in the early fall, it burned the shit out of his hands. Everything was mist and smoke from a piss-poor lightning fire still smoldering after rain. A last fiery limb crashed down right in front of him, and a few dead trees now and then collapsed inside themselves and flung their sparks into the sky. Like over there, where something always burned, even inside the sopping monsoon jungle. Muck there, muck here; fire there, fire here. Hard to keep straight which part of the known world he was inhabiting at any given time. A pack of wild dogs bayed down in the valley, a moiling, frantic sound of lives gone suddenly so strange they couldn't figure out which way to run.

The house inside the gate loomed through a dense orange haze. He couldn't see what-all was there. Looked like parts of it had maybe burned once long before and fallen in. He threw some dirt on the back side, where some of it still smoked again, then walked all around it like he'd seized the Castle of the Black Knight or some such.

"Hunters never go there, climb's too steep. It's like everyone's forgot the fucking thing exists." Jimbo's eyes dreamy in the flares' unearthly light. "Mold all over everything, like digging up a corpse. Dumped all my weed seeds in the side yard. Years of them. Should be shit enough to stone sixteen battalions. I'll take you there when we get back."

Danny found one room he could live in, dropped his duffle. Home.

That signaled Dog to come from somewhere in the mansion's bowels. He heard her before he saw her, her claws tick-ticking on the marble floors. Took her stand in the foyer, a midsized, deer-colored bitch like Pawpaw's hunting dogs. Growling, snarling. Something alive in Hell besides just him.

He'd grinned at her, crooked his right arm chest level.

"Dog! Yeah, you. C'mere."

Slapped his arm to goad her.

"Yeah, I'm a fucking loony but I like you lots. C'mere."

He feinted toward the dog. Once, twice. When she lunged, he grabbed her muzzle with one hand, wrapped his free arm around her body, dragged her to the floor just like he used to wrestle Pawpaw's hounds. Flipped a leg over her and started in petting whatever of her he could reach with his free hand.

"You like that, my hand all in your neck fur? You like the way I rub your belly? Yeah, you like it so much you don't want me to ever stop."

His voice was even, soft, his mouth close to her ear.

"You put on a big show like you're some kind of hellhound, but you're just a hungry little bitch at heart. And you need me to love you, only you don't know it yet."

Danny cocked his head toward the valley and the pack of wild dogs, grabbed her harder.

"Assholes down there, they throw you out? Looks like they didn't let you get too much to eat."

He lay with her still pinned beneath his leg on the stone floor, worked his fingers through her fur, spoke softly in her ear for a good while. At last he took his hand off her muzzle, pulled a Slim Jim from his pocket. He bit the paper open, stripped it with his free hand, fed it to her.

"You better like it. That shit was my dinner. Dumpster's finest."

She gobbled it down and he rocked her in his arms.

"Yeah, you're my dog now. All mine. You belong to nobody but me."

Whispered it in her ear over and over, till finally he let go his hands and she stayed down beside him and the two of them just fell asleep right on that marble floor and let the fire burn out around them.

"Dog?" His one word now muffled by the snow.

Danny holds the gate open, purses his lips, calls her with little sucking sounds. She doesn't come.

"Dog? Okay, see if I bring you any Slim Jims next time."

He's got nothing for her this time, maybe that's what's wrong—greedy bitch only shows up when she smells food.

"Dog, you're acting no better than a human, which has knocked you down a fair number of pegs in my opinion."

He wraps the chain loosely around the gate, leaving enough space for her to squeeze in if she wants to. Snow's starting to clump on Jimbo's reefer plants, on Danny's fruit trees. Apples, peaches, pears, he runs his fingers along one of the small branches of a pear tree, brushes off the mounding snow. *"Apples, peaches, pumpkin pie, something-something don't know why."* He needs to recollect the other words, sing it when he works on them in spring. Memaw always said green things do like being sung to.

"Yeah, you need me, all you trees. Need me to keep care of you."

He can feel, more than see, the smooth progression of the early light, even behind the clouds and snow. Something else he's picked up over time. He is one smart fucker, for whatever good that gets him—smart even among those city-shit frat assholes that one year at the college. Walking up through the orchard takes more time but, truth be told, he likes coming home this way. Makes him feel like he owns the place. Because he does, no matter what shitass's name's gathering dust on some forgotten piece of paper in some other state.

Yeah, he likes it. Likes how the broken driveway sweeps wide from the orchard and that's when you see it. Gatsby's house, just like old F. Scott wrote it.

Three stories. Limestone white as bones—what crazy fuck would haul limestone up here? Wide-ass lawn in front, mountains spread out behind like torn scraps of faded blue tissue paper. Standing here in the early dawn, you can't tell it's a ruin. Can't see the broken windows, raccoons nesting in the sofas, whole top floor caved in. Sometimes you can't tell when you wade across the lawn that's grown up almost to your chest. Sometimes not even when you set foot on that first, and still unbroken, slate porch step. And if you're careful where you look, sometimes you can't tell till you're standing at the door.

Because until then you are something very like a ghost and you can almost see them. All those skinny girls in their thin, flowery dresses and that slicked-down flapper hair; the men in white suits and wide ties striped like store-bought candies. You can almost see them dancing with their knees and elbows angled out, almost hear them.

"There was music from my neighbor's house through the summer nights. In his blue gardens men and girls came and went like moths among the whisperings and the champagne and the stars."

Danny can still quote whole passages, who the fuck knows why? Maybe because Jimbo could and it got to be a contest with the two of them. Maybe because he just craved to be there, someplace so different from anything he'd ever known. At first he thought he was Carraway, because they both knew how to keep a watcher's distance. Then one day it hit him like a block of that damn limestone: He's Gatsby. Got to be—it's his house, isn't it?

The massive oak door sticks in damp weather, same as the door on the Old Man's cabin, Dead Lady's cabin now. Before Danny gives it his usual running shove, he rests his forehead on the wood, breathes in its piss-smell of old mildew.

"Dog?"

He lets out one last whistle and this time she comes, dashing up the drive and lunging into him as if he himself were the stuck door. It gives, and they all but fall into the house, her on the marble entry floor, him on top of her, his nose in her fur. He rolls around with her, ruffles her up.

"Where you been, lady? You get a little?" Her fur smells of pine needles, wet leaves, other dogs. "You think you're well on your way to a wolf's life, don't you?"

Hugging her warmth against his own chill bones, he carries her into the ruined library, won't let go. She sniffs his pockets.

"Nothing there. You got nothing here but me. I got nothing here but you. We're two against the world."

He drops with her onto his rain-stained mattress and sleep falls on him, sudden and heavy, wraps him in the dog's soft fur and imagined fireplace warmth from yesterday's cold embers. His last thought is of the Dead Lady, dragging all she owns behind her up the trail.

The Cabin

She dreams rarely anymore, maybe once or twice a year. This dream is a good one that she doesn't want to end. She feels well in it, which hasn't happened in a long time, and stands in an open space under a gnarled old tree. A wind so high up she can't feel it flings itself against the tree's top branches. They boil into the sky like clouds from a gathering storm. She will continue to be well as long as she stays where she is and doesn't wake, she knows this. But it's cold and it's morning; she should open her eyes.

And let familiar terrors seize her. Where is she? She doesn't know this place. Is it a hospital? Did she collapse somewhere and get brought here?

She can't remember.

Is she hemorrhaging? She feels around inside her mouth, inside her clothes, looks at her hands. Nothing. Oh, dear God. What if she's in some warehouse for the insane? She guards against it and it's never happened, but there's always a first time. She remembers she does not remember things too well. Remembers her strategies on these occasions. Stay calm; assess the situation, one piece of verifiable information at a time; try to breathe normally.

First things first. She can't have died, she hurts too badly. In all the usual places, also the soles of her feet and the muscles in her upper arms. Unnerving, this hurting in odd places. That's how new symptoms happen, they just show up and stay.

There's a window in the adjacent wall and it does not have bars on it. A good sign. Outside there are trees, a great lot of trees. Maybe more trees than she's ever seen all at one time. A bird she doesn't know the name of trills from one of them, a lovely sound—she hardly knows the names of any birds, much less what they sound like. This one is gray, but then they all are, aren't they? Or brown. Except bluebirds and cardinals and jays. The room she's in has stone walls, rough wooden ceiling beams, and a hard, austere beauty, like an old church. A poor church with nothing extra, only dignity. Some things are beautiful, no matter what.

Beauty. Seven out-of-focus Polaroids. They gave them to her at the closing. Somehow she got here, to the pictures, then she slept. With all her clothes on, even her red coat. This is her first morning. All this she is now certain of. Something else: An animal breathed outside her wall last night and frightened her. Of this she is less sure.

On the floor, beside a trestle table halfway across the room, is a pile that looks like everything she dragged into the forest in her sleeping bag. In it there's a gun, which when you get right down to it is why she's here. She can shoot herself today, right now, and get it over with. A quick, clean end to things, not like with the pills. She slides her hand down in her coat pocket, feels the six hard, reassuring lumps of bullets tied inside their bandanna. So simple, easy. Bang. The thought causes her breath to come in strangled gulps.

Or she can wait—a day, a week, a month or two—until her pain's too great to bear.

She slides out of her sleeping bag, stands on wobbly legs. Balancing first with one hand against the wall and then by clinging to the edge of the trestle table, she makes her way to the jumble of her belongings, picks up the gun between two fingers, shoves its hard, cold barrel into her mouth. Being. Nothingness. No thingness and therefore no pain.

How badly does she want it?

Not yet badly enough.

She replaces the gun among her more innocent possessions. By electing not to shoot herself this morning, she can spend the whole day living here. Wriggle into her boots, hike to the privy, bring back firewood and put food on the stove, eat something so she won't feel so weak. Maybe then heat water for a bath. These options turn the room quite bright, the edges of things crisp and clear. She puts on her warm wool sweater and her boots, goes out onto the porch.

And beauty truly is there all around her. So much more than in the photographs, or even on the trail. Beauty that slams into her hard. The cold air smells sharp and clean and makes her want to take in greedy gulps of it. Last night's light snow glistens on the porch railings and lies delicately inside curled dry leaves on the ground. Bare winter trees sway slightly in the light wind, like blades of grass. They're different among themselves. Their shapes are different, their barks are various colors, not the same, and their limbs bend at different angles. The small twigs at their tips appear to wrap the sky in delicate, dark nettings. She makes a frame out of her thumbs and forefingers, examines sections of the woods before her; each is equally lovely. A large, rust-brown bird perched in a tree not twenty feet away spreads its wings and flies off with a harsh cry ending in a dying fall. Katherine watches the soaring bird until it's out of sight, a bird so large she might ride on its shoulders.

Along the privy path she clings to trees. For balance, but also to experience the textures of their barks. Once there, she finds her pain's no more than she can bear—one can bear a lot more of a lot of things than one imagines; also, if you bite down hard on the soft part of your hand, but not so hard you make it bleed, your simultaneous pain in some unrelated body part will not seem quite so great.

Or if you distract your thoughts from it. What animal breathed against her wall last night? A deer? There should be tracks. Small, deep holes in the wet ground, like in her *Child's Book of Forest Animals*.

She looks for examples on her way back to the cabin, finds none and turns to picking up wood—small, damp stove-wood branches to sundry on the porch, a few larger ones for the fireplace later. Wet wood smells beautiful, but it's heavier than it looks. Collecting it's something she didn't plan for, something she must do each day.

Best shoot yourself as soon as possible.

That's not funny.

Oh, but it is. Here you're tramping around in the middle of nowhere picking up sticks so you won't freeze to death, when all you came for in the first place was to die. Small wonder skeletons all grin.

The trail forks here. Last night she hadn't noticed. The broader path leads back to the cabin, past a briar thicket she dodged earlier, its thorny, meandering sticks easy to spot. The narrower path she remembers from the plat as a thin, wavering line that leads out to the pond and then the meadow. Magical to see it come alive, that slender blue-ink thread. She can't help but follow it, no matter how she feels. Drops her wood in such a way it points her to the cabin, moves tentatively onto the narrower path, again clings to trees to save her strength. There's the walking back to also be considered, mustn't forget that.

But already here are cattails. Cattails at the bottom of a tangled bank. A jutting rock she can almost get to. Can get to. And sit on.

Close up, the water smells reedy and cold. Shadowy fish dart beneath its surface. One leaps, flashes a silvery rainbow, sends concentric circles over the dark water. As if on cue, a pair of mallards explode out of the marsh and squawk themselves into the sky—as if they, and the fish, are part of some perfect nature print she has magically wandered into. How can such beauty exist with no one to observe it? Do people take these sights for granted? Her time's too short for that.

Around the next bend, the meadow is a blowing field of wild grass and pine seedlings grown up past her knees. As she walks into it, waves of small, startled birds rise up ahead of her then drift back down a few feet farther on. Surrounding the meadow's center is a rusted fence. Its fragile gate swings open easily. Inside, the worn-down ridges of old furrows rise beneath her feet like ancient graves.

Hard to say how large it was, this fenced-off garden, what fraction of an acre. Large enough for whoever lived here. Now it's the wind that lives here, in the grasses. And it sings, that's all she knows to call it. Long, low notes, like breath blown across the slender neck of an empty Coke bottle. The grass smells of sunshine, the wind rushes into her open mouth. At the far edge of the meadow, a large tree with a thick trunk and branches reaching to the sky stands with the morning sun behind it, not unlike the tree out of her dream. She closes her eyes, extends her arms, turns once around slowly and smiles.

"The perfect place to die."

What a dreadful thing to make of it. An ad.

Ad that would win a Clio. Old habits die hard.

She laughs. It has a different ring when there's no one to hear it. Fuller and unguarded.

Hiking back, arms filled with still-damp branches, she rounds a bend and, for a disorienting moment, in the same way one experiences déjà vu, sees the cabin as a place where she lives and belongs. She drops her wood on the porch, goes to the corner where she heard the deer the night before, brushes away the dry leaves and peers at the ground. There's nothing there. No tracks of any kind.

Perhaps she doesn't yet know what to look for.

Perhaps her deer's a spirit deer that floats.

Hardly. More likely is that fear can prompt hallucinations, aural as well as visual, and there was nothing outside her wall last night at all.

Inside the cabin, two cabbages, huge and green, lie with everything else on the floor beside the trestle table. They are everything she sees. When she picks one up, it's cold and alive between her hands. One leaf, two leaves, three leaves, so sweet you chew them slowly. Now, sit here on this bench, breathe quietly. Oh, miracle! She keeps it down.

Lying on top of her sleeping bag on the sun-warmed floor, she closes her eyes for her midmorning nap, the low point of her day. No one naps mornings except people like her. Damaged, sick, dying. Outside, what has to be a mockingbird sings whole long songs, never repeats itself. They sing because they're lonely, so the guidebooks say; they sing because they're looking for a mate. If she lives out her remaining four months of allotted time, she'll be here when it finds one.

She'll be here when the trees take on that first green haze of spring and then leaf out. Growing up, she used to watch for it out her bedroom window. The year she turned eleven, a small gray bird built a nest in the top branches of the tallest tree, where she could see it. One morning while she was in school the bird hatched three sky-blue eggs. It seemed magical, a miracle, because she hadn't been there.

IT WAS THAT SAME time of year, when she began once more keeping watch over the trees, that she met Michael. She was sixteen, like all her friends, the lot of them just starting to go out with boys in cars, living for the musty smells of Packards and Hudsons when their dashboard radios got hot, the scratch of wool upholstery through their thin spring skirts. The air was wet and heavy; their winter coats were not yet packed away in cedar chests. It happened fast. He was three years older, out of school, which made her feel all at the same time very young and very old and very special. He had played football and she knew even back then who he was, the way you know a movie star. Now he was in the Army, saving to pay for college. In April they had their picture taken at her junior prom under a cardboard archway decorated with crepe paper roses. He had his arm around her. They had only just come from frantically tasting each other in the back seat of his car; anyone could see it in the photograph, in their eyes. She can't remember if she knew then he was leaving.

Of course she wrote him every day; he wrote her every day he could. In June, after the trees all got their leaves, the phone rang.

Okinawa. A hideous and unfamiliar word. The details didn't matter, only that he was dead and all the life in her died with him. Their plans. Because there had been plans, there had not been any question he'd come back and they'd get married. And so they saved themselves for it, that future, even the night before he left. No one so young imagines anyone they know will die.

They wouldn't let her see inside his coffin. Wouldn't remove the flag, pry up the nails. Her mother had to lead her from the church when it was over. Because she could not move for sobbing, no one would take her to his grave. When she got home she tore the dress she'd had on into little pieces, gripped the pieces with her teeth and ripped them once again, threw them in the garbage. Would have burned them had she been alone.

How she got through her senior year she can't remember, only that she marched down the aisle with all her classmates in a white cap and gown, hating herself for still being alive. That fall, she rode the bus downtown to night school. Sat at desks struck by shafts of dust-filled late-afternoon light, memorized shorthand squiggles, learned to type. *Now is the time for all good men to come to the aid of their country.* Banged the keys so hard she bruised her fingertips.

When you latch on to learning desperately, as a distraction, it's easy to rise to the head of the class. Easy afterwards to get a good job, then a better one, then a still better one at a place like Clopton Advertising. On Christmas Eve that year, she came home to find her mother lying on the kitchen floor, dead beside their open refrigerator. An enormous turkey sat defrosting in a dishpan on the bottom shelf, below an array of small brown paper grocery sacks filled with green beans, sweet potatoes, cornmeal for stuffing, oranges and flaked coconut for the ambrosia. The way her dead mother's hands curled under her chin like a small child's stayed with her. And how she looked so small lying there, as if her whole life had been of no consequence. A husband who left her for no apparent reason, a career selling cosmetics in a second-best department store. Katherine feared her mother's circumstances were hereditary; she herself had already known great love and tragedy and there seemed nothing left. When Tim Clopton asked to marry her, she let him.

When she got pregnant, the baby kicked hard early on and she came back to herself in a fierce way, determined to give this child love enough that nothing in the world would ever harm him. Yet somehow she hadn't, and the harm had been grievous—proof her capacity for a great love was used up.

If her dead son were here now, alive, he'd be four years old and she would give to him the singing grass, the squawking ducks, the leaping trout, the cabin.

* * *

SHE GETS UP FROM her sleeping bag, sits at the table gazing at her heaped possessions near her feet. Their presence pleases her, suggests she'll have a life here in this place, a future even if it's short. But now they must be put away. On pegs near the door, in storage bins by the fireplace, in the kitchen pie safe with its lovely punched-tin doors. Here's the hatchet, so comfortable in her hand the day she bought it. If the hatchet is a good man with strong arms in a plaid wool shirt, then the gun's a twitchy hoodlum talking out the side of his mouth: "Yeah, baby, I'll take care of you."

And here's her brand new notebook, the single thing she is most glad to find. She's been two days without it, long to go without one's memory. Because that's what they've become, the notebooks. Of necessity. Until three years ago, she could lie in bed each night and run the whole day she had just lived through her mind like a movie she'd already seen. Then gradually her mind's projectionist grew sloppy with his splices, prone to walkouts, shutdowns, packing up his reels and leaving town with only a few snippets, single frames, forgotten on the floor. She is still good with far-backs and once-upon-a-times, but yesterday, this morning, even five minutes ago, can fly away from her just like the little birds out in the meadow. The notebooks fill in the blanks. Sometimes even one or two words written in a notebook can bring back an entire reel of film. Sometimes. But not often.

On the first page of every notebook, she has always written what she fears she will forget in an emergency: name, age, address and phone, place of business, family doctor. At some point she began listing her bizarre array of symptoms, alphabetically to keep up with them: bleeding, confusion, exhaustion, fainting, headaches, inflammation (gastrointestinal, genitourinary, some talk even of her brain swelling), nausea, seizures, and the last one, pain—in expository writing, as in the Rule of Three, the point of greatest emphasis is always last. Thus pain is permitted to defy alphabetizing. There were new symptoms with each notebook; none of the old ones ever went away. She used to list someone's name to contact in the event of an emergency but quit after she sold her interest in the agency; there was no longer anybody to write down.

But this notebook is different. She writes her name, Katherine Reid, no longer Clopton, not for a long time. And her age, thirty-eight, then realizes she no longer has a place of business, nor a doctor. Nor even an address, only a narrow trail off a dirt road any postman would ignore. After some thought she writes, *I live in the stone cabin past the end of the turnoff by the Wickles Store. If I am alive that's where I need to be and I can get there. If I am dead, dispose of me as you will; I apologize for any inconvenience this might cause you. Please reimburse any expense from my possessions.* At the top of the second page she writes today's date, *February 14, 1967,* pauses a moment, then adds, *Valentine's.*

In the notebooks she writes small and with no margins, keeps her notations spare and to the point. She allows herself a page a day, front only. Each steno book lasts her three months; she has brought only the one. She runs her hands over the page she has just dated, likes the feel of the notebooks, how their cardboard covers make them hard to bend. *Arrived last night. Immediately to bed. Something, a deer, breathing outside my wall. Woke midmorning. Tolerable pain.*

She means to write next about gathering wood and the importance of maintaining both the stove and hearth fires, but something in the jumbled pile in front of her distracts her. White-edged rectangles, bright as quilt pieces with vivid spots of color in their centers, are scattered through her drab possessions. Where did she get them? Why? She doesn't quilt. Frightening she can't remember.

As if lifting a dead mouse by its tail, she picks one of the squares up by a corner. It's made of paper. Stiff, white, coated paper framing a rather well-executed watercolor beet.

Seeds. A small packet of beet seeds.

And she's brought lots of them—three, four, seven, nine, one dozen assorted envelopes of Thompson's High-Yield Vegetable Seeds. They gleam so insistently her breath quickens. The one day her notebook was packed away out of her reach, she ends up with twelve envelopes of seeds she can't remember buying.

And four hours she can't place.

Occasionally, when she tries hard to think of something it will come to her, a scrap of film left on the floor. This time there's nothing for a long while, and then only a mind's-eye view so odd it makes no sense. An Adam's apple sliding up and down in a man's scrawny neck, a man who brings with him the memory of a pervasive smell of oil on metal, and of rubber.

Her tire. The Mustang, suddenly muscular and with a mind all its own, bouncing and flap-flapping up an isolated mountain road. The spare flat, too. Flagging down a car—"Please tell someone." Tow truck, service station, clattering of tire tools dropped on asphalt, hissing of pneumatic lifts. Both tires too far gone to mend. Her sitting outside on an orange crate, dizzy and shaking in the weak late-morning winter sun, noonday sun, afternoon sun. Wanting a cup of coffee and afraid she'll throw it up. Waiting for someone to bring new tires from some other place, perhaps another town.

Her missing hours. Such a relief to have them back.

But that doesn't explain the seeds. Nor the Adam's apple.

Wait. She got up off her orange crate, something to escape the stink of gasoline and engines. Walked down the sidewalk on one side of the street for an entire block and then back up the other side. Moved slowly, sometimes sliding her hand along a building's wall for balance, past stores—grocery, Rexall with a lunch counter, clothing, hardware.

The hardware store.

Where she bought work gloves, the candles she'd forgotten—beeswax, they burn longer and their smell's so lovely—took her purchases to the cash register and laid them on the counter. The clerk looked her up and down and she stared at his swooping Adam's apple, knowing what he saw: an emaciated woman with dark, stringy hair and incongruous new jeans already falling off her hipbones.

"Yew come up from Atlanta?"

The way he curled his lip said at best "summer people." More likely "dirty hippie," though she's at least twenty years too old. They're children, hippies. The Beats were much more interesting.

A senseless fury gorged up in her then, mixing with the store's oil-on-metal stench. She wanted more than anything to spit at him that she was not some city dweller come up for a weekend taste of winter cold, that she was here for the duration. Instead, she swiped her hand across the nearest display rack and slammed a random dozen seed packets—bright watercolor vegetables—onto the counter.

"And that shovel up against the wall, I'll take that, too."

Later, she left the shovel in the car because it was too hard to carry, slid the seed packets into her sleeping bag. Now she collects the shiny envelopes and props them on the mantel. They're pretty there. Cheerful.

Lunch is late, more cabbage and then once again a period of sitting quietly on a bench beside the table. This time, though, a nap's out of the question. She's got to get a fire burning in the stove, dinner cooking, and a second fire laid in the hearth to light at sundown. She's thought a lot about this. If she always keeps the stove fire burning she'll have live coals and not use up her matches. If she burns a hearth fire every evening she'll save candles. From this morning, little twigs and bigger twigs, small branches and larger, all separated by size and laid out on the porch, none of it as dry as she had hoped. And she's got no old newspapers this time, no loose paper at all, just the "How to Use This Book" parts of her guidebooks. But a fire's essential, otherwise she'll almost certainly die sooner than she is prepared for. (She could, of course, just go ahead and shoot herself this afternoon, but she's already covered that one.)

So. Crouch at the firebox with your matches. If the floor bruises your knees, take off your shirt and wad it under them. Pretend nothing hurts. Pretend you have infinite patience. Your plans, your life, depend on what you are about to do right now. Lay twigs and your few nonessential book pages, twisted tight, inside the firebox. Strike a match. If its flame dies out too soon, then strike another. And another after that. Lean forward, breathe your mouth-breaths long and slow into the firebox. Like the wind that sings among the meadow grasses.

The tiniest flame curls the edges of one of the book pages; the flame ignites a twig. The twig's bark smolders, flames, and then the small light dims, winks out. *Oh, don't, don't go, don't leave me.* But another has lit in its place and fire licks all around it. A small branch catches, then a larger one. Slowly the stove's black surface starts to warm. She's done it.

Now she runs water in the larger of the cooking pots, dumps in brown rice and lentils on blind faith. She's never tasted either, bought them on some book's suggestion: "Nourishing foods to take into the wilderness." Her legs and arms are trembling. She should stop, sit on her sleeping bag, lean back against the wall. But the trees fling out late-afternoon shadows that let her know she is afraid, and that there's one thing more she needs to do.

The gun's dull silver makes her think of snakes. Not interesting and harmless ones like hoop snakes. Poisonous ones, like rattlesnakes. Normal good sense says keep the gun within arm's reach of where she sleeps, to guard against intruders. But what would intrude here? She runs through her memorized litany of animals she might encounter in the wild: Bears won't show themselves unless there's food left out, wildcats won't come near you, and cougars have been extinct up here for years; wild dogs attack in packs but bark out warnings, deer are shy and run away, and turkeys, as best she can tell, are just plain stupid. Raccoons, opossums, squirrels, and rabbits are all small enough to fear her.

And there are no people. Yesterday along the trail she saw no cigarette butts, bullet casings, campfire ashes, empty Vienna sausage tins, no sign of any human being but herself. Saw no sign of anything as large as she except a shadow high up on a ridge.

That quicksilver wisdom that trumps good sense says store the gun where it can best protect you from whatever you most fear. What she fears most is not intruders, animal or otherwise. It's the sudden impulse, dream, memory, or fresh, sharp pain that might lead her to reach for it before she needs to, suck its barrel into her mouth and fire. Very like what happened with the Valium, but final. No, the gun goes on the high shelf near the ceiling, where she will have to take some trouble to get at it, take some time to think things through before she brings it down.

Strange in her present circumstances that should matter. Yet it does.

THE SUN IS GONE and the air has once again grown cold. On today's notebook page she's added, *Unpacked. Found seeds I'd forgotten, along with my lost hours—had to buy two tires. Built both fires, a challenge. Cooked beans, rice; tasted not too bad; threw them up returning from the privy. Stored gun and bullets out of reach. If the deer comes back tonight, I hope not to be afraid.*

She crawls inside her sleeping bag and, before blowing out her candle, looks around. All things being relative, she's settled in. Does this mean she harbors some faint hope she'll be here for a while?

Impossible to say. Hope is like what happened with the seed rack in the hardware store: Something uncontrollable that's done by your left hand.

5

Danny's Refrain

It's not 'cause I need to,
it's not 'cause I like to,
It's not 'cause I have to,
It's just 'cause she's there.

Just like with the possum,
just like with the she-bear,
Just like with the panther,
it's just 'cause she's there.

IT'S HIS OWN LITTLE DITTY, MADE UP JUST LATELY TO THE TUNE OF some old-timey song he can't recall. He's sung it patching holes in Gatsby's roof, spreading leaf mulch on Gatsby's fruit trees, scraping rust off Gatsby's gate. Now he's all morning humming it inside his brain where nothing else can hear him, climbing down the mountain once again to pay another covert visit to the Dead Lady. Who don't look near as like to keel over as she did three weeks ago.

"Don't look near as like." College-boy grammar's shot to shit. Hung on to it all through Nam and now it's gone. Maybe the books'll help him get it back. If he wants to. Moldy books all around him on shelves floor to ceiling. He's sleeping in a fucking library.

He's got a plan to read them, learn something. All of them; already started on the east wall. East, the sunrise side, where shit begins. Might as well do it that way, they're not in any order. Just stuck up there on someone's whim. He thought to rearrange them so it made some sense, by writers' names or years when they were published, but there didn't seem much point to it. Easier just to start somewhere and take them as they come. More like life that way. Random. Destined.

Same as with the Dead Lady. Showed up fresh out of nowhere right when he was passing by—and fucked up his whole schedule. Cut into his reading time and all his plans for building squirrel traps and the like. It's got to where near about every day he's hiking down to the Old Man's cabin like going to see a friend. A human friend, no dogs allowed. He's trained Dog to stay back when he climbs down this side of the mountain. Not a pleasant thing, but necessary. Dog would have given him away.

Just like with the she-bear, just like with the panther. "Painters" is what Memaw and the old folks called them. *Just like with the painter, it's just 'cause she's there.*

He tracked a painter, panther, once. Back when you used to hear them screaming in the night like haints. But this panther was no haint. Its prints, splayed out bigger than Danny's nine-year-old hand, bigger even than a grown-up hand, ended in claw holes gouged deep into soft red clay beside a trickling stream. He tracked it down one ridge and up the next then down and up again, far out of sight of any place he knew, only to lose it in some craggy rocks. Used the cat's same tracks to find his way back home, just like Tarzan of the fucking apes. Thought the whole time how maybe the cat had also doubled back and was that very minute slinking along some parallel path, watching with its wild yellow eyes. Tracking him.

Yeah, he could track a panther now, for sure.

It's just 'cause she's there.

If the Dead Lady dies he can dig a hole and bury her and move back in the cabin. No one'll ever know. That being said, the fact she's not yet dead causes his heart to rise.

Though it's wrong to feel so, affects the outcome. Who knows but what his wishing she won't die might be the very thing that's keeping her alive, giving her new strength?

And where's that new strength coming from but sapping his?

Die, you dumb bitch, whore of Babylon. You don't mean shit to me. You dead's like a dead possum in the trail for me to step over, that's all.

Yeah, best to keep a lid on things. He doesn't need to be all the time sending his mind down to the Dead Lady's, taking his whole self down there every night and in the daytime, too, letting his house and all his fruit trees go to shit. Because that's what'll happen if he can't stop her from pulling on him, can't stop himself allowing it.

And he does allow it. Thinks about going down there, being down there with her, all the goddamn time. It even cuts into his reading. Yeah, bitch'll make you stupid if you don't watch out.

But right now it's Saturday, and Saturday's okay. It's not like it's a special trip. It's just him stopping by on his way to hit the grocery dumpster. So what if it's got to where he's spending near the whole damn day down there and then the whole night and then Sunday, too, and doesn't leave her side till almost Monday dawn? He still makes it to the dumpster, doesn't he? And it's only once a week. Allowed, planned, part of his routine life almost. It's all those other days he's got to watch out for. The nights don't count. It never counts when she's asleep.

So this Saturday he sets out from Gatsby's well before the sun's climbed high, but that's okay. He's carrying a canteen, a Slim Jim, a squashed Little Debbie Snack Cake, some rotting book by Hemingway, and two joints. Fat Saturday joints. He takes quick breaths, sucks the smoke in deep. Watching stoned's the only way. Like reading stoned. Stoned lets you set up camp inside somebody's soul.

Just like with the panther, it's just 'cause she's there.

He's starting to know things about her. Like where she hurts and how she hurts at least a little bit all over all the time. Like how she moves so as to keep parts of herself off separate, like little nests for pains. She's not as old as he once thought. Took a while before she showed him that, kept it hid away inside her suffering.

One time, hiding behind an open door, he heard Memaw say how you could tell if a young girl's even once been with a man, how her hips are suddenly all the time rocking like a porch swing. He took Memaw's words for gospel, since she had no idea he was listening. In high school it proved out. He could always tell. With this woman, though, the Dead Lady, he's not so sure. Over there, he saw women that lived day to day with their men, then saw them with their men dead in their arms, saw the moment when that sadness seized up in their hips and there was no more rocking in them. The Dead Lady's hips are stiff from all her hurts, so he can't tell if she's been with a man or not. Or if she liked it. He can't explain her. And it makes him crave to watch her all the more.

Today he hears her before he gets anywhere near the cabin. An axe—halting, staccato, lacking a man's smooth rhythm. The thrill of finding her outdoors, someplace where he can watch her for a good long while, rises in him till he has to slow his breath. Even so, it catches in his throat when he truly sees her out behind the cabin, chopping firewood on an old tree stump. Yeah, here's a woman no man ever taught to swing through with an axe, or that strength comes from momentum. He could step out right now, out from behind this very tree, and put both arms around her, both hands on her tensed-up wrists, teach her to trust the axe's arc. How many steps? Seven? Six? Five?

But only if he's someone else, not Danny. Danny must never touch again.

That's why God gave us reefer. Long as you've got reefer, you're never alone. Reefer and books, the Dynamic Duo.

He moves in close, at an oblique angle where she'll not likely look. Between the trees, behind the rocks, and finally, his sounds covered by a sudden gust of wind, he stretches out in a laurel thicket. Then everything else falls away and there's nothing but her. And him watching her, the way you chew that first meat when you've been a long time hungry.

Yeah, look at how she stands up on her tiptoes just before she swings her axe, then bumps back down on her heels when she hits wood. And look at how she wipes that hair out of her eyes with the back of her wrist. Look how that hair falls right back down into her eyes and makes her brush it back again. How she does it always the same way.

In his intensity of concentration on the Dead Lady herself, Danny misses something. Her pile of limbs has dwindled. She props her axe against the stump and goes to look for more, takes short, quick strides straight toward him. He can't move, can't breathe. Lies flat against the ground, the dead leaves under him a mat of slick, wet sadness pressed into his cheek. It's all over now, him watching her. Done for and gone. Without her, what's he going to be? Already any life he had before she came is life he has forgotten.

She aims her Dead Lady eyes straight at him. Danny braces for her screams. If she kicks him with those stiff, new work shoes, he'll roll into a ball. If she runs he won't run after her. Whatever, the whole thing will end. She'll go back to wherever—she's nothing but a rich-bitch Lady Brett Ashley anyway. He'll get back to living in the cabin, eat pond fish, get his world back. Happy, happy.

Why, then, has this sad hole fetched up inside him like a seep?

And why, when the bitch keeps staring at him, looking through him, looking past him, passing by him unseeing on her way to find more firewood, does he get a jolt of joy so pure she might've shot it straight into his veins?

Joy so complete it brings back a big thing he has forgotten. The free pass of watching. If they don't sense your presence, if you're that good at what you do, they won't ever see you. That's a proven fact. People only see the things they're looking for. You can bang an entire shivaree of pots together, set your fucking hair on fire, and if they aren't looking for you they won't find you. The Dead Lady looked straight at you and she never saw.

You've still got it, Danny Boy. Everything your Pawpaw taught you. Everything you brought back home from over there. Nothing in this world's so bad it doesn't net you something.

Still, he can't have what just happened happening again, her coming up on him like that. There's a sure way he can fix that, but not one he craves to implement. It changes things, and that's not good. Change something just a little and, by definition, you won't be watching anymore what you set out to watch. By definition. Change things and you affect the outcome, change their world. And yours.

He finishes out today's watch scrupulously, by the book, cataloging it all in his head. She's got on what she always wears. The too-big work pants, leather work shoes not yet broken in, red wool shirt, its sleeves rolled twice, extra shoelace tying back her hair. Keeps hold of the axe like it's a walking stick. No extra movements; still stiff and coddling all her pains. But not as stiff as a few days ago. Maybe not as stiff as yesterday, except he's got no way to know—she'd finished all her outside chores before he got there, gets up earlier these days.

She ties the wood up in her jacket, carries it back to the cabin, duck-footed from its weight. Soon there's smoke coming out the stovepipe. Danny digs in his jacket pocket, pulls up his Little Debbie Snack Cake, eats it so his stomach won't growl. He misses the Old Man's fish. Pulling fish out of a pond's a damn sight more dependable than counting on rabbits and squirrels. But rabbits and squirrels are all he's got now. Small price to pay for watching the Dead Lady. Still, he might ought to build a few more squirrel traps. Except that's time away from her.

Tonight, like every night, the sun can't set too fast. He stares at it till it blinds his eyes, as if to speed it behind Panther Mountain by sheer force of will. This is the hardest part, her inside but with her lamp not yet lit and it not dark enough for him to move in close. Can't even see her pass before a window, all he can do is wait. And take a quiet piss, maybe his last chance till morning.

Yeah, you're going to mess with her world, aren't you, make it just a little different.

She'll never notice. What harm can it do? Nothing but make her life some easier, though that's not your intent. So what does it matter?

You're not fighting a fucking war these days, you're just watching one dumb whore who came up here to die.

Still, you hadn't ought to do it for another reason, hadn't ought to go around touching shit you know she'll touch. Puts you just one step away from touching her. One step. Every man walks down the road to Hell just one step at a time.

But not Danny. Danny has the power of his will. Danny will obey his almighty first commandment. Never touch again.

Shadows getting long, his favorite time except for pitch-black dark. Time when nowhere you might cast your eye is necessarily what it seems. A hollow stump might be a bear, might be a fender from a rusted-out Ford Fairlane. Might be Danny.

Danny loves the twilight, even though it's nighttime gives you the best edge to move in close. Tree to tree, silent as a shadow, he sneaks toward the cabin. All the way up to the corner where her sleeping bag lies on the other side. He squats, sits, the stones cold between his thighs, hugs them loosely with both arms, rests his cheek against them. Through the broken mortar is the Dead Lady settling down. Yeah, this is what he came for, the small sighs and whimpers that give way to whispered breaths of sleep. He times his own breaths to them— can't get much closer to someone than that—stays by her through the night. He'd kill for reefer strong enough to let him see her dreams.

When a stiff breeze stirs itself near morning, he uses it to cover his few sounds as he gets up and makes his way some distance, toward the tree stump where she left the axe. Creeps beyond it in a wide arc, past the thicket where she almost found him. Moves the deadfalls away from his hiding place, out to where she can get them easy. Moves other branches in close from the woods.

Changes things.

It ain't 'cause you have to. It's just 'cause she's there.

Spring

6

Seeds

SOMETHING'S WRONG. SHE HARDLY NAPS ANYMORE, MAYBE TEN OR fifteen minutes and that's all, finishes her routine tasks in half the time with energy to spare, rarely throws up her food. It's been a month; she's been told to expect by now the start of organs shutting down. Every day she checks for signs, but they don't come. From the looks of things, she's not dying according to schedule.

To say this is worrisome is not quite accurate but close. Closer is to say it's a situation that demands strict vigilance. Because it's producing change, an unfamiliar dilemma: She has time on her hands, time when she wants more than to sleep, or sit and stare, a luxury she can't remember and hence did not plan for. And time on one's hands begs to be filled.

When there aren't other diversions, one's mind answers the call. And hers has stepped up to the plate to fill her empty hours with craziness. Today, as is increasingly the case, the sunrise moved her to a whole morning of joyous tears at the mere fact of her continued existence. But in the afternoons, when shadows take on a certain length and shape, she cowers, keeps away from windows, certain she is being watched. Nights, she dives into her sleeping bag before it's dark enough to light a candle; who knows what its bright flame might draw? One joy, one fear, is as foolish as another, she knows this. Nonetheless, they come.

To defend against them, she invents activities, distractions bordering on obsessions. From her tree book she has learned, as best she could in winter, the names of all the trees she can see from the cabin and along the privy path. Excluding the dogwoods, which she came here knowing, the chestnut oaks were easiest: huge Aubrey Beardsley concoctions, gnarled and black, with thick trunks and twisted, horror-movie limbs. The other oaks she mostly told from acorns or their brown leaves rotting on the ground. White, post, red, scarlet, black, pin, chinquapin—amazing how so many can exist in this one place. The poplars are straight and tall, the hickories less so, the branches of young maples angle like calligraphy. Her favorites, the delicate and slender beeches, keep their parchment leaves all winter and stand gathered in low places like clutches of people talking. For several days she had a mystery tree, then pegged it as a serviceberry, known for its "ragged, white, wedding-bouquet blossoms with a languid scent." She's sketched in her notebook—on the backs of pages—every tree, its shape, and a leaf when she could find one.

There's a bright-colored snake lives in the privy. In the warmest part of the day it stretches out where the floor meets the wall, like the piece of decorative molding she at first mistook it for. When she reached out to touch it, the snake convulsed against her hand—its skin smooth, not at all slimy—then streaked away. Back at the cabin she looked it up in her *Child's Book of Forest Animals*, the wafer-thin booklet she bought only because she thought it might fill the last space in her sleeping bag. Unlike larger, more thorough guidebooks, it told her in a hurry everything about snakes she was in a hurry to find out, mainly that the privy snake, a corn snake, would not kill her. The *Child's Book of Forest Animals* did not tell her why, considering her prognosis, she thought this fact important.

Now she watches for the corn snake in the privy the same way she listens for the deer at night outside her wall. But these wonders aren't nearly enough to fill her empty hours. In all her advance planning she never allowed for time. Not the time she has left—that's a black crow perching always on her shoulder and she counts its feathers last thing every day. No, it's this other time, this time-on-her-hands time, leisure time, she failed to consider. Today, after resting maybe fifteen minutes, she simply gets up and sits on one of the benches. There's nothing left for her to do. The house is clean, clothes and dishes put away, four days' worth of firewood stacked by size out on the porch, more under the woodshed overhang. She's eaten lunch, picked some dry weeds on her privy walk, arranged them in her extra cup and set them on the table. It's too early to build up the fire for supper, so she sits, hands folded in her lap.

Her little cabin has the simple, functional beauty of a thing created over time with loving care, a life's work. Even the knobs on the storage cabinets take into account the grain of their wood. The trestle table and its benches, though perhaps crafted more hurriedly, show a similar sensibility and belong here in this place. The same holds true for the "few good things" she brought. Even the seed packets belong, as they gleam from the mantel. She stares at them a long while, then gets up and brings them to the table. A dozen lovely envelopes, each different and all chosen by a random sweep of her hand. Even the backs are pretty, with their pastel diagrams of planting zones. Her cabin is in zone seven.

She fans out the envelopes, arranges them by the colors of their vegetables: parsley, kale, broccoli, green bell pepper, sage, cabbage, lettuce, turnip, yellow summer squash, golden winter squash, carrot, beet.

If their names make a litany, their various planting directions are a poem:

Plant in late winter.
Sow after the last frost.
When the ground is warm to touch.
In full sun.
In partial shade.

In small hills.
Scatter soil one-eighth inch.
Water in.
Thin at two inches.
Harvest at sixty days.
Ninety. One hundred twenty.
Let the ground lie fallow until Spring.

Her work in the meadow starts innocently enough. No more than poking around, tugging up a patch of weeds here, kicking a rock there, examining the rusted fence. Something to do, a distraction. There's a spading fork in the woodshed with a handle not too rotten. She uses it to poke between tree roots, under slick mats of last fall's leaves and leaves from other falls before them, down to the dark, loamy soil. *We are not here long, any of us.*

It's not a plan, standing inside the rusted fence at various times of day, turning in all directions to determine angles of the sun, amounts of shade from trees at the forest's edge, prevailing winds. Nor is dragging limbs and branches from the woods and piling them beside the fenced enclosure any sort of plan. It's not a plan a few days later hiking to the car, bringing the shovel she bought at the hardware store, digging up each weed and seedling inside the enclosure until her every move is agony and bruises black as orchids bloom on her arms apparently from no more than the strain. It's still not a plan, laying the collected limbs inside the fence in rectangles narrow enough for her to reach halfway across, or washing out the privy slop jar, using it to bring soil from the woods day after day until she's filled all the rectangles. Nor is it a plan upending one of the picnic-table benches, dragging it to the sunny side of the front room, filling its box-like underside with small stones and loamy soil for seeds that call for indoor starting.

Not even on a windless noon, when she tears a tiny corner off the turnip envelope, shakes its granules out onto her palm, and sprinkles them into the vastness of her first raised bed, is it a plan. Mere specks that cannot possibly grow turnips. Turnips she may never live to see.

No. It's not a plan. A plan requires a future.

* * *

ANOTHER TWO WEEKS GONE and she's developed a new symptom: a focused, trance-like state, some variant of a daze. Her vision's grown quite sharp and she looks only at right now.

It's in this daze she turns over the other bench to make another indoor bed, and keeps on building outdoor garden beds for all the other seeds she owns and seeds she doesn't own but can imagine owning. It's in this daze she stops and listens to a pair of crows quarreling at tree line for a length of time so long it can be measured by the changing angle of the sun. Or lets the wind into her hearing, until it no longer sounds like traffic on some not-so-distant freeway but only like itself. This morning, as with all others now, she stokes her kitchen fire in darkness, rolls up her sleeping bag and sits on it to watch the dawn light filter through the trees; shows up ahead of time as if she's bought a ticket. Later, she eats slowly. Her foods are few, but every day their tastes intensify. And nearly every day she keeps them down.

This wilderness that so recently was merely nameless trees on nameless ridges has grown infinitely complex and subtle. She writes in her notebook: *Spring is felt before you see it; buds swell in the cold. My seeds sprout in a green fringe so frail I'm frightened for them.* After dinner she waits for the sun to set just as she waited for its rise. Its afterglow flames up and fades; the birds grow quiet. If she looks away, when she looks back it's dark.

This night she awakens to the sound of gentle rain that drowns out the deer's breathing, imagines how her seeds will swell like small, expectant bellies, then drops back into sleep knowing she has prayed a prayer.

THE WEATHER'S WARMER NOW. In the garden a few days ago, she spied on a single ant most of a cloudless morning, as it marched along one of the stacked branches enclosing a just-planted bed. The ant disappeared periodically into patches of shade from the branch above it, only to emerge seconds or minutes later farther on. Mostly now she takes each morning one ant at a time. Works in the garden, dreams of harvesting full-grown vegetables, plans long walks, imagines sitting on her porch in moonlight.

But she does not, in fact, sit on her porch in moonlight. Something that surely has to do with seasonal changes in the slant of light, the length and shape of shadows, how they move, has put a thick, black smear inside her mind that spreads and clings like oil. On the few days she's lingered in the garden past midday, this inner dark has come on her at what seems the same hour. And always suddenly, like a current of chill air that brushes against one's skin on a hot afternoon. Or the intensity of something's sudden gaze, something watching. She makes a point to tend her garden, chop her wood, perform all her outdoor chores now only during mornings, dreads her last hike to the privy in late afternoon. Afternoons, she doubts even the deer—she's never found its tracks.

Perhaps it really is no more than fear of shadows, the way they move when wind blows through the trees. If this is so, then there will be some time of day that she has not yet noticed, when things become all right again and that black pall inside her thins and disappears. A point where it is safe to go outside, at least a little while. Perhaps some precise moment, just before the sun slides down below the trees. That time when all the shadows merge but it is not yet dark. That's when she'll go down to the privy.

Now.

Throw on her coat and run, if she still can. If she knows she can run, perhaps she won't be so afraid.

It's probably quite normal, her abnormal fear, a hardwired survival mechanism we all share. In cities you're supposed to be afraid. It makes you lock your doors, stay out of alleys, keeps you safe. Perhaps the fear that keeps you safe in cities gets kicked into overdrive by isolation.

And yet come summer, she won't be able to see three feet to either side of her on any of the paths. Even now, with all the trees still bare, if something crouched on the downside of a ridge less than three feet away she wouldn't see it. In cities, someone is always near enough to hear you scream. Who would hear her in this lonesome place?

And there is something out there. Now. Twenty, thirty feet beyond the path, something she can't quite see but hears. Or perhaps only senses—its eyes crawling over her skin. It's moving parallel to her, causing changes in the light. Around the next bend is the privy. She runs toward it, dashes in and bars the door.

Takes comfort in the little bit of light that leaks in from a screened vent near the roof. Takes comfort even in the enclosure's rank smells—and how someone improved upon the usual hole by inserting a slop jar she can empty. But the sun is almost down; she can't stay here all night. Even assuming whatever thing that's out there eventually slinks away and doesn't bother her, if she stays she will almost surely freeze, catch pneumonia. Die—and not in any way she planned. She unbars the door, steps outside, runs.

To the cabin—the porch, the door, and then inside. She shoots the bolt, stands panting.

But it's not over. What if the thing got in while you were gone?

Too frightened to move anything except her eyes, she stands with her back against the door, looks all around. The cabin's full of places she can't see. She crosses the room—on tiptoes, what good will that do?—lifts the lids on both the storage bins and peers in, cranes her neck to see up the hearth's chimney, tiptoes to the kitchen, checks even the pie safe. Nothing.

There is one more place something could hide, if that something knew how to climb up there. She's never once been in the loft, gave it only a quick glance her second or third day. Heights dizzied her when she was in the best of health; they terrify her now. And the loft steps are steep and narrow, more ladder than stairs. She would have to climb five of them to see up there.

Fear makes you weak. Fear also makes you strong. Two steps, three steps, four, one more.

Quick, look. Empty.

Nothing is hiding there. Nothing is hiding anywhere. She is a foolish woman. Her terror is all nonsense. Nothing more than a new symptom, something else to not give in to, to ignore.

7

A Journey

Swaths of violets bloom against the ground and buds have popped out on the dogwoods. She has not only lived into the spring, she has outlasted her provisions. There's hardly any food left in the house and only half a candle.

This morning she flipped back through her notebook entries, slid her index finger down each page. On the face of it, she's hardly dying. Certainly seems strong enough to hike out to her car, drive to Elkmont.

Tonight she unrolls her sleeping bag in the same corner by the fireplace, curls deep inside it as the dark rolls in. In her safe shell she rides the night from sound to sound. The owl, whose soft call only deepens silence; sometimes a larger animal—a bear, a boar—crashing among more distant trees. But the sound she waits for, longs for, is that breathing, so in rhythm with her own, that leads her to believe she has an ally.

She has grown to think whatever animal is there protects her—from whatever other animal it is that terrifies her. Most nights it comes. Always at first she fears it but then settles down and lets it lull her into sleep. If she wakes in darkness it's still there, a doe that steps so lightly she makes no sound and leaves no tracks.

On the few nights the doe does not come she sleeps more fitfully. Sometimes in the darkest part, as if in some dream, a wild cry echoes off the mountains with such a human sound it chills her. A bobcat, certainly. Nothing to fear. Nonetheless, she stares up at the cabin's trusses, makes herself a stowaway on a sturdy ship rocking secure and out of reach on a calm sea.

She sleeps then, and all the night's mystery seeps into her bones. It's still there come morning, even sounds she has forgotten.

A DAWN MIST SHIMMERS among the trees and the hike out to her car is easy. She has lived to see the dry text in her guidebooks come alive. Hard, pale humps of edible fiddlehead ferns push up through the soft ground by the stream; tiny peeper frogs, drawn to wetness, sing out one at a time and then in chorus; a huge and beautiful pileated woodpecker, with its sleek red head and jungle cries, sweeps through the trees. *Pay attention. You may never see these sights again.*

She squeezes her hand around the list she carries folded in her pocket. Post office (rent a box), bank (open an account), supermarket (rice, beans, squash, cabbage, salt), hardware store (nails, screws, screwdriver, a second inside lock for the cabin door, candles, more bullets for the gun), bookshop (small paperback on gardening), dress shop (two cotton shirts—she failed to bring clothes for warm weather). A rocking chair would be so nice, but there's no way she can bring it in on the trail.

The mist is burning off and she takes strong, sure strides. The ground, with all its textures, moves fast beneath her feet. During her time at the cabin, her sense of smell has grown extraordinarily keen. A strong scent of dampness leads to a cache of delicate boletus mushrooms on a decomposing log. She marks it with a cairn of stones; her guidebook says they're good to eat. Not much farther on, she glimpses in the valley far below a sudden flash of too-bright yellow through the trees. Her car, neglected, mud spattered, its roof covered with small twigs and dried leaves, a city car that never once put in for this, poor thing.

Her reflection in its windows is a shock. Had she glimpsed it un-awares, in some downtown building's plate glass, she might not have recognized herself. She looks like an Indian. Thin, but not emaciated, her face firmer, tanned, the cheekbones more pronounced. Her eyes seem a deeper, blacker brown, their gaze alert, direct. She stares into them as she might into a stranger's, the 'stranger that this wilderness has made of her from some race only it remembers.

But when she opens the driver's-side door, its signature creak floods her with forgotten city memories. Inside, her car smells of all she used to be: a woman who hung lavender sachets in her closets, daubed Arpège on her wrists, flung her expensive briefcase on the seat beside her. A wave of dizziness assails her; this new sharp-eyed woman reflected in the window glass is nobody she knows.

Rolling down the window helps. The engine rumbles and dies the first three times she turns her key in the ignition. Should have hiked out every week, started the car to charge the battery. Stupid to assume she'd not be needing it. On the fourth try the engine catches. On the highway, she steps on the gas; the needle climbs to forty, fifty, sixty on the straightaways. Speed feels good. How can she have forgotten?

If you drive fast you can make it to Atlanta in three hours.

The thought surprises her, but only for a second. It's crazy living here alone and frightened, without even a rocking chair.

She can drive back this very day, check into a good hotel, order dinner. Rent a small apartment in one of those new, tall, downtown buildings—with windows that look out on other buildings filled with people, or on the green mist of a park—and live there for however long she has. With lots of chairs.

Die in a hospital, like you're supposed to.

"We'll see." She speaks the words aloud to the farmhouses she speeds past. What her mother often said when Katherine wanted something—a ruffled party dress, a radio all her own. "We'll see."

Sometimes she got the thing she asked for right away and sometimes not at all.

And sometimes she had to wait for later. Right now she has a list of things she needs to do.

The clock in the courthouse tower reads eight forty-five. Elkmont sparkles in the morning sun, its streets still deserted. She parks by the square, drops two quarters in the meter. Small, rough acorns litter both the benches under a bare chestnut oak. Brush one off and it's a good place to eat lunch.

The day's already warm. Across the street, a dark-haired man in khaki pants and a plaid shirt buttoned to the neck steps out of the feed store, dumps a bucket of soapy water on the sidewalk and jabs at it with a push broom. Katherine watches him with total concentration, fascinated by the way he jerks his broom or moves his shoulders, this first human being she's laid eyes on in a month. His pavement glistens.

But in spite of the clean sidewalk and the sunny day, the air around her smells peculiar, artificial, as if concocted from the odors of orange marshmallow peanuts, roof tar, and those cake deodorizers that one finds in service station toilet bowls. Small waves of heat rise off the asphalt street. The other day, down near the privy, she caught the scent of a bear, or someplace where a bear had been. The blackberry bushes all were crushed and broken and beside them was a paw print. The ground around smelled like the biggest, wettest, foulest dog imaginable had wallowed there. A rank scent, but she'd trade this one for it in a heartbeat. She takes a deep breath in a futile attempt to clear her head, which has begun to throb. She has errands, needs to finish them before she can move on. She made a list.

8

Need

HE CAN'T SLEEP, TOO GODDAMN COLD. NOT COLD IN THE HOUSE, NOT even cold out there with Jimbo's reefer plants and Gatsby's fruit trees. It's cold that's in him and hadn't ought to be, and that his moldy blanket can't do anything about. Cold curling through him, through the whole damn room, like some weird, twisting, dry-ice smoke.

Here, Dog. Don't stand there and stare at me with those sad-mama eyes. Come lie down beside me, warm me up so I can get some sleep.

Okay, fuck you, don't then. Get on outside.

He gives the dog a good non-contact kick, then lights a joint, cups both hands around it, draws the ash-end to bright yellow. Even that won't warm him.

He could read something if he had a lantern; candle won't give light enough. Start the next book on the shelf. Jimbo was a reader. Taught Danny what it meant to be one. Jimbo lived in town, in a house full of books. Books he loaned to Danny. Because Danny had taught Jimbo how to beat up anyone that picked on him. One good turn deserved another. Danny and Jimbo—they played Robinson Crusoe, Natty Bumppo, Jason and the Golden Fleece, Tarzan. Later, he was Sal Paradise to Jimbo's Dean Moriarty—in high school, in college. In the war. But by then they weren't playing, that was who they were. Danny and Jimbo. Friends for life.

Yeah, well.

Eastern sky's showing a thin line of morning light. A hair more and he can climb down to the cabin, watch her walk out to the privy, come back and eat her breakfast on the porch, feet tucked under her long red coat, whatever. He's never been by her this early, doesn't know her morning ways. Yeah, something different, that'll do the trick. Watch her stoned out of his mind, let the sun come up and warm his bones.

He pinches out the joint and drops it in his shirt pocket, ties his boot laces together, drapes the boots around his neck and scrambles down the mountain. Barefoot, quiet, grabbing onto saplings, sliding over rocks. *Just like with the she-bear, it's just 'cause she's there.*

He's later than he means to be; the brassy sun's already showing through the trees along the ridgeline. He sets up watch high in the rocks, but as he stares down at the pitched roof of the little cabin, that cold inside him gathers strength. She must still be sleeping—sick people sleep a lot. He tests the wind, fires up the half-smoked joint. Time to wake up, bitch, Dead Lady, Dead Lady Ashley.

But there's nothing. Nothing when the sun silvers her window-panes, nothing when the jays swoop down raucous and hungry. No privy trip, no chimney smoke, no breakfast on the porch. The cabin's emptiness rolls into him. Where the hell is she? Where the hell can she go?

Then it hits, tears out of him a wolfish howl his hands over his mouth can't stop. The Dead Lady can go anywhere she goddamn wants. She's got a car.

A goddamn, fucking car.

He runs along the trail with no thought now for silence or for cover, snuffs out the joint on the move. Looks for her car so hard, that spot of yellow with its ass end backed into the laurel, he runs past where it ought to be. Gets halfway to the highway before he knows it's really gone. Then he's shaking so hard he has to sit down in the middle of the road.

She hiked out to her little yellow car and drove away. Left him, just like that.

Weird how he'd quit thinking she might do it. Quit thinking about her dying, even. Like she was going to be right there in her little cabin for the whole rest of his life. He takes the roach out of his shirt pocket, cups his hands and lights it one last time, sucks frantically. A red ash falls into his beard. He swipes at it in a panic—burning hair smells like a lot of shit from over there. Worries a thorn in his big toe with a thumbnail. Fuck. The roach has burned a blister on his lip. Her gone, it'll be just like before. Endless string of days stretched out ahead of him, each one no different from the rest.

He grinds out the last of the jay on a rock, scatters it on the ground. He is a ghost, is Danny. Leaves no sign. Stands up, the thorn still in his toe, and sets out running back the way he came. Just like with the fox cub, just like with the she-bear, just like with the panther, squirrel, blue jay, fat-ass woodpecker bigger than a goddamn hawk. Except this time she isn't there.

He got used to it, is all. Used to his mind's eye seeing her inside the Old Man's cabin, cooking her little meals, eating them at Danny's picnic table, sitting on the extra bench he made just like he knew she was coming, knew she was already on her way, just like some kind of prophecy. Bench for him, bench for her. Surely she won't leave him.

Daisy did. Left that Gatsby fucker flat. Him and his whole house full of goddamn shirts, yard full of people, vault somewhere full of money, too, most likely. Bitch just up and split. Who's to say this one here hasn't done the same?

Got to know. Got to know *right now.*

He skitters, wolfish, to the cabin, hiding first behind the pointed rock, then behind the two-trunk chestnut oak, then flat on his belly in a dry wash. Finally, the heart-pounding run across the clearing at a place where she can't see.

Presses his hot face against the mortar chink in the cold stones beside her bed and listens. Nothing. No Dead Lady breathing. No Dead Lady feet pad-padding through the house. No sound of any Dead Lady at the table, clinking her spoon against her bowl, setting down her cup. No sound. Safe to go in, take a look-see. Find out where the hell she's gone. But first, one major, unavoidable precaution—reefer stinks up your clothes. He sheds his shirt and pants, kicks them beneath the porch, stands naked in the dappled light. Climbs onto the porch the Old Man made, but even this can't soothe him.

He gets past the shiny brass door lock with a few flicks from the sharp point of his trusty utility knife—"leave no mark"—shuts the door softly behind him, stands still, breathes deep.

He can smell her everywhere, same as if she was here beside him. The acrid odors she came in with that first day are gone. In their place are smells of air and sunshine, clean-scrubbed wood. Memaw's smells. He knows now the real reason he left his reefer clothes outside. Stays there a long time, eyes closed. Not till he's got her scent all through his blood does he open them, start moving through the house. "Fuck you to hell, Dead Lady." He presses his thumb and forefinger in the wet corners of his eyes. He is Odysseus, Natty Bumppo, Jake Barnes. He is *in control.*

The midmorning sun shows everything inside the cabin. The Dead Lady left a lot of shit behind. Tin plate and cup on the table, book about weeds, one of those little notebooks secretaries use. Shirt and jeans folded just so on a shelf. Everything so neat and orderly his heart hurts from it. Sleeping bag unrolled in its corner, something, a nightgown, folded, laying there on top. White with blue flowers no bigger than his pinkie nail. Its bright afterimage lingers.

Her pots and stuff take just one kitchen shelf. The rest are bare, except for two near-empty paper sacks. One holds half a handful of beans, the other about the same amount of rice. Enough for a day, maybe. Burnt-down coals in the firebox, but the nearest stove eye is still hot to touch. The warming oven holds a plate piled with cooked beans and rice, slices of some kind of deep-gold squash.

She's coming back! She left herself a meal!

"Bitch went to Elkmont to buy fucking food."

He flings his arms out, head back, grins wide at the ceiling.

Stops.

She might still be gone for good. Just up and left, like on a whim or something. Anyhow, she got away without him knowing. Can do it again, just hike out to her little pissant car, crank it up, take off. Someday soon she'll go for good. If not today, someday.

Or maybe not.

Back in the front room, he sits down at his table, picks up her little notebook. Her handwriting's hard to read, like it's some foreign language that's a lot like English. Name: Katherine Reid. "Ka-ther-ine." He says it out loud, sounds it out, the Dead Lady's name. Ka-ther-ine. All wrong for her. She wants a simple name. Rose, like his Memaw. Blanche, his mama's name. "Age: 38," same age his mama'd be. He presses the open notebook hard against his face. It smells of the cabin and the wood in his table. Smells, too, of her hands, her skin.

"Ka-ther-ine."

In the corner, a shaft of sunlight falls across her sleeping bag. He goes to it, his bare feet on the slate floor make no sound. Kneels on the canvas, picks up her nightgown, buries his face in it. Ka-ther-ine. Keeps hold of it, traces the throat of the sleeping bag with his right index finger, stops at the zipper, works it slowly down till there is room for someone, Danny, to slide in. He zips himself inside, then curls up like a baby, clutches her thin cotton nightgown close. Her clean-washed smell is all around him till he wants to fucking weep.

Get up, Danny. You can't feel anything for them. You're nothing but a ghost that watches. Go put your clothes back on. Get your ass out of here. Lay her fucking nightgown down and back away.

Before he leaves, he takes a small stone from his pocket. A white oval with one deep ochre vein that sometimes means there's gold nearby. He got it at the pond his first day in the Old Man's house, kept it. Now he pushes it gently into the ground beside the porch step, close to her but where she'll never find it. He has deliberately violated one more of the cardinal rules of watching: Leave nothing of yourself behind.

He laces his boots, sets out in a run, shocked back into what he has to do. Runs through the woods to where her car should be, then on. How could she leave and him not know? He knows how she fucking breathes, for Chrissake. Running along her tire tracks now, his head large as a pumpkin, aching how it used to when some shit exploded right above him in the air. Then there's nothing, not pain nor any sound except the wind, no thought but words that mark the cadence of his running. *Fuck you, dumb whore, fuck you.* And whatever things his eyes see do not register. His mind's gone to some other running long ago.

Him running home from his first day of school on chubby six-year-old legs, Memaw at the door. "Your mama's gone." Him, sure she's just walked into town, starts in running to catch up. Only, his Memaw ran faster, caught him, lifted him high in her old arms, his little legs still churning.

"She couldn't stand not being with your daddy." That was all she said.

He didn't cry, not even at the funeral. Because the coffin had its lid on and he didn't know it was his mama in there till days after.

Fuck you, dumb whore. Runs like an animal, not making any non-essential sounds.

Stops, finally, at the "Elkmont, pop. 4,017" sign to get his breath. Strolls along Main Street trying to look normal. Stares up at the sky, down at the street—he'll blow it if he meets somebody's eyes, they'll see him for the spook he is. Just walk around the courthouse square, past the gun-colored parking meters. And, yes, there it is, her dumbass little car. Yellow. The Golden Fleece.

He has to sit down on the nearest bench from how the Mustang's brightness slams into him, weakens him in the knees. Although finding it's no more than he expected. Yeah, expected. A world ahead of "hoped."

He stares into its window-glass reflections. Granite courthouse, too-blue sky, maples with buds swelling on their twigs, Danny himself sitting on the bench. Bitch's got no idea what he looks like. He can wait here in the open till she shows up and drives away. Rarely do you get to watch where they can see you. It's as much a luxury as good food or a clean, soft bed.

9

Lonely. Home.

THE SQUAT BRICK POST OFFICE SMELLS OF STAMP PADS AND STALE cigar smoke. A round-faced woman behind the counter looks her up and down as if she doesn't often see a stranger.

"May I help you?"

Katherine ponders each syllable individually, as though it were a perfect swirled-glass marble falling from the woman's mouth. They are the first words anyone has spoken to her since she walked into the forest.

"I need to rent a mailbox." She shapes her own syllables precisely.

The woman hands her an application and she completes it in a shaky hand. The clerk looks it over, checks her driver's license, and hands her a key. Katherine stares at it. P.O. Box 2609. She has an address now.

Even if she's never coming back, she'll need it. Everybody comes from somewhere and she'll need it to show where she's been. With the cracked ballpoint pen chained to the counter, she draws a line through the first item on her list. Her headache's growing worse.

The Elkmont National Bank's institutional blue-green walls and carpet, coupled with muffled voices that set off a roaring in her ears, make her feel as if she's under water, drowning. On the lapel of the teller's dark blue jacket is a small red enamel pin shaped like a drop of blood. A sign on her counter says she participated in the bank's annual blood drive. "I gave life. I gave blood." Katherine tries hard not to stare at the sign or at the blood drop. She is dizzy, feels unwell.

"I need to open a savings account."

Yes, even if she's leaving on this very day. Because the cashier's check clutched in her hand is all the money she has in the world and it is for a fairly large amount and she might lay it down somewhere and just forget it. She is capable of that. She meant to deposit it on the drive up and forgot. She will deposit the check here today and transfer the money when she gets down to Atlanta; that way she won't lose it. All this was clearer on the trail; now it's all jumbled.

Except that soon she'll climb back in her car and drive back to Atlanta, that much she is sure of.

Isn't she?

During the transaction she stares at the teller's nimble hands, her stubby fingers so like, and yet so different, from her own, these first hands that are not her hands that she has seen in weeks.

Her next stop, the grocery store, is old and dark, with cracked linoleum that stinks of Pine-Sol, rotting vegetables, and an unpleasant suggestion of dry-cleaning fluid from the laundry next door. Her list says *dried beans, rice, cabbages, winter squash, cornmeal.* Staples; they'll all travel well. At the last minute she grabs a can of salted peanuts for the trip. She'll tell them at the agency that California didn't suit her, something, couldn't stand the air. They'll hire her back, to do illustrations if for nothing else. While she waits for the garrulous woman in front of her to charge her week's worth of supplies, Katherine crosses "bank" and "grocery" off her list. She could just throw the thing away.

Except she took the time to make it, this list of tasks she needs to take care of. Because when its words are all crossed off she'll have completed all her business here and can go anywhere she wants. Because for now it comforts her to feel it in her pocket, clutch it in her hand.

At Nora's Dress Shoppe, which smells like artificial flowers might if artificial flowers had a scent, the white-haired saleslady addresses her as "dear" in a soft, musical voice that makes her want to stay, maybe ask if she can organize the clothes on the sale racks, which really don't need organizing. Maybe the saleslady will ask her to stay for lunch, join her at that round table with the two chairs in the back room behind the not-so-carefully-pulled curtain she can see from where she's standing. Katherine can talk with her and eat the food she brought. She is suddenly so tired of eating lunch alone.

But the white-haired saleslady does not ask her. And Katherine has other errands, needs to finish them.

The bookshop down the block is narrow, dark, and quiet, with a side room given over to a weaver's studio. Katherine peers at it through the open door.

"It's okay, go on in. Have a look around."

The proprietor, seated at a small desk near the rear of the store, presses his rimless glasses back up on his nose.

"It's my wife's. She's just gone out a minute."

Katherine nods, steps through the door, then stops. Going farther seems an intrusion akin to reading someone's exuberant, chaotic mind. The bright, sunny room is pleasantly in disarray and smells of nothing except wood and wool. In it, her dizziness subsides. Bins of yarns the colors of grasses, flowers, the dirt along the trail, are stacked halfway up the opposite wall. Taking almost all the floor space are three large looms on which a rug, a blanket, and something still too narrow to identify are coming into being. On the only wall lacking a door or window hangs a dramatic and unfinished woven rectangle suspended inside a giant square of hefty nails resembling a child's potholder loom made large. She walks over to it, studies it.

Her cabin has a large expanse of empty wall. But it's too late, she won't be living there.

City apartments have all kinds of empty walls. Have to—they back up against other apartments.

"Do you think she would sell me some yarn, your wife?"

She leaves with a dozen skeins stuffed in a paper bag with two jute handles, along with the gardening book she came for. Out on the street, dizzy again and queasy, she rummages a hand inside the shopping bag, tunnels her fingers through the wool and keeps them there.

At the hardware store she buys a sturdy hammer and two pounds of their largest, longest nails. Tenpenny nails, that's what they're called, she's told. Likes knowing it. The man with the Adam's apple isn't there, will never know how right he was a month ago when he implied she wouldn't stay. Screws, nails, a trowel, a lantern, candles, another door lock, seeds for tomatoes, lettuces, green beans, she brings them to the register. The seeds she'll plant in pots on a balcony, or in window boxes. The nails, the lock, the other things, they're good to have on hand. And now her list is finished, she's done all she set out to do. Now she can drive back to the city.

As she dumps her purchases onto the car's back seat, the trowel's sharp point jabs her palm. She blots the blood off with a corner of the red bandanna tied around her lunch, looks up to see a thin young man sprawled on the nearer of the courthouse benches staring at her. Stringy blond hair grown past his shoulders, camouflage jacket, jeans ripped across both knees. His visible boot sole has a hole in it. He smiles, flashes a peace sign she at first takes for a rabbit in a shadow play, and his eyes meet hers with such a fierce and inexplicable intensity her face grows hot. She does not walk over and sit down on the other bench to eat her lunch, as she had planned. Instead, she locks the car, hurries away.

The sun's high and the courthouse clock is chiming noon. The street has grown shimmery; she fights to keep her knees from buckling. A young man and woman, both in jeans and soft, well-worn twill shirts Katherine yearns to touch, come toward her from the opposite direction. Laughing, looking only in each other's faces, they nearly run into her then skip aside like fawns to let her pass. Katherine turns and sees them stop to look into the window of a little gallery, how they lean into each other, bodies perfectly aligned, with the fluid grace of something they've done many times. In Katherine's chest comes a quick pain, as if a thorn has tweaked some memory she can't recall.

Suddenly, she does not want the lunch she's brought. She wants something else entirely, something she can't imagine.

Perhaps simply to get out of the heat. Down the block, a neon sign
proclaims "Rexall Drugs and Luncheonette. It's cool inside." Inside it
is indeed cool. A cloying, custardy smell from years of people wiping
up spilled coffee and ice cream mingles with odors of perfumes and
medicines—all drugstores smell the same. She takes a seat at one of
the small fountain tables and immediately realizes she should not have
sat facing the plate glass window—sun deflecting off the parked cars
blinds her. A waitress in what looks too much like a nurse's uniform
comes toward her brandishing a menu.

It ought to feel so *normal,* stopping in a place like this, something
she's done since childhood. It's what she wanted from this place, to
feel normal and to cool off from the sun, that's why she came inside.
Only, it doesn't feel normal: Walls appear to slant toward her (all those
soda glasses lined up on the shelves), the floor seems to lurch beneath
her feet, and what's real is no longer anything to be depended on. She
shakes her head to clear it, but that does no good.

"Excuse me. Dizzy. Need some air."

She runs out and retches on the sidewalk like a drunk outside a
bar. Ashamed, she swipes a hand across her mouth and walks quickly,
guiltily, away. Someone will bring a bucket of water and a push broom,
scrub it off; the sidewalks of Elkmont are very clean. But that's scant
comfort.

The stringy-haired young man is gone. A part of her wishes him
back, in case she needs some sort of help. She can't stop shaking, can
barely unlock her car.

At a filling station just off the square, the gasoline fumes gag her.

"Wash yer windows? Check yer oil?"

"No time. Just fill it up. Got to get home."

Strange word, "home." Same long, mournful "o" as "lonely."
Lonely. Home. She circles the courthouse, drives past the Atlanta
road, does not notice this until she's heading back the way she came.
Got to get home *now.*

Mustn't, mustn't miss the turnoff. Peeling clapboard grocery.

Wicks? Wick's? Wickle's? "The Wickles Store" with no apostrophe. "Colonial is Good Bread," "Drink Coca-Cola."

She's back to dying, isn't she?

At the road's end she grabs one of the grocery sacks. She'll come back for the rest of it. Tomorrow. Sometime. Maybe. Forgot to buy more bullets for the gun.

On the trail she retches once again and feels better enough to fear the afternoon's long shadows, whatever makes the blue jays shriek, the peeper frogs go silent. Trees creak in the wind. She draws up her shoulders to hide the exposed back of her neck, its thin, vulnerable hairs.

Just after the sun has set, she climbs the single step onto the cabin porch. Inside, she sets down her grocery bag and, with an unsteady hand, lights last evening's half-burnt candle. This is not where she thought she would be this night, but it is where she came.

Lonely. Home.

She slides down to the floor and weeps into her hands, as the stubby candle gutters in the window.

10

Danny's Errand

DANNY IS GONE FROM THE FOREST PRETTY MUCH THE WHOLE NEXT day and night, doing what he has to do. Far beyond the hour when the wind blows cold through his thin jacket. First night—in how long he can't remember—that he hasn't stopped there by the cabin, hoping to eavesdrop on her dreams.

11

The Cart

TWO DAYS LATER, SHE HIKES BACK TO HER CAR TO GET THE REST OF
what she bought. It's muggy and overcast, a March day that belongs in
April, as quiet, moist, and warm as the day before it had been raucous
and cold. Shreds of drifting mist envelop her and wetness drips from
the trees, small, muffled plops in the hushed, comforting stillness.

The walk is easy. And a good thing, too; it'll take two trips to
bring back everything.

Getting sick in Elkmont was a one-time occurrence, had to be.
She caught a stomach virus. Or ate something the night before, some
poisonous weed nestled among the salad greens, a lesson to take more
care.

Or just to get the hell out, drive back to Atlanta like she'd planned.
Buy food in supermarkets, eat in nice restaurants, live like normal
people who aren't dying.

As she skirts a jutting rock she sees in her mind's eye for no apparent reason the iron pot on the cabin stove, recalls how old and alien she'd thought it that first day. For weeks after she came, her mind's projector showed her only city pictures: odd, ordinary scenes, most of which she could not remember having noticed when she lived there. The white stucco house with the crank-out windows she drove past going to the agency; the downtown alley where a small neon sign identified a shop that cleaned and blocked men's hats; the flat, wooden arms on her easy chair, wide enough to hold a coffee cup and saucer. A longing for the previously unremembered thing would squeeze her heart each time.

During those days, the skyline in her mind showed itself crisp and white as origami under a della Robbia blue sky; the agency became a sparkling carousel of a thing that spun in its own cloud of noise and cigarette smoke and excitement; and her home looked as it did when she had lived there, including all its furniture. Lately, though, deep sunset shadows hide most of the downtown buildings, when she thinks of them at all; she walks through a silent agency as unacknowledged as a wraith; and her home has been refurnished, its exterior indeed repainted Restoration blue.

Or else she sees the woodpile by the privy, the cast-iron pot. A change of scene.

The hike feels shorter even than two days before, a measurable indication of improving stamina, despite her setback in the town. She stops everywhere to look at everything—a startling patch of bright waving daffodils, a wild azalea with blooms orange as fire, the bleached and peaceful skeleton of a small rodent. Already she's reached the rock outcrop where far below she'll see the smudge of yellow that's her dear little car, its rear end backed into the laurel. But not today, today it's hidden in mist. She grabs on to a series of small saplings, scrambles down the bank. Her car is just the other side of that thick clump of rhododendron, she can see it now. Only, something's wrong. She stops, stares. The perspective's off. Her car looks too low to the ground.

"Oh, dear God."

Her shirt's gone damp with a cold, prickly sweat. She hugs her elbows, bends over out of fear she'll faint. Someone has shattered all her car's windows, headlights, taillights, beaten in the roof and all the doors until they look like crumpled sheets of paper. Both bumpers and all four tires are gone. Rims, hubcaps, everything. And the hood is up.

She runs to her poor yellow Mustang—its doors won't even open—thrusts her head in through the glassless window on the driver's side.

Inside, all the seats are slashed, the floor mats cut out. The door's ripped off the empty glove compartment and the radio is gone. There's nothing in the trunk; they took the jack. Under the hood are gaping holes; what's left is smashed, slashed, twisted, bashed in, broken.

A mourning dove coos far back in the quiet woods. The sound's incongruous peace unhinges her. She lowers herself onto the ground, leans her forehead against her wrecked car's left front door, pounds hard on the crumpled metal with both fists and screams.

Afterwards, she fishes her red bandanna from her shirt pocket, wipes her eyes and blows her nose, gets up. She will need to go back to Elkmont in another week, and the week after that, and the week after that. Because a week's worth of food is all she can stuff into her backpack, carry in her arms. She can't live here anymore. But where else can she go?

Standing quite still, hugging herself so tight she moves only her eyes, she studies the brown weeds around her ruined car. They're tamped down but they hold no footprints. There are no footprints anywhere but hers. She turns her upper body, twists her head, looks in a circle. Against the wide trunk of a chestnut oak something gleams silvery and incongruous. She forces herself to look at it and a fresh current of fear runs through her. It's a cart. Packed full, and large enough someone could crouch behind it. It's taller, leaner than a grocery cart. Narrow, with wire sides. There's no one hiding back of it, of course. They're gone.

But they left everything she bought behind.

For that's what fills the cart. Vegetables, yarns, bags of rice and beans, the lantern, trowel, hammer and long nails, even her sunglasses from the glove compartment.

Why would anyone do that?

She starts to shake as if from cold. Stripping the car is something she can understand; it's a crime, impersonal. But why remove all her belongings and leave them for her in a cart? Why didn't they just dump them? Or carry them off with everything else, eat the groceries, sell the hardware items? And why did they take the time to shatter her car's windows, bash its doors, slice through its upholstery? It's senseless. Crazy. Terrifying.

She should leave immediately, run as fast as she can into town and catch a bus back to Atlanta. That's the only sane, sensible thing to do. She knows this, and at the same time knows she will not go, knows she would not have gone even the other day. In this wilderness, and only here, she feels as if she isn't dying. Dares not carry this thought further. Dares not hope. And dares not go.

Still wary, she creeps up to the cart on tiptoe. There are no footprints here either, except now hers. She runs a hand over the vehicle's wire frame, yanks at its rubber-covered handle, pushes it a few feet along the rutted road, pulls it a few feet back. Perhaps she can push it all the way to Elkmont, pack it with food enough to last two weeks. Might even, with those rubber tires, get it back to the cabin.

The flat, gray sky has grown dark, threatening a storm and turning the air suddenly wintry and cool. Katherine throws her pack onto the cart, jerks it up the steep bank, and sets off pulling it along the trail at a terrified run.

The thing looks so new, not a dent or scratch.

And so useful. As if whoever stripped her car bought it especially for her.

12

Gun Love

SHE'S DIFFERENT NOW. ALL KEYED UP AND WATCHFUL. CARRIES HER little weapon everywhere she goes. On the alert. For Danny. The thought squeezes his insides in ways he never wants to stop.

Yeah, the gun makes it better. Makes it how he likes it, that's what it comes down to. Like that day, him just a little boy, tracking that panther up and down those ridges, wondering was that panther tracking him.

Just like with the panther, it's just 'cause she's there.

And, man, it's good. Him watching sometimes from his hidey-hole up in the rocks, sometimes crawling down to get in close. Her coming out into the early morning when the light's still soft and fine, tripping down the privy path toting that gun in her left hand. Silly bitch, she's right-handed. How's she going to kill him quick like that? And her so pretty anymore, it puts a smile right on his face.

He could sneak up behind her, put his arm around her, take the gun out of her left-hand fingers, gentle so she wouldn't be afraid. Put it in her other hand and show her how to hold it right. Times like this—hell, every time he thinks about him touching her—he has to hold his breath so she won't hear. His Dead Lady, Katherine, keeps him moving, that's for sure. Twists him all around.

Too bad it scared her so, him stripping her car like that. But he had to fix things so she couldn't drive away. Never wants to go through that again, her gone and him not knowing where or why. Or whether she's all right or ever coming back. And her new fear just keeps him sharp. One eye on her, one eye on the gun. No chance to tune out now. He's even cut back on the reefer. Doesn't want to leave her side to toke up.

Because that's what it's like now—him right there beside her all day, every day, then most of the night. He's put himself on short sleep rations. The before-dawn hours when he knows she won't wake, that's all he's allowed. He's rolled away his flea-bag mattress, taken to the floor, among his piled-up books. The pain of this hard bed wakes him in a couple hours, three at most. It's what he wants.

Because she needs him all the time now. Needs him to breathe with her throughout the night to calm her down. Needs him to stay by her throughout the day to be a witness to her fear. He's living in a frenzy now. Like over there.

It's him that's changed her, too. Broke the rules and made her scared, but there's times you need to. Got to keep your quarry in your view. In time she'll come around, leave her little gun inside the cabin once again.

And anyway, selling that shit off her car got him four hundred bucks. Told the junkyard dude the car'd been his ex-wife's. ("You know how that goes.") Son of a bitch knew he had old Danny by the short hairs. Still, you can do a lot with that much money. So much he hardly dares to think about it.

Well, look at that. She's put down her gun to split her kindling, balanced it on a tree root. Ought to make herself a holster for it. Wear it like Memaw wore her handbag, slung around her neck. Or just stuff it in her waistband, keep the barrel all snug and warm.

When she goes back inside the house, he thinks about her being there, the things she does that he can't see. Sometimes he'll pick just one, imagine himself with her while it's happening. Her stirring dinner in that big iron stew pot. Rabbit, deer meat, something he's killed and brought her. Her standing at the stove just like his mama did. Him watching there beside her like his mama's little Danny Boy. Her, his mama, asking if he wants to lick the spoon.

Later, them sitting opposite each other at the table sopping gravy off their plates with soft white bread. Him trapping her narrow foot between both of his. She's not his mama now.

13

On Foot

WHOEVER STRIPPED YOUR CAR WON'T COME BACK. No, THEY KNOW coming back's a very foolish thing to do. And anyway, they're not the sorts of people who go tramping through the woods. They're people who hang out in bars in seedy neighborhoods. Or at stock car races.

How, then, did they know where to find your car?

They didn't. They came upon it by accident. It was a crime of opportunity.

But why were they driving down a road that leads nowhere in the first place?

They took a wrong turn. They were lost.

Then why did they go to the trouble to buy a cart and unload all your stuff into it?

Because they have some sort of moral code, after all. It just doesn't include not stripping cars.

Maybe they thought the car was stolen and that someone had abandoned it, so whatever they chose to do to it was perfectly okay.

Maybe. Maybe so. .

It all churns in her head night and day, causes her to startle at familiar sounds, makes her more tired than she has been in weeks. She hates carrying the gun and still won't load it. If it were loaded she might well be afraid to pick it up, terrified of holding something in her hand that could end someone's life through one small, inadvertent movement on her part.

Banking on hard work to clear her mind, she builds three more raised beds inside the garden. In this way pass several sunny days she barely notices.

THEN SHE'S RUNNING HER hand over all the shelves in the dark recesses of the pie safe, looking for beans that might have spilled out of their sacks. There aren't any. Well, three. And not a thimbleful of rice. And there aren't dandelion greens along the privy path, garden path, or pond's edge either, as her irresponsible guidebooks more or less had promised. Too early. And too late to thin the fringy little garden plants and eat the excess, she's already done that. Hard not to eat the larger ones as well.

She must learn to keep up better with the rice, the beans. Should have bought more, more of everything, before somebody stripped her car. Should know by now to plan for change, loss, the unexpected. Fill the back seat, trunk, passenger seat with beans, rice, nails, seeds, candles, winter squash, cabbages, anything she might remotely need. You never know what's going to happen. Best plan for the worst right from the start.

She sits on a bench, her shoulders hunched, and stares at the cart parked by the door. She's pulled it, full, uphill over the trail, the roughest ground she'll need to cover. Good to know, but she has never walked to town. How far is it? How long will it take? Does she have strength enough to get there? More importantly, does she have strength enough to get both there and back?

Maybe it doesn't matter. As she sees it, she's got two choices. She can set out tomorrow before the sun rises and try to make it back before it sets, or she can stay here and starve. Six weeks ago she might simply have stayed and snuggled up next to the gun. Now, however, that does not look like a particularly useful option. In fact, it's an option she can scarcely comprehend.

She goes over to the cart, shakes it, bounces it lightly on the floor, bends down and checks its wheels, spins each, kicks one. Tomorrow's Saturday, country folk come to town and day-trippers from Atlanta. Strangers will see her pulling the cart along the highway. Strangers who might be the ones who stripped her car.

Enough. They took everything they could pry loose. Not likely they'll be coming back for more.

This evening she reads by candlelight in her *Weeds and Wildflowers* book until her eyes sting in the dimness. An oil lamp would be nice; she could buy one in town, wrap it in something so it can't get broken on the trail. She blows out her candle, listens to the tree frogs. Deafening as they are, after a while you cease to hear them. They're still singing, you're just used to them; a person can get used to lots of things after a while, no longer notice them. Maybe someday she'll get used to living so alone, used to feeling like she's being watched. In the small patch of sky visible out her front window, she can see Orion's Belt. Tomorrow ought to be fine weather.

IT'S BARELY LIGHT WHEN she starts out. Last thing, she slips the gun into the empty rice sack, lays it in the bottom of the cart. It'll frighten anyone she points it at, no matter that it isn't loaded. On the trail she is alert to danger, looks and listens to make sure she isn't being followed. Sniffs the air. Detects a flowering redbud, a grove of blossoming dogwoods, long before either one comes into view, lifts her chin with pride at this new skill.

Yet a different and troubling odor has begun to seep in underneath the wild, familiar scents, like an unpleasant thought that will not be repressed. It's oily and acrid, as if from a fire, except she can't see any smoke. As she nears the highway, the smell grows more pervasive, adds to itself a sickening sweetness that's a mockery of flowers; then something else, a fool's idea of cake. Up ahead's the little clapboard grocery, she can see it through the trees. What she smells is exhaust from cars, trucks out on the highway, perfumes and lotions worn by customers in the little store, cellophane-wrapped snack cakes. People.

The highway's asphalt surface sparkles, hurts her eyes and dizzies her. When a huge silver Oldsmobile streaks past blaring "I wanna hold your haaand," she springs aside in panic, nearly toppling the cart into a ditch. Soon as she can, she runs across the road and walks facing the traffic, a safety rule she knew until this moment just from books. Nonetheless, long before she gets to Elkmont her muscles ache from tensing every time a car speeds past.

The town coalesces gradually out of surrounding farms and woods, until suddenly there's the square, with its columned courthouse and its granite monument "To Our Confederate Dead." As she crosses the street the courthouse tower clock strikes nine. She's made good time.

Hardware store, post office, grocery, she rushes through her errands; she is not self-sufficient, never will be, a disappointment she'd rather not dwell on. She does not visit the bookstore or the clothing store and does not stop to eat the lunch she's brought. She is tired; her body has begun to hurt. She wants only to get back to the cabin, forgets once again even to glance down that part of the highway that leads out of Elkmont and into the wider world.

The hike back home is longer, hotter, dustier than the same distance had been in the early morning with an empty cart. She tries not to look at the shimmering road and does not stop to rest. When she turns off at the little clapboard store, the smell of cheap cake swells her throat. She jerks the cart behind a large red oak and retches on the ground, hikes the rest of the way panting and drenched in a cold sweat. At the cabin she heats a pan of water, strips off her clothes. With a new bar of Ivory soap she scrubs the residue of Elkmont from her skin, then washes her fake-flower-smelling garments.

When it's done she still feels disoriented, as if her true self has wandered far away.

14

In the Snow

THE NEXT MORNING THERE'S NO SUN. AT THE PRIVY SHE POKES AT
her belly; the old hurts are back. She has expected this. When she
stands the air is ice against her skin. Yet she doesn't move, stays still a
long time inside the small enclosure as if in a frozen trance. Throughout her illness there have always been strange, isolated days, peaceful
as the eyes of hurricanes, when she felt almost as good as anybody else.
The only difference this time, there were more of them.

Back at the cabin, she stays in bed and shivers until the pewter sky
begins to darken, gets up only to light a hearth fire. Moves her sleeping bag in front of it, then burrows deep inside, pretends her own
breathing is that of something else, until at last she sleeps.

But it's a ragged sleep, filled with shreds of dreams and memories.
Her father closing the apartment door behind him that last time so
carefully it didn't make a sound; her mother's fingers digging into both
her shoulders like claws, "Don't run after him." Later, in that same

too-hot afternoon, her mother's foot furiously rocking the sewing machine treadle, Katherine's new blue sundress taking shape too fast from pattern pieces on the floor.

Toward morning Katherine dreams the deer has come and she can see it lying in the snow outside her cabin wall, then wakes so cold even the sleeping bag can't warm her. The fire has died to embers, the moonlight turned to dawn light, but with that same eerie, blue-white glow. The wind that moaned last night shrieks now, bending the skinny trees like grass. It's snowing. Hard. In the third week of March. She slides out of her sleeping bag, steadies herself against a dizzying wash of nausea, stokes the fire. Crawls back inside her sleeping bag. She can pass this one day without going outside.

The rest of the day she shakes with chills and throws up periodically into a pot brought from the kitchen. Memories of Elkmont's odors rise into her throat. Outside, the wind screams like a live thing being torn in two. Finally, a thick, viscous sleep draws her into its red-edged darkness and she curls up like a baby.

She dreams she holds her baby as he turns to ice—Where had she been? Why was she not paying attention?—and wakes to find the hearth fire gone to ashes and the walls slicked with grease-colored light from the late afternoon. The room stinks and the gray-green cold is everywhere. She shivers violently, tries to sit up. A wavering darkness beats behind her eyes.

Yet she sees all she needs to. She is out of wood. Even the fire inside the kitchen stove has died.

You'll die, too, if you can't make it to the shed and bring back more.

Does it matter? Dying's what you came for; here's your grand chance. You don't need to raise a finger, death without culpability. Who knows what slender shred of time you might gain otherwise? Perhaps only hours. Perhaps only pain.

So, does it matter?

There's only one way to know.

Her clothes are near the door—her flannel shirt, jeans, boots, gardening gloves, her long red coat with its ridiculous fur trim. When she gets up to go to them, it sets the room to whirling. When she tries to put them on, their coldness steals her air. She throws her coat over her nightgown, steps into her boots, takes her backpack from its wall hook. The human body can perform amazing feats when summoned. A lone mother lifts a Volkswagen to rescue her trapped child—you read about these things. And she, Katherine, can open a door, make her way across a porch and out into the wind and snow so she won't freeze and die.

If you plunge your hand in boiling water, for that first split second it feels cold. Snow's the opposite: It burns. This snow drives at her mixed with hard sleet pellets that hiss and sting and stick to her gloves. The woodshed path is white, hidden, but it runs right of the chestnut oak.

Or does it?

Her feet sink into drifts that force her to step high to keep from falling. Inside her coat, her body is thin, hot metal. A sharp pain in her chest reverberates with every heartbeat. She is so small, to a bird high in the sky no more than a red berry. She is not healed; why should it matter if she gets where she is going? The bird always flies on.

But now, ahead of her, a faint patch of pale gray inside the swirling white. Please let it be the woodshed. It does matter if she gets there. It matters a great deal. One step, another, straight ahead.

Inside the lean-to's shelter, her stillness hurts her much more than the walking. How pleasant it would be to sit here on the ground and rest, but there's no time. Time only to pile the driest stovewood into her backpack, all it will hold. When she shoulders the pack, its weight slams her to her knees. To rise again takes all her strength—for such a little bit of wood, hardly a day's worth for the stove and nothing for the hearth. To stay warm she'll need to sleep in the kitchen, far from the deer's reassuring breath.

And if she sleeps somewhere distant from its breathing, she herself might cease to breathe. Who's to say that can't be true?

If she turns her coat into a sling, she can bring logs large enough for the fireplace. Her not wearing it won't make much difference— going back will take less time than getting here, she's left a trail. And anyway, the effort of carrying the wood will keep her warm; people don't freeze to death in five minutes. She strips off her coat, throws three heavy fireplace logs into it, draws its edges up around them. After the first few shocking seconds she no longer feels the cold.

Except in her feet, which hurt more than she could ever have imagined.

But the snow is falling harder, already filling in her footprints. She shoulders her backpack, drags her improvised tote with both hands and starts for the cabin, pushing hard against the wind. The wind pushes back. Peering ahead into the swirling snow is like staring into an endless maze of rooms, the forest rooms that beckoned her that first day. But unlike those woodsy rooms that let her walk on past, these snowy rooms are irresistible. She enters one and gauzy curtains close behind her, thicken into walls. The spaces these snowy walls enclose are small—alcoves, anterooms—but open into larger rooms beyond.

She's less conscious of her pain now; her whole body's growing numb. Everything's gone calm and dreamlike as she leans into the wind. When she topples into a drift, she sees no reason for alarm, lets go of her coat, watches its wood scatter, black against the snow, the unconscious artistry of it something to remember.

Smart to quit walking when she did. No point to it. She can rest in this small room until the weather clears. That's what it's for: a waiting room. Granules of snow collecting now inside the folds of her nightgown, as is their nature. She closes her eyes, at peace in her four walls, waits in this white room, this waiting room.

For what? Not for the snow to stop, she likes it here, her feet have even ceased to hurt. No, she waits for something that's supposed to happen, the reason why she's here. She waits for Michael to come bringing her child, carrying it in his arms. Hers and Tim's child, which should have been hers and Michael's. Let the dead carry the dead, isn't that the way it goes? She has vomited up everything inside her that is sickness. Now she is pure enough to go to Michael, pure enough to hold her son. In this white waiting room, snow swirling all around them.

"Get up."

Her numb heart lurches. "Michael?" Spoken so soft he'll never hear.

"Get up, lady. Get up."

Snow sifts into her hair.

"Ka-ther-ine, get up. Go home."

He's said her name. Michael is in the adjoining room, she sees his shadow. Yet he makes no move to come to her. And he has not brought their son.

Clumsily, slowly, she gathers the spilled wood back into her coat, ties up its corners, pushes her hands deep in the drifted snow and tries to rise. Stands at last with a cry of pain that shatters all the snow-white rooms. Cries out again with every step, until she drops the coat and all its hearth wood, closes her hand around the porch rail of the cabin.

Later, this will be the last thing she remembers.

15

Danny's Long Dream

TOUCHING HER, EVEN A LITTLE, IS THE MOST DANGEROUS THING HE can do. If he does it, even just to pick her up out here and carry her inside so she won't freeze, he breaks his number one commandment. If he breaks his own commandment, he will go to his own hell. A whole goddamn hell just for him.

Well, shit, what's he supposed to do? Leave her here to die not ten feet from her door? If she dies that's the end of watching her. And all he's done to keep her here won't go for shit.

There's just one answer: He will operate under *new rules*. Special rules just for today. Because today is an *extenuating circumstance*. By these rules he still can't touch her. Not really, not her bare skin. And that includes her face and hands. Even her hair that falls by accident over his wrist when he carries her inside and lays her down. He shrinks from it, shakes his hand free.

He probably *should* touch her. Take off her wet clothes so she won't catch pneumonia. Zip her in her sleeping bag so she'll stay warm. As it is, all he can do is go out for more wood and build a huge and everlasting kitchen-stove fire, drag her sleeping bag beside it, pick her up off the front-room floor and dump her in there on her side so her wet clothes'll dry.

The cotton of her gown feels soft and velvety, like the outside parts of his own ear.

She's shivering from the cold, passed out and frowning. He spreads the damp coat over her, the only cover he can find. Empties out the pot she puked in.

Get out, Danny, before the dumb bitch comes awake.

And yet he stands a long time in the kitchen doorway, looking at her and at everything around her. Thinking how nights she'll cook herself a meal in that big cast-iron stove pot, eat it off that pewter plate there on the shelf. Eat sitting at his picnic table. He backs out into the front room, sits on the only bench he comes to. Stares across the room at the other bench, turned upside down under a window, full of dirt with green shoots coming out of it. Wonders what it means and why she did it—the Dead Lady's full of mysteries. On the table there's a burned-down stub of candle in a little metal holder, that book about weeds. His mind's eye sees her sitting on that other bench, across from him, her head bent over the weed book, reading by the candle's light. Her dark hair parts at the back of her neck, falls forward past her shoulders.

It's not like the Dead Lady, Katherine, turns him on or anything—she's the same age as his mother. It's just, he's gotten used to watching her. It's just, the day before she drove to Elkmont she squatted on the ground, clawed through the dead leaves and pulled up everything green. Violets and creasy, curled-up ferns, all the little spring things. Stuffed them in her mouth with both hands like a goddamn vole. How hungry do you have to be to gobble that shit down like that? It sent a shiver through him that he'd seen her do it. He liked it, seeing her like that, is all.

Sometimes over there, when he'd been stoned and watching some gook days on end, when he'd been waiting to do whatever he'd been sent to do, he'd get to feeling the gook knew the score. Like it was all some dance, them moving to the same rhythm like lovers in some black-light jungle disco-hole. When he threw a stone into a patch of creasy that day and she turned toward the sound like he intended— went for the creasy without wondering, much less knowing, why—in that moment that's the way it felt with her. Just like with the gook.

Get out, Danny. Get out while you still can.

Outside, he rubs his tracks out with a pine bough, starts up the mountain. Keeps turning around, looking back, until her cabin disappears inside the falling snow.

BY THE TIME HE gets to Gatsby's house, snow's mounded on his fruit trees, on what's left of his driveway, on his slate-floor porch with its marble columns. Snow has sifted into his grand entrance hall and through the broken window in the library where he sleeps.

Dog meets him at the front door, paces, maybe wants something to eat. Danny digs in his pockets, pulls out a Slim Jim.

"Here, you sad-eyed bitch. This was supposed to be my supper."

She eats it noisily, barks once when she's through.

"Nah, you're not getting any more. That's it. It for me, too."

He peels off his wet jacket, canvas pants, flops back onto the mildewed mattress. Dog curls up on the floor. Danny's right wrist still tingles where the Dead Lady's, Katherine's, hair fell over it. He rubs it with his palm.

"If you're going to San Francisco, be sure to wear some flowers in your hair."

"Try to set the night on fiiiii-errr."

The hippie girl's blond hair splayed out over the California rocks, daisies crushed beside her ear. He hadn't even come. Wound his hands all through her hair, so long and silky like Janelle's, thinking that would make it happen. Because it was supposed to happen. Because it was his first time. Because he had waited, his whole time over there. Then there comes the part he can't remember. Only afterwards, crouched, determining which way to run, did he see the other couples there among the rocks and trees, sliding over each other's bodies in what passed for love. He ran then, so fast no one looked up.

On the Greyhound, he stashed his rucksack in the seat beside him, squeezed his hands around his elbows so his trembling wouldn't show. At some jerkwater town in Arizona, a Mexican woman tried to get on without paying. He pressed his ticket into her damp palm and walked away. Took him three months in a rusted-out trailer, howling into the hot desert sky, before he got back on a bus again and headed east and did the only thing he could do. Gatsby's house, just like the cabin, stood right where Jimbo'd told him.

He pulls a ratty blanket over him up to his neck and his hands remember the soft feel of the Dead Lady's clothing.

In three years going with Janelle they'd never done it. "The Golden Couple," every high school has one. People he went to school with actually called them that. Danny and Janelle. Janelle and Danny. They weren't supposed to do it, were expected not to. Good kings and queens live up to expectations, so they didn't. Time for that when they got married. It's what kept him sane out in the fucking jungle, thinking how he would come back a hero, spread out his medals for her on a velvet cloth. That, and the reefer that hollowed out a room inside his head where he could shut the door.

And his all-day fantasies that kept him safe from dying.

Because he'd never heard of any man in all recorded history to fetch up dead on any battlefield, his cold hand squeezed around his dick.

Danny's hands slide down his belly, along its centerline of soft, pale hair. Over there, the point of his every daylong dream was just to take it slow and keep it going, that's how it saved you. It had just one rule: You have to start from where you are. And whether it's some dung-heap jungle village or it's Gatsby's burnt-out mansion, that same rule still applies.

Over there, his every long dream started with him crawling through the jungle back to camp. Then the usual Army bullshit, discharge papers, and at last the Huey rising out of its own dust like some huge, glorious bird that had swallowed Danny whole, and the killing and the dying turned to silent smoke puffs on the ground. In the beginning, lots of times he shot off there. He couldn't help it.

Later, in Saigon, he'd meet a woman, strike up a conversation, buy her steamed fish in a French restaurant. Buy her coconut ice cream that she'd let melt on her tongue, slide out the corners of her mouth till he was forced to look away to where her heart pulsed in her wrist—you got to get the details down, that's how you stretch a long dream out and make it last. He left her on a bench beside a busy street to catch his plane. And him still safe, still saving himself for Janelle.

In his long dreams over there, it was always night when the plane they put him on crossed the Pacific, and he slept deep, drowning, stateside sleep there in his seat, lulled by the engine's hum. The high school girl sleeping beside him sighed when his arm brushed against her coat. When the plane landed in San Francisco, he got off and kissed the tarmac. Sometimes that's when he came.

He used to spend sweet long-dream time in San Francisco, a mistake. Should just have let himself catch the Greyhound right away, then maybe the thing in the park would not have happened. Should just have let himself drink in all America outside his window—desert, grasslands, delta floodplain. He always slowed the bus down when it got to where the ground grew trees and where blue mountains, his mountains, rose up like mist on the horizon. Sometimes a song from Memaw's church came to him then. *"With arms wide open, He'll pardon you. It is no secret what God can do."* He believed it, every word. When finally he let the bus pull into his hometown, sometimes real tears rolled down his face there in the jungle. Other times, he shot his wad from no more than the cosmic thrill of seeing everything that he remembered.

When you start a long dream from Danny's burnt-out mansion, there's not nearly so far to go. But if you walk it takes the same amount of time. You notice everything. A farmhouse woman in her side yard hanging clothes out on a rope line tied between two sweet gum trees. A tractor rusting in the damp shade of a willow grove. A fast-running creek where water sings inside a hollow stone. Nights, you curl up on the warm ground. Once or twice you stop to eat the bread and cheese you carry in your pockets or an apple off somebody's tree. One day you fall in step with a redheaded girl Janelle's same age, but all you give her when you part ways at a crossroads is a closed-mouth kiss.

It all takes you to the same place, no matter where you start. Walking from Gatsby's house, you cross a railroad bridge and you're on the outskirts of the town. When you used to start from Nam and took the bus in San Francisco, it let you off just one block farther on.

It's always early morning when you get there, the sun's first rays warming the downtown's squat brick buildings. Everything smells fresh. You're the only person on the street, no cars. And it's so unearthly still you can't hear your own footsteps. The granite office building across from the courthouse has its upstairs windows labeled "Bobby Brownlee, DDS" and "Matthew Hingle, Accounting." Downstairs, on the tall window with the green shutters, the one that looks out on the square, gold script letters edged in black read "Daniel J. MacLean, Attorney at Law." Inside, there's a Chinese rug, brass lamps. Good furniture, like at Jimbo's dad's office that time he sewed up your cut foot. All of which is very weird, because you joined the Army after freshman year and never once got near a law school. But that doesn't matter. Nothing matters in a long dream except holding on.

So you walk on by, because you're getting close now. Almost to where the houses start. Mimms, Beasleys, Rowans, brick houses set on good granite foundations, shaded by magnificent old oaks. You pass through a strip of woods you don't remember. Thick woods, on both sides of the road. Then you round a curve and there it is. A big house, two stories, white and frilly as a wedding cake, with a wide porch and a cupola like Janelle always dreamed of. It sits back from the street behind a picket fence. And all the grass inside the fence is green and purple flowers edge the walk and nothing there can ever harm you.

You turn in at the little gate and you can hardly breathe for wanting all of it right then. But you got to slow it down, hold on—this is the best, the most important part. Up the walk, up the steps, across the porch boards painted shiny gray. You're trembling so hard your rucksack bangs against your legs and you can barely ring the bell.

Don't move. Whatever you do now, don't move.

Used to, in your daylong dreams, footsteps echoed down the hall. Then the door opened, and you caught a flash of Janelle's gold-blond hair inside the hall's cool darkness. You reached out to take her hand, so you could lead her down the hall and up the stairs. To the bedroom, your bedroom. Your own brass bed you slept in with your mama when you were a little boy and your daddy was gone off to fight the war.

You never made it. Convulsed there on the porch before you even touched her. Every goddamn time. Bit your lower lip to keep from crying out. And then the sun was going down and you'd got nothing left to give her, but you'd kept yourself alive another day. Because there never once was any death inside a daylong dream.

Till he got Janelle's fucking Dear John about how she'd got engaged to someone else. After that, nothing worked right anymore. No one opened the door and Danny just stood there on the porch, his dick in his hand and nothing happening, real tears running down his stupid face.

He kept on trying for a couple months, then gave it up. Because there wasn't any point to it, it was like something inside him had quit paying attention. He got scared then, decided maybe he was nothing but a ghost and didn't know it. That maybe that's the way you tell, your dick gets hard and nothing happens. That's when he knew for sure his number had come up and he was going to die. The men knew, too, wouldn't go near him, left him to move day and night inside his own cleared space. All except Jimbo.

Then one bright blue-sky October morning Jimbo got blown up not ten feet from him. A smear of pink brain froth on Danny's forehead pointed him out sure as any finger: That hit was meant for you.

He screamed for seven days, then tried to shoot his trigger finger off. The Army sent him to a hospital. After that they sent him home.

But the long dream didn't work there either. Not in the desert, not in the Old Man's cabin, not here on his moldy bed in Gatsby's house.

It doesn't work again tonight, but the end is different—the door opens. He doesn't see Janelle's blond hair, but the hallway isn't empty. There's something in there, he can hear it breathing close enough to touch.

Maybe just another ghost like him.

Or maybe not—his right wrist tingles underneath the covers. From where whatever-it-was brushed against him in the dark.

16

The Ones Who Went West

SHE IS ALIVE IN A WARM ROOM, AMID SOUNDS OF DRIPPING WATER. The kitchen sparkles with the bright, wet light of sun on melting snow.

She does not remember how she got here, only the heaviness of the wood she carried through the blizzard's white-walled rooms. And Michael commanding her to get up, go home. And so she must have, and with strength enough to build a fire inside the stove and sense enough to lie beside it. There, though, her resourcefulness seems to have deserted her. She is still in her wet nightgown and her boots, and huddled under her damp coat. But it was enough, what she did. She can save her own life, take care of herself. Alone.

Her starving eyes devour everything in sight. The twined bas-relief tulips on the stove's firebox door, the dull sheen of pewter plates against whitewashed walls, the floor's earth-colored slate. She is alive in the midst of beauty. How could anything be wrong?

Yet something is. She pokes with stiff, exploratory fingers at her throat, chest, stomach. Nothing. It's as if she has gone numb. A pure, clean terror seizes her. Has she had a stroke? Have parts of her—organs, appendages—frozen from exposure? Did she die out in the snow? She moves her right arm, right leg, turns her face to the right, repeats it all on her left side. Everything still moves. And she can feel the damp sleeping-bag canvas balled up under her, its zipper tongue gouging her thigh—not a characteristic one associates with afterlives. Yet something is absent. Something that used to fill every empty space inside her—spaces between joints, in and around organs, seemingly even inside cells—as recently as yesterday.

Pain.

For this one minute all her pain has ceased.

Don't move, don't breathe. And whatever else you do, don't weep. It's just one moment out of your life's sum total of moments, one vagary in the countless vagaries of your condition. You are not healed, don't think it; name one thing you wished for from this illness that came true.

She lies motionless until her muscles cramp, yet her familiar hurts do not return. Not when she stands, nor when she walks across the kitchen floor so solid beneath her feet. All the air smells moist and new. She bends down to pull on her boots and when she raises up she is not dizzy; when she hikes out and uses the privy, no hot pain lashes through her; when she stoops to pick up firewood, nothing clenches in her lower back.

Walking as if on eggshells to preserve this wondrous state, she lays a new fire in the stove, takes giddy pleasure in small, silly things. The shape of the iron kettle, the growing weight of a tin cup filling with water. The sound of her warm blood coursing through her veins when she sits still and listens.

In the warming oven is a mix of beans and rice left from before she went to town. It's hard and dry, and she eats every bite while she heats water for a bath. Afterwards, clean, rubbed dry with a rough towel, every inch of her tingles as if she's a snake that has just shed its skin.

And she is still hungry.

*   *   *

THE SNOW MELTS IN one day and it is truly spring. Seeds sprout in the garden like an edging of green lace, the soil smells rich, and earthworms wriggle everywhere.

She has gone six days without dizziness or pain, alive with an energy and attentiveness akin to some strange state of grace. She seems to have lost need of irony, of looking askance, standing aside. Spends time instead absorbed in the small things of the moment, contained by them. Her days have narrowed to activities she counts on the fingers of one hand, yet within each is infinite variety. She rises when it is still dark, stokes the stove, makes tea, then sits at her front window watching for the first hint of new day, awaits it leaning forward like an acolyte at prayers. Yesterday she held a small branch in her hand, studied it for what must have been an hour.

In her notebook she still keeps a written record of her days, but for their mystery and beauty, not because she needs its prompting to remember:

> *Wednesday: Thinned carrots,*
> *found two quills from a blue jay.*
> *At night, gentle rain.*

Entries spare as haikus. Nights, she sleeps inside the deer's soft, even breathing, but she never writes of this and she does not know why.

She loves the clear, fresh mornings in the garden, where there's always a surprise. Lately, among the weeds, a patch of spindly, dry tendrils with a nostalgic fragrance has turned out to be mint. She moved some to a cracked pot she found back of the woodshed and placed it in her south-facing window, so she can drink mint tea. This afternoon she pounded all the long nails from the hardware store into the heart-pine wall that separates the front room from the kitchen. They form the outline of a square, and now she has a loom.

So quickly, so hungrily, she is coming to believe in her new situation, to accept it. Not as health, not yet, but as a feeling of well-being, something that someday she might take for granted, build upon. A thing even now far beyond what health once had seemed.

And she wonders: What did happen to the ones who went west in the covered wagons, signed on to the ships that sailed around the Horn, or found some other change of scene and were not heard from?

This?

17

Awakening

FOR THE FIRST TIME SINCE SHE GOT HERE, SHE FEELS SAFE, EVEN IN the afternoons, a phenomenon she can't adequately explain. Nonetheless, she hasn't lost the sense that something watches her, her one symptom that didn't disappear with all the rest. That's why, though she can't bear to load it, she still keeps the gun with her. The gun is hideous; it intrudes on all her thoughts. She stuffs it behind a rock when she works in the garden, so the tender plants won't sense its threat. Today, to wean herself away from it, she leaves it on her porch. If whoever stripped her car has not shown up by now, he likely isn't going to. And if she were being watched by something out to do her harm, by now it surely would have harmed her, or have tried.

Perhaps her fear has lessened due to what she tentatively considers her recovery. Or perhaps because her days are full. Lately, after twice seeing a brown rabbit scamper back into the woods, much of her garden time has gone into repairing the old fence. All its cedar posts are solid in the ground, but much of its barbed wire has rusted through. The pliers she bought are barely adequate to cut and twist new wire from the coil out by the woodpile. And even as she mends one break she spies two new ones someplace else. The work causes her wrists and fingers to both ache and grow strong.

She has already thinned the earliest seedlings. The tiny plants, all of them, tasted of her joy at being alive and eating food she's grown. She gardens with her sleeves rolled up to feel the soft breeze on her arms. Writes in her notebook:

> *May fifth: Salad greens!*
> *The cabin smells of sunshine.*
> *Started a large weaving, "In the Garden."*

In the same way her life here is now woven into everything around her, she weaves the fabric of her days onto her loom. A storm cloud boiling over Panther Mountain, a silver fish sliding through the pond's dark water, the wild green growing things thrusting out of the ground around her, all show up as dark, ragged wools, delicate silk threads, dried weeds and grasses that pull her life together and interpret it. With no shuttle it's slow work winding each strand through the warp with her fingers, yet it compels her. Some days it seems that every breath she draws gets woven, and that the thing taking shape between the square of nails gives no more than the crudest hint of all it stands for.

Wild animals come near the cabin now. One morning she surprised a raccoon sleeping underneath the porch; several times she's seen an opossum slink out from the woodpile by the privy; she's started leaving little bits of beans and rice for a red squirrel who comes begging. And, yes, there are deer. More than once outside her window she has glimpsed a doe standing at tree line, a doe that leaves her tracks. At the pond one afternoon, a buck with antlers so magnificent he seemed unbalanced by them stared at her from across the water for a full minute before stepping away as if he had behind him an entire retinue. And once at dusk a bear lumbered purposefully past her porch on its way to someplace else.

Her first weeks here, she talked out loud a lot and in her arrogance said words to birds, animals, even insects, as if she expected them to understand. Then in those first days following the snow she spoke no sounds at all, an exquisite, encapsulated time in which she listened fiercely to the forest, a time that humbled her and cleared a space for her to notice her surroundings in deeper ways than she had heretofore imagined. She knows now she misses ninety-eight percent of what goes on.

With her new sense of well-being, she dares venture farther from the cabin to forage for wild foods. And for the loom: Her once empty shelves are stocked with a prodigious array of weeds, feathers, vines, and grasses, in addition to the yarns she's bought; she sees everything in terms of texture, dreams of intense, new, hairy yarns, strong silks, fine white sheep's wool dyed with summer flowers. And so today, as an experiment, she plans to hike someplace she's never gone. It's not a path, not really. No more than a suggestion of a gully cut by spring rains sliding over rocks and around trees. She's seen it often, this subtle ribbon twining up the side of Panther Mountain. When she thinks of it, excitement rises in her chest as if her heart stands at attention.

She ties her shirt at her waist, knots her hair at the nape of her neck, wriggles into her boots. It would have been easier, more useful, wiser, to have walked the perimeter of the pond. There's good eating on the other side—no end of cattails, maybe fennel or wild asparagus where the pond-marsh peters out among the trees. And all kinds of reeds and grasses. Nonetheless this climb is what she wants. Maybe she'll find a patch of fiddleheads and fill her backpack, but that's not the point. The point is the climb itself, that it's an adventure, not just a mosey on flat ground.

And that she wants it; she has not wanted an adventure for so long.

She runs at the start of it, up the first mild slope. But too soon the path grows slicker, steeper than it seemed. At the first turn she slips, slides backwards, clutches a maple sapling to break her fall, and thinks dark thoughts about the possibilities for injuries. This is a path to scratch and scrabble up on all fours, not a path for walking. Yet once she gets the hang of it, she has no trouble finding workable handholds and footholds among the rocks and roots. Invariably they are right where she needs them, as if some animal has come this way time and again.

The sun's grown warmer, almost hot. She stops under an overhanging rock, checks for snakes with a long stick, then crawls inside its shallow cave to catch her breath, cool off. Below stretches a panorama of the clearing: her stone cabin, the privy, the garden, the pond, the paths connecting them. Through the trees' new leaves, she can make out a small, shimmering sliver of the pond's surface and the jutting rock at shoreline. In winter she would see more. She imagines she can see a tiny Katherine moving through her outdoor chores, a Katherine she can hold in her warm palm.

A Katherine something might watch.

Dry leaves blown in by autumn winds carpet the ground beneath the overhang. Something has crushed them. Perhaps some animal sleeps here, perhaps her deer. From what she's read, there's not sufficient privacy for bears. If a bear had hibernated here, the place would reek of it, that overpowering wet-dog scent. Instead, it smells only of the earth, moldering leaves, and some faint, smoky sweetness she's unable to identify. Nonetheless, she feels herself a stranger here, uneasy.

She should turn around, go home, but it's too early. She planned this walk to fill a morning. So she continues up over the rocks, where it's impossible to look at anything except the next niche where her foot will fit, the next root or rock she must grab hold of. A breeze rustles the slender trees that grow above her. When she reaches them she'll feel it, catch it, let it cool her. But always by the time she gets there the breeze already has moved on. She climbs higher, but the breeze stays always just ahead.

She's panting now, arms and legs heavy from exertion; she really should turn back. Something clatters toward her from above. She looks up too quickly, causing the trees to slant at crazy angles in the too-bright sun. A stone nearly as big as her balled fist hurtles past her.

Something has dislodged it, some animal climbing ahead of her, hidden by trees. What sort of animal? She pulls herself upright with the aid of a skinny poplar growing between two boulders.

"Hello? Who's there? Is anybody there?"

She claps her hands—once, twice, three times—high in front of her to ward off bears. "Shoo, shoo. Go away now!"

Scrambles down the way she came, fast as she can, following the narrow gully past the overhang and down into the clearing. She stands on her porch, panting, gripping the gun and looking toward the path. Whatever thing was up there in the rocks above her has not followed.

She should have taken the gun, stupid not to. But not doing so was somehow part of the adventure. Anyway, her waving an empty revolver would have meant nothing to a bear. So it makes no difference, if she never loads it, whether the gun goes with her or goes back inside the cabin. She knows this now, but keeps the gun close for a few more days whenever she's outside. Eventually she leaves it in the cabin, and finally puts it back on the high shelf, where it belongs.

SHE GOES EARLIER OUTDOORS as the days lengthen, stays longer, wants to know this place as thoroughly as the wild animals that live here, to know what things mean. To this end, she pores over guidebooks; makes intricate notebook sketches of leaves, pods, fungi; glues on feathers, strips of bark. She no longer starts at every shadow. Many afternoons she sits an hour or more on her rock that juts over the pond, stares into the water, listens to her thoughts, which are now mostly of the cabin and the land around it. The porch and kitchen rafters are festooned with small, fragrant bundles of herbs hung up to dry. Last night she ate steamed cattail blossoms with brown rice and a chickweed salad, gourmet fare. The rare evenings she doesn't weave, she stays long at the table, maps where she has found things. In this way passes the gentlest month she has ever known.

And the most disturbing. New life sprouts everywhere. In the garden, in the woods, beside her porch rail. New leaves curl out of dead, fallen trees. Pods burst, filling the air with downy seeds, and the pond teems with tadpoles, water striders, and silvery fish. Birdsong fills the daytime air; wild animals cry out at night, wake her to lie there with the deer outside her wall.

On a spring day years ago she sat in her high school biology class, waves of heat flushing her face, while the teacher drew on a blackboard the reproductive cycle of the mosses. Primitive plants as sexual as people; even their parts looked embarrassingly the same. That wondrous thing she so often had imagined for herself with Michael was no different from what happened with the mosses—just as blind, just as imperative. These days she feels again that rush of heat.

Even before her baby came into the world so cold and still all her desire had fled. Now it's as if once again she has a seed inside her, a seed that's grown a tiny curled-up shoot that's pressing to get out as if her body were the dry and crusted earth. Its presence rules her thoughts, causes her to pick a fuzzy leaf from off a lamb's ear plant, rub it lightly against her cheek, the insides of her wrists.

Her whole body quiets around that insistent shoot. She stares into flowers, pulls off petals and caresses them between her thumb and forefinger. Nothing, not even silk, has so soft a texture. Some distance off the privy path a princess tree languidly drops its lavender trumpet blossoms. She picks one off the ground, thrusts her index finger into its long throat to taste the pollen, sticks a pair of them into her nostrils. Tusks.

Late one afternoon she lights a lantern in anticipation of the evening, hangs it from a brass hook on the porch, then makes her way down to the pond. She keeps a bar of soap there now, wedged under a rock. It's easier and more relaxing on warm afternoons to bathe there in the cool stillness than from a pan of water in the cabin. She parts the dense branches of the budding alders—and stands motionless, stunned. The air above the pond has turned into a swirl of iridescent spangles. Mayflies. So many they have dimmed the copper sun.

She's read how they survive for years as larvae in a pond and, as adults, live only a few hours, long enough to mate and die. They will die without once having eaten; the implication of it steals her breath.

Seated on her rock, she gazes at the hordes of tiny insects that swarm frantically, far as her eyes can see. Their ecstatic music is a high-pitched whine that fills the air. She turns her face up to them, whorls of mayflies spinning in the sky like Van Gogh's stars.

She cannot look away from them, can think of nothing else. What if one loops down to touch her? Will she feel it? Will it make a sound? She shucks off her clothes, balls them into a pillow, lies back on the sun-warmed stone. A light breeze plays over her body and she brushes her fingertips across her breasts in imitation of it. If a mayfly touched her there, what would she feel?

She stares upward, through the swirling insects, until the rock she's lying on appears to move, to slowly turn and rise into the sky. Her abdomen's soft as the underside of a new leaf. Her hand moves down and she was wrong to think no skin could be as delicate as flowers.

That new, green shoot inside her swells and pushes to escape, for it has grown so large. Overhead, the mayflies fling themselves into the air. What is in her shimmers, taut and exquisite, then bursts. She has pressed her fingers deep into the throats of flowers, and the sounds she makes are hideous and beautiful against the whirling sky.

Afterwards, she weeps from the newness of it. For it is not something come back as it once was, but something she has never known.

The mayflies circle black against the sunset's afterglow and the pond's water washes her skin cool. An owl hoots from the tall pines as she gathers up her clothes. The lantern on the cabin porch glows like a beacon in the twilight. Everything is a gift.

18

The Why of It

HE SAW.

It's all he can think about. Can't for one second put it from his thoughts.

Like right now. He's sanding the age-rough floor in his library-bedroom, running the block over it time and again. Take him months to finish, but if he can get just one room decent so people can live in it, maybe two, then he'll have something. And working on it makes him feel good, like he's the Old Man building his hickory cabinets or some such in his cabin. But even then she's in the forepart of his mind.

He's quit the reefer. Doesn't need it anymore, she gives him that much peace. And fire, a steady glow that's warmth he can depend on. Except sometimes when it feels like the whole forest blazes up inside him. Only, like Moses's burning bush, it never gets consumed. Just burns and burns and he lays on his bed and lets it.

Yeah. He lets it burn.

He picks up his hammer, pounds a finish nail into a loose board, on the diagonal, where the next board's groove will hide it. Feels the Old Man smiling down on him, carpenter to carpenter. Maybe Jack London built his "Wolf House" for his "mate woman." Yeah, Danny's burnt-out old house nobody wants to live in but the possums and the coons needs him to fix it up. His fruit trees need him if they're going to thrive. And her, she needs him most of all. In ways she doesn't even know about, ways no one's ever needed him before. Day after day he has to choose. He always chooses her.

He only goes to town when she does now. Won't leave off watching over her to go in stores. Sometimes he wishes he was like the Old Man, needing nothing but a cast-iron sink, wood stove, little bit of roof tin. No, he doesn't really wish that. Needing her's become too sweet a part of him.

He drives another nail into another floorboard, but it's one nail too many. The noise, vibration, mess with his head. After Jimbo died, Danny made a point to never plan for any kind of future. Homage to the dead, or maybe only superstition. Keeps his mind's door shut against it at all times. Never thinks about tomorrow, does what wants doing at the moment and that's it. Right now his floor needs fixing, that's all he needs to know. The why of it will come to him in time, if it's supposed to.

So will the why of her. And what he needs to do.

Summer

19

"*Please, Won't Somebody . . .*"

SOME GIFTS ARE WASTED IF THEY CAN'T BE SHARED.

Her food is running out, so she hikes to Elkmont once again, walks with perfect posture, as if pulled by her own heart, through a forest filled with beauty, signs, and wonders. But when the gravel road turns to blacktop and she sees the dingy clapboard of the Wickles Store, everything changes. The odors from the store and highway are so strong she ties her red bandanna, outlaw-style, over her nose and mouth to block them, removes it only when she gets to town. There she rushes through her errands, wanting only to be gone. On her way home she retches once again behind the oak tree past the little grocery, by now an unwanted ritual, then straightens up, her mind seized by the Rule of Three:

"Three strikes, you're out."

She's been to Elkmont three times now, and every time she's become ill. It's always the same. She feels well in the forest, sick when she ventures out among people. She grew ill in a city filled with people, got better once she left.

It can't be true. It's coincidence, and nothing else. How can anyone be made ill by proximity to people? It's perverse. As if she's been somehow singled out to serve as an example. Or is being punished for some grievous sin she's either unaware of or has yet to commit. Or perhaps there is only chaos and her number just came up for this one, could as easily come up again for something worse or better.

Back at the cabin she wanders aimlessly inside its rooms. If it's true, her conclusion, then that evening by the pond was only cruel. She had come to love the forest because she thought that someday she would leave it, but it's the forest and its isolation that sustain her. No longer merely what she chose, it's become a necessity. And that makes all the difference.

The trees, dense now with summer foliage, have so quickly turned into impenetrable rows of sentinels, separating her from every being but herself. Lest she miss the point, the animals no longer come around. The raccoon, the squirrel, the possum all have better things to do. Sometimes she hears them in the distance, their grunts, cries, groans. They so gloriously have each other. She has no one.

NONE OF US—NOT THEM, not she herself—is meant for solitude. We crave attachments. When we can't make them among live things we attach unnaturally to something else. And so she stands watch this night over a last burning nub of candle as if she were waiting by a sick friend's bedside for the end. The little flame wavers in the still air, winks out, and she cries inconsolably. Lately, it saddens her to see even wildflowers die; she no longer picks them for her table.

The next time she goes to town she behaves erratically. Although she knows now she must hurry before sickness overtakes her, she talks too long to shop clerks, stares too intently at everyone she passes on the street—at their amazing faces, hands, fingers, opposable thumbs. A swarthy man in a sweat-stained shirt and overalls stares back boldly and she doesn't look away, imagines he might follow her, reach out and touch her, so she might experience it for a moment, then remember: the touch of a man's hand.

Her loneliness sometimes approaches frenzy. Nights, she can't sleep for it, kins herself to the melancholy mockingbird outside her window, who throws his songs relentlessly into the darkness. Days, she makes an exhibition of herself for no one, rolls her hips for no more reason than it stanches for a while some nervousness inside her. When she stops, she's worse off than before. Please, won't somebody . . .

Won't somebody what?

There's no one.

DESIRE CAN BE A comfort to slide into, a warm bath that gently nudges you and rocks you. But when it quickens, it's a knife. Today, amid the garden's green profusion, a fury seizes her. She dashes across the meadow, rushes blindly at the massive chestnut oak, beats her fists on its hard trunk and screams. Stands crying soundlessly in its impersonal and dappled shade.

"Please, won't somebody . . ."

She whispers it into the forest's endless green chambers, is answered only by the still air.

In the cabin she takes the gun and all its bullets down from the high shelf. It's cold in her hand despite the summer heat. Sits on a bench and spins the chamber, peers down the barrel. Unties the bullets from their kerchief, hefts one of them in her hand, examines it. Is this the way one dies from loneliness?

She is unnatural, cursed, has merely traded one disease in for another.

She hurls the gun across the room.

20

Sin-Cleansed

IT'S JUNE, JULY, SOME MONTH HE CAN'T KEEP TRACK OF. THE GARDEN near midday. He loves to watch her in the heat. The way she moves now, looser in the hips. And something about her eyes, how large they are, and moist. The hot temperatures expose things she kept under guard in colder weather. There she is, wiping her damp hair off her forehead with the back of her hand. Impatient, like she's some little kid. Impatient for something—what?—to happen. If he was back in grammar school he'd let her be his girlfriend on the playground, stay by her through high school, let her wear his football jacket. Pick up some work, maybe do home repairs. Buy himself a car, take her out riding, to a movie. Afterwards to get a burger. Later to some dead-end road where they could park. With her around he'd never once have looked at old Janelle.

If he was back in college, she could be his teacher. Teach him about Gatsby and Daisy, Lady Brett Ashley. Joanna Burden and Joe

Christmas. Huck Finn. That Greek bitch with snakes for hair. Teach him other things as well. He'd take her out, even with her some older, spread a blanket by the river, watch the full moon in the water. Always they'd find some private place so nobody could see her, get her fired. Yeah, if she'd been his teacher he'd have never ended up in Nam. He'd still be in school, with one year left to graduation. There with her.

Hiking back up the mountain after being with her through the night, passing through his orchard in the dawn, he's struck again by how his peach trees need him. He's who relieves them of their burden of ripe fruits. Each fruit's a little rising sun, begging to get picked so its sweet gift won't go rotten on the ground. Mounds and mounds of peaches, so many more than he can ever eat. Dog won't eat them, even fed by Danny's hand. Who's to eat them?

Who?

NEXT MORNING, DANNY'S RUNNING flat out along the Elkmont highway. Him with far less beard and his hair cut best he could with a dull razor and a piece of shaving mirror. All the little birds and animals scattering to the four directions—Danny's coming. Him not knowing the why for any of it, only that he badly needs something in town, and needs it now.

He's not at all sure what, just that it has somehow to do with all the peaches on his trees, his burnt-out house's rotting books and partly sanded floor, the woman in the Old Man's cabin. Yeah, her most of all.

Pine needles crushed under his running feet smell like the woods in back of Memaw's house, and he feels good about the world and all that's in it. So good even glary, noonday Elkmont can't bring him down.

For he has willed it. Once upon a blue and waxing moon God lets him will such things.

At the edge of town, he puts on his boots, starts walking like he knows exactly where he's going, what he needs to do. In the hardware store he buys more finish nails, more sandpaper, a handsaw. But these aren't the reasons why he's here. Buys himself a pocketful of Slim Jims at the market. Cardboard box of cupcakes he eats sitting on the courthouse bench, wishing he was waiting for her, Katherine, to come get in her little car. But it's not food brought him here either. He can live on weeds and squirrels, summer fruits from Gatsby's orchard. No, food's not the thing he's after.

He dumps the empty cupcake box, takes another walk around the square, goes down the side streets, all of them, a second time, looks in all the windows. His last chance. Third time, folks start to notice you. He'll find out this time what he's come to do. Or else it stays the fuck undone and that's the way of it.

In the Rexall the newspaper headlines all scream "Vietnam"; he looks away. Buys himself a new razor, little pack of refill blades, big double bar of soap. Coming out, that's when he sees it. Right across the street. Next to some fancy restaurant, sharing the same rocking chairs on a narrow wooden porch. Little store with a classy three-side window, skinny little mullions like the Old Man might have made. "George Stockman and Sons," sign hanging from a porch beam by a brass link chain like for some lawyer's office—maybe Danny's own law office someday ought to have a three-side window, little wooden sign, porch with some rocking chairs.

He can't quit looking at it. Under the "George Stockman" part, in such little-bitty letters you need to climb up on the porch to read them, it says "Men's Clothiers Since 1926." Since before his own mama and daddy were even born or Memaw's hair turned white, this Stockman dude was selling clothes. He tries looking in the window but can't see past his own reflection, a smiling, sunlit Danny gazing at him from the other side.

A small bell above the door tinkles when he enters. Inside, it's cool and dark and quiet, smells of lemons. Lots of racks and shelves, all red cherry wood shiny as glass. Looks like right now he's the only person in the place. He could just as easily swipe something, run. But he doesn't need to, he's got money. And anyhow you don't swipe something from a place like this. You buy it.

He checks his hands, makes sure his fingernails are clean, starts flipping through the racks. Suits. Suits everywhere. Last suit he had was some dumb short-pants thing Memaw made him wear to church. Only place he's seen men wearing suits except in movies. Bought himself a sportcoat at the Goodwill when he got to college. Shit, maybe this is not the place he needs.

Nonetheless, George Stockman and Sons, Men's Clothiers, is some sight to see. He strolls up one aisle and down the next, pauses at. a stack of silly sweater vests like he knows what he's looking for but he's not finding it.

Whoa, wait just a minute. There's stuff here on the back wall. Jeans, shirts, boots. Pair of leather mocs that fit his feet like they were made for him. And what's this here? Some kind of weird shit nobody'd buy but gooks. Gook suits. Loose pants you tie up at the waist, long shirts that flap around your ass. All made out of cotton soft as peach skins. Yeah, here's what he's come to town for. Shirts, jeans, new boots, that pair of mocs. And, yeah, that gook shit, comes in black, white, khaki.

That's what he needs. The white one.

"Young man, can I help you?"

Old guy sneaked up so quiet on the carpet Danny jumps. Sneaked up on old Danny, not many can do that. White hair, thick white moustache, voice like he's talking on the radio. Old George Stockman himself.

"I want to buy this stuff."

Old guy eyes him up and down. Just that. Not like he's scared of him or anything. More like he's eyeballing his shirt size, inseam. "You'll want to try it on." Waves him toward a couple doors in the wall to his right. "To make sure the sizes fit."

Danny nods, goes. Needs to do this right. The old guy yanks open a door, ushers him into a little room with a big mirror, shuts him in. Little rooms freak Danny out. Mirrors too. He pulls on the pair of jeans, buttons the fly, throws on a shirt. Opens the door with a shaking hand.

"Yeah, they're fine. How much I owe you?"

At the register, the old guy pushes aside Danny's filthy camouflage and torn-up army boots. "Want to just leave these here?"

Danny takes a long breath, lets it out slow, casual-like. "Naw, I'll just keep hold of 'em. Never know what you might need."

He counts out upwards of ninety dollars, leaves the store. Yeah.

Good to be outside, take off his new boots, head for home. He's got what he came for.

BACK UP THE MOUNTAIN, he stops at his rock overhang for one quick glance down at the cabin. Then in Gatsby's house that smells now of new sawdust along with the old, sour fire smoke, he puts on the white gook suit, stows the rest of what he bought in a warped chifforobe. The gook shirt has little buttons carved out of some kind of tree wood he can't recognize. He's never worn anything so fine.

When he goes outside, Dog wants to follow. He gives her a Slim Jim, shoves her in the opposite direction. Language she can understand. The afternoon's warm with a breeze. Barefoot, he hikes to a noisy creek a half mile on the mountain's other side, water that doesn't flow down to the cabin.

There he takes off his new, white clothes, folds them carefully and leaves them on the bank. Naked, carrying nothing but his hunting knife to protect him, he wades out to where the creek cascades over a large, smooth rock and lies down in the middle of its flow. Spreads his arms, opens his legs, stares up at the angled sun till it blinds him.

"Lord Jesus, I beseech thee, wash my sins away."

He says it over and over, right hand wrapped around his knife—Lord Jesus, Lord Jesus, Lord Jesus, Lord Jesus—for what seems like forever. Says it till it seems enough. Then he lays there, trying to feel what it'll feel like having all his sins gone. Especially his sins in San Francisco, if that's even possible, and sins he committed halfway across the world. But all he can think about is her.

Katherine struggling up the trail that first day in her Sunday coat, a dung beetle dragging everything she owned behind her and reeking of Dead Lady sick. Katherine out every morning chopping wood, tending her garden, mending her fence. Katherine toting her little gun around. Katherine stretched out naked on that rock that time, how bad she needed him. How bad she needs him now.

Sweet Lord Jesus.

Water's for-shit cold. Numbs every part of him, but he'll stay in it till he can't stand it, till he's all but too far gone to rise. That's the kind of time and water it'll take to cleanse his sins.

Still, Lord Jesus ought to send him down a sign, pure white dove or some such, for when he's laid here long enough that he can stop. His arms and legs are tingling from the cold, starting to ache. Parts of him shiver on their own now and again. He lays quiet as he can, his burning eyes still staring at the sun. Then tears run down his face and he is singing.

> *"With arms wide open, He'll pardon you.*
> *It is no secret what God can do."*

Knows it for what it is, his prayed-for sign. Sings it over and over, till he's hoarse and can't sing anymore and it's enough.

Still clutching his knife, Danny staggers off the rock, picks up his folded clothes and puts them on and climbs back to the house under a sky the color of his peaches. Cutting through the orchard, he picks a windfall fruit up off the ground, holds it high and sees it all but disappear against the heavens. God's gift, to let him see a peach that way. He brings the fruit close to his face, touches its soft skin to his lips. Then smashes it against his open mouth, grinds its wet flesh into his teeth. He clamps down hard on the porous seed, sucks out all its sweet juice. Oh, how much the good Lord loves him. To give him such a precious gift.

All Danny needs to do is take it.

This night he rushes to lie on his bed, hardly waiting for the dark. Rushes to his Long Dream. In it, he crashes through the underbrush, runs all the way. From his moldy mattress in the partly sanded library of his burnt-out house to the center of his old home town, he runs. Thin branches whip his ankles, calves.

It's first dawn when he gets there, streets all still in shadow. He runs like a thief. Past the courthouse parking meters, past his law office with its three-side window and porch rocking chairs, little brass-link-chain sign. Past the fat brick houses with familiar mailbox names, the little strip of woods. Rounds the curve, unlatches the white picket gate, dashes up the walk between the green grass and the beds of purple flowers, takes the porch steps two at a time.

Door's stuck. He barrels into it with his shoulder. It flings open and he lurches in.

Inside, it's not the house he's used to, with its long, dark passageway. It's the Old Man's cabin, heart-pine floors and huge stone hearth. Her sleeping bag's spread out in the same corner he embraces every night. God's gift. God's sign.

She stands beside it in the dim light, barefoot in her white nightgown with all its tiny flowers. Her gaze is steady, unsurprised, as if she's been expecting him. He moves toward her till he's just arm's length away. This close, her eyes are gold, a thing he did not know. He reaches out and grabs her wrist with his left hand.

Danny shudders and can't stop. Won't. Has to finish what's begun.

He bites down hard on his left wrist, but even that can't choke his arcing cry that spirals into the dark and echoes down the mountain.

21

The Gift

DREAMING, KATHERINE GIVES DANNY'S CRY TO A HUGE BIRD CIR-
cling high overhead. In the morning she opens the cabin door to find
her porch is covered with ripe peaches. And, at her feet, a moldering
copy of *A Room with a View.*

She picks up a fruit wedged against her left foot, bites into it.
Can't remember tasting any peach so thoroughly. Someone besides
herself is in this forest. Another person. Someone who brought gifts
and disappeared.

She should be frightened, of course. Sucks the rough seed dry and
slips it in her pocket, picks up the book, heads down the privy path.
She has again begun leaving the door open so she can see the mountain, leaves it open still. Because nothing's changed; on some level she
knows this. Whatever's here has simply been made manifest. She's in
no more danger than she's ever been. Who left them? A young girl?
An old woman? Who would she like this other one to be? A man

would not announce himself that way. Men are straightforward; he'd just knock on her door.

In the garden, her hands are sure among the plants, pulling peppers and cucumbers, yellow summer squashes, picking beans off their vines with two swift fingers, cradling ripe tomatoes on their stems until they fall into her hands. A book! Something to read in the long summer evenings. She fills the lopsided basket rescued from behind the woodpile, pulls the army of small, tender weeds that every day encroaches. Then she rubs a couple radishes against her jeans to get the dirt off, pops them in her mouth; their heat's a wake-up call. Next she eats a tomato, then a small green pepper. Breakfast. It's all so simple and yet not. She is part of everything and everything is part of her; how can she not have known this all along?

Perhaps that's why, when she looks up and sees him standing there under the chestnut oak, clad all in white and staring at her like some fierce blond angel, she is startled but is not afraid, simply gazes back at him for what her eyes can know. Much as, a few days earlier, she gazed at an exotic luna moth, pale greenish white, large as her open hand, that pressed itself against her window screen.

"Hello," he says in a voice too deep for a boy so thin and doubtless barely out of high school. "I live over the mountain. I'm the one brought you the peaches. And the book."

He sounds so serious, perhaps afraid.

"Thank you. I ate a peach, it was delicious." She smiles. "You're sure you didn't bring too many?"

"I got lots," he says, still staring. He looks like he hasn't eaten in a year.

"You could sell them in Elkmont, you know. I could pay you what you'd get there."

Something, fury, flashes in his eyes.

"I didn't bring you them for pay."

"Well . . . thank you again. Thank you so very much." She gestures awkwardly. "Please. Take some vegetables. I've got more than enough."

"I don't eat vegetables much." He shifts his weight, looks around at all the garden beds, turns back with a faint smile as if from some pleasant memory. "But I might trouble you for one of those bright red tomatoes."

"Of course. Come in and pick one. Pick all you want."

Her voice sounds schoolmarmish, patronizing, to her ears. She takes a step toward the gate to undo its wooden bolt.

"No!"

He barks it like a wild thing, startles even himself. Takes a ragged breath, tries to smile.

"You got to pick me one yourself. One you want me to have, and put it by the fence there. Then go back to where you are, smack in the middle. I'll come get it."

"Oh. Yes. I can do that."

He looks so frightened standing there, as if she'd threatened to strike him. She picks the largest, ripest tomato she can see and lays the red fruit gently on the ground outside the fence. Then she returns to the center of the garden, stands there motionless. The young man dashes up, grabs the tomato, scuttles back to the meadow's edge, a feral dog too watchful to eat. He runs his hands over the red fruit, eyes it like some hard-won prize, then looks back at her with that strange fervor.

"I come by here sometimes on my way out to the highway. Come up along that ridge yonder."

Was he the shadow that she saw that first day hiking in? Did he see her?

"Sometimes I stop awhile and watch you in the garden." His words rush from his mouth. "It brings me peace, seeing you working with those growing things. You mind?"

She shakes her head quickly, feels uncomfortably warm. "I don't mind."

"I'm glad for that. Can I stop by again sometime? Stand out here and watch you work? I won't come any closer. I swear I won't."

Why not? Why won't he come close enough to touch her? "Yes. I mean . . . it's all right. And you're welcome to come into the garden if you want."

He looks at her, nods once, slightly but with significance, as if some understanding of which she is as yet unaware has passed between them. Then he turns on his heel and strides into the trees.

So young and alone, holding his head so high. She tries to bring her mind back to the plants around her, but her concentration has been shattered. All she can think of are the sharp wings of his shoulder blades inside that soft white shirt, when he turned his back on her and walked away.

22

"It's. All. Right."

STUPID. STUPID. STUPID.

He hadn't meant to do it, any of it. He'd got out of the creek water, put his clothes back on, started for home so cold he couldn't feel his own skin. And everywhere he looked was ringed in rainbows.

When he got close to Gatsby's house, none of the burnt parts showed. From this side it looked whole and perfect. And he, Danny, looked perfect, too, in his loose white clothes. So perfect he imagined Katherine standing on the other side of that enormous lawn, alone and staring at him, a light breeze playing in her hair.

His feet left bloody prints on the slate porch steps from burrs he'd stepped on without knowing. Pinecones. Thorns.

That's what got to him, her standing there across the lawn, what pulled him through his Long Dream to its rightful end. Later, he woke in darkness, his thin fists jammed under the blanket. Lit a lantern, headed out, his still-sore feet seeking the soft, damp orchard earth, his hands seeking the ripe peaches that weighed down its trees.

It's all right.

Climbing back up the mountain, he can't get the words out of his head. What she said when he asked her could he stop back by again. "It's all right." He turns it around inside his mind. Never dreamed her voice would sound so soft.

"It's all right." So much more than "yes."

It's. All. Right. His feet beat time to it. Each word and all that it suggests. Pooling, spreading.

It's. Contraction of "it is," a hurry-up word tumbling out as if she couldn't wait. *It:* Noun, subject. On the face of it, him coming to her in the garden. But who's to say? "It" could mean anything. Or everything. *Is:* Verb, to be, exist, exist as. Equal. "It" equals "right," that's how she said it. Old Professor Beckham would adore his redneck ass.

Right: Good, perfect, proper, correct, permitted. Encouraged? Yes. Desired? Yes!

All: The key word, meat and heart of the matter. Danny says it out loud, slowly pushing the *A*'s long airstream from his chest, curling his tongue around the double *L*s. If "all" is a noun, then "all" equals "it," and "it" truly does mean fucking "everything." Whole, entire, complete, be-all and end-all, alpha and omega. Universe. If "all" is an adverb, then "it" is "right" in every way.

Case closed. Any way you look at it, according to the woman in the garden, everything he wants to do with her is right and good all through it.

Danny climbs the mountain tall and strong. *It's. All. Right.* His sins are washed away.

His whole way home he keeps care of her tomato like it's made of glass. Then he sets it on the center of the mantel in his sleeping room, well out of Dog's excited reach, and stares at it. Katherine held it with her own two hands. Not just touched it, or brushed it with her fingers. Carried it, her hands all wrapped around it, set it down outside the

gate. Before that, grew it out of nothing but a seed she'd pressed between her thumb and forefinger, her soft flesh surrounding it before
she dropped it in the ground. The red fruit smells of sun, other plants,
the earth that grew it. And of Katherine. Who smells also of those
things. The thought's a heat inside him.

He has placed the tomato in a square of sunlight, watches it across
the room all afternoon. Watches the light move over it and then away.
He takes his knife out of its sheath, same knife he took into the water,
held all through his sin-cleansing so now his knife is sin-cleansed, too.
Goes to the mantel, slices the tomato lengthwise down its middle with
his sin-cleansed knife.

Lord, it's the prettiest thing inside. He's never really looked at one
that way, how it makes a pattern you might find inside somebody's
heart. He slices a piece off one of the halves, flicks the wet seeds out
with the knife point, then pushes them with the blade into a wet little
pile. If he spreads them out, dries them, keeps them till next spring
and plants them, he'll have tomatoes that came out of hers. The idea
rips through his insides, clears a space for his recollection of her voice
to thrum, like a hollow reed you hold straight out to catch the wind.
Should maybe have brought her some other book this morning.
Maybe *The Secret Garden*. Would have fit better with the peaches. But
it's for children. That Forster book's got romance in it. And other silly
things that women like. People riding in carriages, sitting in drawing
rooms. That sort of shit. So maybe it's okay.

He can't sit still. Attacks his floor with the block sander so furiously Dog runs out the door still hungry. Sawdust rises in the air, then
falls. He brushes it into neat little piles with his index finger. Yeah, he
could live out a whole life of days like this one.

Only, it's not wise to be too happy. Happy is the orange you get at
Christmas—you prize it because you only get one once a year. He
mustn't go to her too often. In the broad day. In the garden. Needs to
hold it back till he can't stand it longer, him being away from her like
that.

He falls asleep in the late afternoon in a hot square of sunlight, so
its darkening will wake him, let him know it's time to head down to
the cabin once again to be a silent witness to her dreams.

* * *

TONIGHT, WHEN HE WRAPS his arms and legs around the corner where she lies, places his cheek against its still-warm stones and joins his breath with her soft breathing, he feels a quickening inside him—made out of her voice; and the tomato; and the July sun. The last time he had a day so perfect, it was with his mama.

She'd packed cornbread and beans for just the two of them, hiked with him to a laurel slick, led him through it by the hand and out the other side into a meadow. There she spread her shawl for them to sit on and they ate the lunch she'd brought, drank water from the creek out of a mason jar. "You look just like your daddy," she had told him and he liked that. He went to sleep there, his head pillowed in her lap. The last day before he started school.

That blond hippie girl in San Francisco, she'd looked something like her.

"With arms wide open, He'll pardon you."

It's. All. Right.

23

"Unbraid Your Hair"

AFTERNOONS BRING FAR-OFF THUNDER, NEVER ANY RAIN. NIGHTS, she lies awake, breathing with the deer and staring at the moonlight on the floor. Days, she passes at once calm and oddly jangled, wanting to sit still yet far too restless for it. She feels too alive, imagines things too starkly. The tiny Jack standing so proud and erect, not preacherly at all, in each Jack-in-the-pulpit plant along the trail. A humming-bird's invisible, fast-beating heart. No matter how she tries, she cannot weave the day the boy came to the garden. All she gets is something white, with here and there thin lines. Some straw-colored, a few dark red.

He'd looked not much older than Michael had been. Blond like Michael, thinner, more hawklike in the face. If she and Michael had made love and she had had his baby, he'd be close to this boy's age. Perhaps resemble him.

Outside, on the cabin porch, peeling and slicing the ripest of the peaches, tossing the peels to birds gathered in the nearest trees, flies circling the leavings. Inside, standing over the iron pot, cooking the fruit down to a sweet, thick syrup that will keep awhile, sucking it off her fingers, licking it out of the spaces in between. Why does she keep thinking of him? He lives alone, has no one. No wife, father, mother, brother, sister, child. She's not sure how she knows this, just that it rises off him like an odor.

The next day in the garden she senses his watching as a soft cloak settling around her shoulders, but he does not show himself. His presence, even unseen, relaxes her. In the same way she believes he lives alone, she also believes he will not harm her. She picks the largest of the yellow squashes, runs her fingers over it before laying it gently in her basket; knows exactly where her womb is, traces it outside her clothing.

Of course this is nonsense, the kind that comes of living much too long alone. She doesn't know a thing about him. Except his being here means she should load her pistol, carry it whenever she sets foot outdoors, point it at him, tell him to keep the hell away. She also knows she will not, cannot, do this. Instead, she stays longer in the garden, invents tasks. Wishes even there was more work needed on the horrid fence. A day goes by, then two. He said he lived over the mountain. Maybe he comes this way infrequently, just every month or so. But he will stop by, he said so. He asked for her permission.

A week passes. She has read the book he gave her. Twice, even though she also read it years before. Is losing hope that he will come again. She leaves the garden early, as before, finishes her half-done weaving, no longer thinks to trace her womb. Distracts herself by paying close attention to a small brown bird that's started visiting the garden, each day lighting on something closer to her—a strand of the wire fence, a tomato stake. Until one day it perches on her shoulder, lets her walk with it, its tiny claws pick-picking at her shirt, her skin. Its soft warbling, so close to her ear, sounds like creek water over stones. Companionship's what she had wanted from the boy, that's all.

How many days now since she's seen him? Enough that she has

eaten all the peaches, even the last of the syrup. Enough that there are wide gaps now between the times she thinks of him. One morning the bird flies too soon away, and she looks up to see the boy there at the meadow's edge, wearing the same white clothes he wore before.

"Hi there," she says, as casually as she can.

"Hello. Am I bothering you?"

She shakes her head. "No, it's all right."

"Yeah, I know."

He looks so earnest, so intense, and also looks like he's about to smile. Someone should comb his hair, it's full of knots and tangles. Someone.

He settles himself cross-legged on the ground, leans his back against the chestnut oak, his hands folded in his lap. Follows her with gray eyes darkened from the shade and doesn't speak for a long time. She tries not to do anything differently than if he weren't there, tries not to look at him, tries not to pick only the vegetables on his side of the garden. Tries not to think how much he looks like Michael. The cicadas' buzzing intensifies the heat as the sun climbs.

"It's pretty there inside that fence. All orderly and green."

She starts, had grown used to his silence.

"Yes, isn't it? Thank you."

He nods. Again that almost smile.

Harder now to concentrate on garden chores, on her fingers picking off the bush beans, dropping them into the basket, cradling the ripe tomatoes. Harder not to look at him, not to imagine how he looks looking at her. He's her nearest neighbor, that's all it is. Another human being like herself, like the man in town that day wielding his push broom.

No, this is different.

"Stand up sometimes where I can see you. When I don't see you for a while it's spooky. Like you're a ghost that disappears."

This time he does smile. At himself, the corners of his mouth turned down.

She straightens, steps out from between the squashes and the cucumbers. "I'm here."

"Yeah, I can see that now."

What is she doing? Why does she just stand there smiling back at him?

"Unbraid your hair."

"What?"

That startling grown-man voice. "Unbraid your hair."

She is afraid to move, to breathe, afraid he'll run away like a wild animal. As if tranced, she lifts her hands to the back of her neck, then slides them down along her single plait to loose its band.

"Look. There's a breeze yonder inside the fence. You see it in one spot, then in another. Memaw used to say a breeze like that's come looking for a present."

Memaw. Used to.

He stares at her and doesn't smile.

"Unbraid your hair and let the breeze play in it."

She looks back at him, runs her fingers through the plaited strands, shakes her head to free them. Her hair lifts gently off her neck.

"Look at that old breeze. That's what he came for."

"My name is Katherine. Katherine Reid." Her mouth is dry. The words come out with difficulty.

"My name's Danny MacLean. I'm pleased to know you."

The first of this afternoon's dry thunder rolls itself around his voice, curls into it. The boy untangles his legs, jumps to his feet as if he means to run to her.

Instead, he jerks his head up, scans the sky.

"I got to go."

He turns away and disappears, his white shirt a brief flash among the trees. And she is once again alone.

INSIDE THE CABIN, GARDEN bounty buries her table. She shoves aside tomatoes to make a place for the small bowl of vegetables and rice that is her dinner, the rice kernels dry and slightly burnt from when her attention wandered.

Unbraid your hair.

She shakes her loose hair vigorously, fretfully, combs her fingers through it. He should have come into the garden.

And then what?

When she rinses her bowl, the water runs slowly from the copper faucet. It's not the first time and it's getting worse. A rusted pipe, a leak, something she should see to.

Unbraid your hair.

That deep voice, its strange, grown-up authority—she burned the rice.

Everything looks all right under the sink. That likely means the problem's in the pipe outside that brings the water from the stream. She needs to go to town, ask at the hardware store what she should do. Needs to see people on the street, hear voices in the shops. Needs to buy a canner and as many canning jars as she can manage, buy more yarn, keeps forgetting to buy bullets for the gun.

Unbraid your hair.

She drops onto a bench and clamps her hands over her ears. Rocks there, squeezing her arms across her belly. Squeezing her thighs to-gether. Wrong, wrong, wrong, wrong, wrong.

To think of him that way.

To think of him at all.

Gets up, goes to the loom, warps it quick in anger. Yanks the weft strands through its middle.

There.

And there.

Brings to life a wild, uneven thing, hairy and terrifying. Dark and bristly hunks of rough wool yarns and stiff dried swamp grass cradling a soft, lush center—purples, corals, reds—yarns like pillows in her hands. She weaves past sundown into lamplight, through the dark-ness. Binds off her work only when the sky grows light, then drops onto the floor. Sleeps curled around the finished weaving, far from the deer's sweet, rhythmic breath.

* * *

WHEN SHE WAKES, STIFF, to a sun high in the sky, she knows what she must do. Roll up last night's work without looking at it, slam it in her cart, then climb into the loft and get the other one, with its spare, straw-colored lines, roll that one up, too. Take them both in to that gallery. Get him out of her house, out of her mind.

On the trail she does not hear the birds, nor recognize the service-berry tree that dropped such sweet blooms back in April. Does not see the dead log where the edible boletus mushrooms grow, nor even note the outcropping where she can look down at her mangled car. She looks and listens for only one thing. Where is the boy? Is he on some far ridge looking down at her? Or is he close, behind this chestnut oak, that hickory, so near she can reach out and touch him? She sees him in every shadow, hears him in every rustling leaf.

Unbraid your hair.

ELKMONT'S SHIMMERING SIDEWALKS DIZZY her in the silver heat. She pulls her cart into the courthouse park to drink at the fountain. He was the boy on the bench that day, the boy with the stringy hair and the hole in his boot, who held up two fingers in a peace sign. It's been going on that long. The realization creates an upheaval deep inside her, a shuddering she has to stand quite still to bear.

When she is able once again to move, walk, drink the hot stream from the outdoor fountain, she makes her way out of the green shade toward the sidewalk. A little boy in a blue sailor suit toddles past on chubby, dimpled legs, heads for the street. Katherine rushes after him, scoops him up just after he steps off the sidewalk. The child's small, frightened heart beats hard against her own.

"You mustn't run into the street like that."

She brushes his fine blond hair out of his eyes. Won't, can't, put him down.

A sour-faced young woman in an orange maternity smock rushes toward her, wheeling a baby in a stroller.

"That's my boy. I'll take him now."

Katherine glares at her with fierce eyes. "He ran into the street."

The woman turns, watches a single car creep past.

"Give him to me. Clyde Junior, let go of the lady's sleeve!"

Katherine relinquishes the boy into his mother's sturdy arms. "No harm done," she reassures the woman, wheels her cart around, heads in the opposite direction so no one can see her anger, or the yearning in her eyes. Because there had been harm. The boy's mother turned away, was not paying attention. She, Katherine, would never turn away.

Unbraid your hair.

In the hardware store she finds a canner and the proper jars. But there's no such thing as "plumbers' tape," and the goop they sell her, "pipe dope," makes her so dizzy when she sniffs it that she asks the clerk to wrap it in three sacks. The thin man with the Adam's apple, who still doesn't recognize her from that long-gone February day, looks at her like she's crazy but not like she's "summer people." Her shoes are much too sensible, her clothes too worn.

In the little gallery by the bookshop, she remembers the young couple who looked in the window, how they stood locked together, pieces in a jigsaw puzzle. Something she has never known. Not with Tim, whose truest love had always been the agency; not even with Michael. Something she will never know. Regret's as real as a taste on your tongue. She unrolls last night's weaving, its wild wools and grasses discordant, shocking against the counter's smooth and quiet maple. A plump woman in a denim skirt emerges from the studio. Her eyes widen as she sinks her fingertips into the weaving's red and swollen center.

She takes both pieces. They will hang now in the little gallery for strangers to look at and buy, and she, Katherine, will get seventy percent. But that's not what she thinks of. Only that the boy, Danny MacLean, is now out of her life as if he never had come into it. Never had stared at her from a courthouse bench, nor watched her from a ridgetop or behind a chestnut oak, had never sat cross-legged in the shade outside her garden.

She is dizzy on the walk home, starts at every vehicle that speeds past, retches as soon as she gets beyond the little grocery, the price she pays for venturing outside the wilderness. On the turnoff road she hears all the birds and names them from their calls, listens to the distant thunder, the light wind ruffling the trees, sees tones and textures all around her, in the dirt beneath her feet. Her life, even alone, is rich and good. She is herself once more.

Until she leaves the road and rounds the trail's first bend. He is not here. He is not anywhere.

The sun, the birds, the trees' bright dancing leaves are only desolation, as she drags her cart behind her up the trail.

Unbraid your hair.

24

$\mathcal{S}torm$

DANNY SPRAWLS ON THE LAST WOODEN PEW OF THE EMPTY CHURCH, before an open window. He likes it here, likes churches in general. They're almost always open, empty, ready when you need them. He used to sleep in them sometimes. After he set up in the desert. Before he set up here.

This one calls to mind the church his Memaw used to take him to, where people fell down in the aisles jerking and wailing when the Lord came into them. Danny sat there every Sunday, waiting to see it happen, terrified it might happen to him. Sat very still beside his Memaw, watching for the Lord to come and wondering how He got inside the church. Especially in winter with it all shut up.

Wondering if it was all some grown-up bullshit to make boys like him do what they said.

He stares out the two-inch window opening he's made, thinks some about Memaw's church, and how churches in books can seem some like it in the way they look. Even faraway churches in Spain or England. Danny also thinks about the Old Man's house, which looked like Memaw's church inside, a thing that hadn't come to him till now. Mostly he thinks about Katherine. From where he sits he can see nearly all Elkmont's stores and such and her pulling the little cart he gave her in and out of them. Post office, grocery, hardware store, some prissy "gallery." He could sit here out of the hot sun all day long just watching her, knowing she won't see him through the colored glass. Her so determined, jerking that cart over doorsills, potholes, broken places in the sidewalk. The sun gains brightness every time she's in his sight. He will never hurt her. Never.

It's Saturday, street's full of people. Sometimes some man turns and stares at her, she's a good-looking woman. But that man can't have her. Danny'll kill him first. Danny's the one watches over her. Yesterday she took her hair down all for him, for no more reason than he asked her to. Memaw never took her hair out of its knot for anyone save Pawpaw. Danny's mama, too. Never took the pins out once after his daddy died, except to sleep.

Ka-ther-ine. He mouths it silently, craves how the "th" makes his teeth clamp on his tongue like it's a little live thing caught between them. Keeps his tongue there. Clamps his teeth down till it hurts, before he lets it loose.

Ka-ther-ine.

Sometimes he thinks she knows everything there is to know about him, reads his mind or some such. Maybe read it long before she ever saw him. That shit happens. You can know people that way without ever seeing them. From the pure fact they've spent a long time near you. Same as knowing some gook's out there in the jungle without seeing him or hearing him. Smelling him even. You know it just because he's near.

And because that gook very badly wants to kill you and you very badly want to kill him first so you can go on living. Yeah, there's got to be deep feelings on both sides, that's what transmits the knowledge. Danny wants to be with Katherine more than he's ever wanted anything in God's great turning world. She wants him, too. He can sense it coming off her even from this far away. How hard a thing, to know he must never touch her. She senses that, too.

But it doesn't matter. She's as much as told him. *It's. All. Right.*

What doesn't matter? What's all right?

Everything.

Yeah, she's got her back turned to him now, heading out of town. He'll let her go a little ways, give her her lead. Can't take a chance she'll see him, she'd recognize him now. Can't let her know he's come this far. He rests his head against the back of the church pew, the wood's comfortable curve. Danny and Katherine; get it tattooed on his biceps. Big heart with an arrow through it. *Danny loves Katherine. It's. All. Right.*

HE JERKS AWAKE TO darkness. Flashes of phosphorus-blue fire, rumble of incoming artillery. Dives under the bench in front of him, curls himself into a ball. He is a ghost again. Jimbo's bone throbs in his thigh, the only life inside him. Jimbo died when Danny wasn't looking out for him.

Ka-ther-ine.

He crawls into the aisle, stands. Runs out of the safety of the church into the growing storm.

25

"Take Me In"

SHE LIGHTS HER LAMP, SITS AT THE TABLE LISTENING TO THE THUN-
der. Closer tonight; please let it rain. Four times these past two weeks
she's carried water to the garden, feared always she had not brought
enough. The air feels heavy, but that's not the same thing as a promise.
All she can do is wait.

For the storm. For the deer, who hasn't come for two nights now.
For the boy at the garden, whom she will never see again. For her
memory of him to fade.

The child she held this afternoon is with her still—in her arms,
against her breast. On her way home, she left the trail to pick a small
red flower, bright against late afternoon's green darkness, so she could
rub a single petal on her cheek to see if it was smoother than that baby's skin. It was not.

Don't hope. For anything. Life is a series of small moments; sometimes they bring a little cooling rain and then it's gone. That's the most you can expect.

Why, then, is she so restless? She goes to the kitchen, takes mint off a shelf for tea. The sink water runs out a rusty brown; maybe that means it's raining somewhere. Now an occasional lightning flash precedes the thunder. Its blue-white bleach makes all the trees, even the sturdy oaks, seem frail. Tomorrow she will weave it, if she has all those electric shades of yarns.

Maybe if she had a rocking chair, its constant motion, she wouldn't feel so out of sorts. She has thought many times how she might get one to the cabin: Take it apart, bring it back on the trail in pieces; then nail them, glue them back together. It would need to be a small one, its seat and back no wider than the diagonal inside her cart. She could bring it in two trips, first the seat and rockers, then the back and legs. Wedge other items—bags of rice, salt, beans, balls of lightning-colored yarns—around it. Maybe that will work. If she can find one small enough.

It's full dark now, still thundering and still no rain. She strips off her day clothes, reaches her muslin nightgown from its hook, pulls it on over her head and stretches out on top of her sleeping bag.

But nothing sleeps in this heat-swollen night. Not the owl, not the monotonous whippoorwill, not the desperate mockingbird flinging his lonely arias into the heavy air. Katherine lies there with her gown hiked up.

Unbraid your hair.

She barely notices the rising wind, the thunder, not even the rain. Until she hears his voice shout out her name—so like a dream lodged in the storm, yet real. She rises, dazed, moves toward the sound. Pulls back the bolt, opens the door.

He stands there on her porch, wild-eyed and shaking. Rivulets of rain slide off his tangled hair. A blue-white flash of lightning, crack of thunder, something struck nearby. A brief pain in her ears. The boy's hand shoots out, grabs her wrist tight as a vise. His eyes bore into her too proud to plead.

"Take me in."

26

In This Quiet, Familiar Place

DANNY JERKS WITH EVERY PHOSPHORUS-FLARE LIGHTNING FLASH. So many things rain down on you out of a sky lit up like that. Bird shit, metal shards, bone fragments, human flesh. All of it on fire. *Jimbo, man, I told you. Stay off the fucking trail!*

Ka-ther-ine.

Words come into his mouth hard as stones. "Take me in."

She steps back and he follows her across the threshold. Her wrist bones turn in his clenched fist.

"I don't mean to bother you." It spurts out all run together like he's on a battle high. "It's just, I got to get inside."

She nods. In the darkness he feels the movement more than sees it. "It's all right."

Her words wash into him, rain sluices down outside. It's all one thing. Her words, the rain, her wrist-pulse banging against his fingers.

She reaches around with her free hand, closes the door and bolts it. Now everything inside is silent. Even the wind and rain seem far away. He is in the Old Man's house, in the Old Man's presence, with this woman he has known such a long time. In this quiet, familiar place, he is suddenly so tired.

She moves toward the picnic table he built out of the smokehouse boards. Table and two benches, a foretelling.

"I'll light a lamp." Her voice soft in the darkness.

"Don't."

He walks her to the corner where he's watched over her so many nights. Pulls her down onto her sleeping bag. Her body trembles in the heat, she is afraid of him. Afraid of Danny. He curls himself behind her. Draws up his legs, his knees against her back. Still gripping her wrist he wraps his other arm around her.

"We got to lay like this. Like spoons but with our legs drawn up. Pull your knees up like mine."

She folds her legs. Danny smooths her gown down over them, his other hand still clamped around her wrist. Her body shivers like she's cold, and she makes tiny, frightened noises not quite words.

He rocks her slightly. "Hush, now. I just got to lay here for a time. I promise I won't hurt you. That's why I laid us with our knees drawn up. So I can't hurt you even if I try."

She nods, still full of fear. *Please, Lord, please let her know I don't mean to harm her.*

"It's just, I can't stand a thunderstorm, especially in the night. I got to have some live thing to hold on to."

His words spill out onto her back, into the dark well between her shoulder blades.

Comes a lightning flash he tightens his arm around her knees, counts off time till the thunder. Thunder moving off, his shakes settling down, muscle aches he gets after the shaking starting to come on. Got to stay strong, she needs that.

"I had a dog that used to let me hold her, but she ran away. I wasn't home too much by then. Couldn't find enough to feed her. She never did take much to dumpster food."

Dumbass. Talking such stupid shit. His words are moist air caught inside the muslin of her gown. Her back is smooth against his forehead and her nightgown smells of sunshine. He rests his free hand against her hair. Won't comb his fingers through it, no matter how he craves to. But he can't do anything about his words, how they keep tumbling out against the warm life of her lying there. And him not even sure she hears.

Words about how his daddy was a laughing man who grabbed Danny by his baby ankles, swung him high into the air, and how that's all of him that he remembers; how his mama's lipstick, when he sucked her titty, made him think of plums; and how he should have cried for her in that hot schoolroom full of other wailing kids so maybe she'd have heard somehow and not have shot herself. He tells how Pawpaw smelled of two-day-old tobacco spit and Memaw smelled of flour and sometimes of carbolic acid she used on the babies and sometimes of mamas' babies dying when she couldn't help them, how he knew from her smell coming through the door which thing had happened on that day and how she felt about it.

He tells how, the day after his mama died, his Pawpaw taught him how to shoot a rifle so he'd have a thing to take her place, and how by the time he turned eight he could already hit a squirrel square in its eye; Pawpaw, who used to ride him on his back when they went hunting so he could keep up, Danny grabbing at his shirt to hang on, the muscles in his Pawpaw's hairy shoulders like riding on a bear, the dogs moiling below him on the ground; Pawpaw, who died when a logger's tree fell on him the year Danny turned twelve. Tells how at high school football games they all cheered "Dan-ny, Dan-ny," because he was the quarterback; and how at college sweet bells chimed the hours so you didn't need a clock and all the radiators hissed and every room he entered seemed a place where he was meant to be.

Tells how once he'd thought to be a lawyer and came home from Memaw's funeral and sat inside the room where Pawpaw's mantel clock still ticked, till Jimbo showed up banging on the door and saying how they should get up and go, just like Sal Paradise and Dean Moriarty, and if they joined the Army they'd get paid for going back to college, maybe even law school. And how, too much later, he realized

Jimbo'd done it all for him, that even growing up with all those books Jimbo never gave a flying fuck for college.

"Now Jimbo's dead and I keep in my thigh a bone from him, from the explosion."

She winces and a silent exultation rises in him that she's heard.

"My flesh and skin grew over it so now it's nothing but a long red welt that aches before a storm. Motherfucker threw me his brains, too, on his way out. Frothy with tiny bubbles like half-melted ice cream. I had to wipe them off my face. Reckon he thought I might have need of them.

"Yeah. Jimbo. He knew how to get things done. Medic tried to dig his bone out of my thigh and I raised up and held my knife blade on him, said, "Leave it alone, man, or I'll slit your throat.""

She shudders and he smooths her gown over her knees to soothe her.

"It's different over there. You try and leave it all behind, but you can't help taking some away with you. Like what drew me to you was you were dying. I was used to people dying, I smelled it on you hiking in, you in your long red coat and dumbass city boots. I wanted to be near you when it happened. If a person's dying smell turns sweet, most times they're gone before the week's out. I waited but yours never did; your dying smell just went away. You beat out Mr. D., and when he came for you again out in the snow I wouldn't let him at you. Took you inside and laid you by the stove and made a fire."

She turns her head and tries to look at him. Storm's moving on. All that artillery flying off to somewheres else. His muscles ache from shaking, still he can't stop talking. Into the forgiving back of this once-dying woman lying in the curve of his right arm.

"Death draws you, but you got to keep a distance from it all you can. Each time you see some poor fucker buy it, each time you look at them, at anyone after they're dead, touch them, smell them, any of that shit, you take a little of their death inside you. Take in enough and you become a haint, a ghost. Like me.

"Over there you're in the death business. There's death everywhere and you can't get away. Some poor shits got to bring the bodies in for counting, load them on the trucks, fly them in the copters. Sometimes there's not body bags enough. You steel yourself to not look and then you look anyway. The dead reach out to you and make you stare. It's their last act with the living.

"I saw myself once in a dead gook's eye. I'd killed him, he was my dead gook, so it was me had to go out and bring him in. I bent down to get him and the sun was shining through the trees behind him and I saw my face inside his open eye, its iris clouding like a mist, trapping me inside that eye forever. I grabbed my knife to gouge it out—it's nothing, taking parts of dead gooks; Jimbo wore three ears around his neck strung on a bootlace—but I couldn't get my hand to do it. I feared cutting myself out of him might kill me. That dead gook took my life inside him through that eye. I looked at it and took his death in me. I reckon that's a fair exchange. Considering.

"That's why I live in the woods. I got so much death in me there's times it takes over my mind. It's mostly people set it off. Their sudden noises, all that talk. The fact they stayed behind. It's just better in the woods, with the wild animals."

The Dead Lady, his Katherine, is shaking violently against his folded knees. Danny tightens his arm around her, pulls her nightgown down some more in case she's cold, then knows she's crying.

And then he's crying, too. The way he's learned, without moving or making any sound. It's got to be the first time he's been cried for. He tries to think on what that means, him being cried for, what the Dead Lady's, Katherine's, tears signify. In this way, so tired, he drifts into sleep.

Later in the night he wakes enough to know the rain's stopped, hears the quiet, moisture dripping from the trees. Maybe halfway up the mountainside a whippoorwill chants in the dark. He's let go his grip on Katherine's wrist and she's no longer curled there with her back against his knees.

He lurches in a kind of panic to get up and find her, but there's something holds him back. In their sleep they have changed places. It's now her arm around him, her knees pressing in the backs of his, him lying there in her embrace. It is a terrifying thing to feel so safe.

Please, God, I laid down in cold-flowing creek water. Do this one thing for me. Please let me, us, stay here like this forever.

She breathes small, regular sighs against his neck, their rhythms as familiar as his own. Now it's him matches his breaths to hers. Which is better, to hold the one you love or be held by them? Danny ponders that, wants very much to find the answer. Nick Carraway went back east to learn "the bond business." Maybe the bond business he took in wasn't that Wall Street shit at all. Maybe it was what he learned from Gatsby, who loved Daisy more than he loved life itself.

Yeah. Maybe so.

27

Morning

IN THE HOSPITAL SHE TOUCHED HER DEAD SON'S PERFECT, PEARL-like fingernails. Last night she stepped back so this frightened boy clutching her wrist could come inside.

That she took him in without a question didn't have to do with anything that happened in her bed before he screamed her name into the storm. It had to do with how he is so thin, too thin to be a man in spite of his man's voice. Thin like a boy who has just come through his last growth spurt, a poor, used-up boy from some hot, harsh country she has never seen. Because she had fallen asleep, because it was his voice that woke her, she is not certain now which was a dream and which was real—her lying in the humid night alone, or this boy lying curled into her back like a sharp-edged quarter moon.

He quivered in the darkness, jerked with every lightning flash, jerked again with the ensuing thunder. She settled her body full against his knees in the hope that this might ease him, and it seemed to. Then she let the facts and implications of his words come into her with all their ugly strength, until at last she couldn't take in any more of it or else there was no more to hear, and so she slept.

She woke once and found he had let go of her and they had turned the other way and she was holding him. Such an easy way to lie. The comfort of it spread in her until she could have cut the word "fulfilled" out of whole cloth if it had not yet existed. With this thought she fell back into sleep. All this she remembers.

Because now it's day and she's fully awake and he has gone away from her, left her belly to resume its emptiness, left her hands, like his, in need of some live thing to hold.

Of course he would go, and without waking her, ashamed both for needing her and for the things he said, this boy so feral and shy he might not come to her again. The possibility brings her close to panic. She can't see any of his clothing, any sign he has been here, not even an imprint where he lay. Yet the house still holds his damp-earth smell, much as it holds her odors and its own, as if they're in some three-way conversation.

It's then she hears small noises coming from the kitchen—rasping, clinking, scratching. Quickly, quietly she gets up, pulls her jeans up underneath her nightgown, throws the gown off, shrugs into her cotton shirt with all its time-consuming buttons. Barefoot, she tiptoes toward the sounds.

He is squatting on the kitchen floor, the brass sink-faucet in pieces at his feet, working a bit of her steel wool scouring pad over some small, round part of it. He looks up when she comes into the room.

"Your water wasn't running right." He flicks his fingernail over a patch of gray-green corrosion on the piece he's holding. "I'm almost done cleaning it. Hope you don't mind."

"I . . . thank you. You didn't need to."

"I know. Figured it's the least thing I could do."

She nods, goes to the stove and feeds the firebox, stirs the coals to steady her trembling fingers. *Don't go. Not so early. Not before I look at you in sunlight. Not before you say my name.*

She smiles at him. "Would you like something to eat? It's rice and beans. Not what most people think is breakfast."

"It'd sure be breakfast to me."

He sits on the floor, bends over his work, has found both pairs of pliers and the small iron file on her tool shelf. She sets the beans and rice in the warming oven, goes back to the front room, pulls one of the picnic benches close enough that she can see him through the door but far enough away he can't affect her. She wants only to look at him without speaking, at the way he moves. After he has gone she'll weave him, his thinness, his concentration, his hands working with the faucet pieces. She's never put even a suggestion of a human figure into any of her work; he'll be the first. It's how she has to think about his leaving, make art of it so she can bear it. She has become a foolish woman overnight. For no other reason than that he held her with strong arms against his thin, hard knees.

After she dishes up the food they sit across the table, both bent too earnestly over their plates. Everything she starts to say seems trivial and so she doesn't say it.

He is the first to speak. "I'm glad you were home last night."

"I'm always home."

"I know."

His words dart through her. She looks at him with a bit more care. For the first time since he pulled her down onto her sleeping bag last night, she feels perhaps she ought to be afraid, wonders why she is not.

"I'm sorry if I bothered you. I won't do it again. I'll get my dog back, get another one. There's a whole pack roams these mountains. Won't be hard to tame one, it's what I did before."

"It's all right. You didn't bother me."

Some bright flame lights his eyes, extinguishes itself so swiftly she doubts what she saw.

"It's more than enough thanks to get my faucet mended. I was afraid the outside pipe had sprung a leak. The one that brings the water from the spring? I had no idea what I was going to do. Wasn't sure if I could even find it. The leak, I mean. The pipe's buried." You're babbling, Katherine. Oh, please shut up.

"From now on you can call on me, that's what."

Him there with his grin, his chest puffed out like a male robin's. She laughs, blushes, stares down at the table.

After too long a silence she looks up. "You live on the other side of Panther Mountain."

"Yeah. Yes, ma'am. I'm working on that house up there. That mansion. The one that burned. Rebuilding it, you might say." He takes a conscious, prideful breath. "It's slow going. Road's washed clean away, so it's not like I can drive a truck of lumber up. I got to carry everything by hand."

"Oh, my. That must be a huge undertaking." More words so silly to her ears she'd rather not say anything.

"Yes, ma'am. It is."

"You don't need to call me ma'am."

"Yes, ma'am." He grins.

Too soon he's finished eating, gets up from the table. He picks up the faucet off the floor, screws it back in place, turns the water on under the sink. Then he opens the faucet, cups his hand under its stream to test the force.

"There." Drying his hands on his jeans. "Good as the day the Old Man put it in."

"The old man?"

"Old Man that built this house. Died and left his homeplace empty. Jimbo told me how to find it, his daddy and him used to sleep in it when they went hunting. That's how I come to be here." Danny smooths a hand over one of the kitchen shelves, along the grain. "Best carpentry work I ever saw. So good you know he had to be that way clear through."

She gets up from the bench, wishes he would touch her, even just her hair.

"Don't go."

Her own words shock her. How has she come so soon to letting them fly out her mouth? Become unable to imagine being in this room, this house, without this boy she barely knows?

But it's true. He should stay here with her. She can make a place for him, knows this. For this poor boy condemned, as she is, to a life alone. No one but she can do it, would do it. Because she's not afraid of him, not really. If only he would touch her hand, her upper arm, her hair.

His eyes fix on her a moment, as if to remember for all time what she looks like. Then he closes them, throws his head back, grimaces like he's in pain.

"Oh, lady. Oh, goddamn you, lady. You're so good. You got no idea what you just said."

He opens his eyes then, and they show so much of him it hurts to look at them. Yet she can't turn away.

"I made that table months ago because I knew someday you'd come. Tore down the smokehouse for the boards the way the Old Man would have done it. Two benches I made. One for me and one for you. Oh, lady, Katherine, I dreamed you long before you ever came."

She sways, can barely stand. How can anyone confess a need so strong?

He stares into her face. "There's something I got to tell you."

She doesn't want to hear, not now, knows this already from the way he's said it. Fights an urge to clap her hands over her ears.

"There was this girl in San Francisco my first night back. She had long blond hair like my mama's and I put my hands in it and don't remember after that. Most times I think I killed her. Yeah, maybe I did." He looks down at the floor, then back at her. His eyes hold more pain than she can bear to see. "I promised God I'd never touch another woman. My whole life."

A blue jay shrieks out in the trees. All her familiar things—her cotton nightgown on its peg, her warped loom, her pewter plate and cup—look strange to her, as if she'd gone outside and come in through a different door.

"You touched me. Last night."

"Not really. Not that way. That's why I laid us down together how I did. So I never could get at you, never hurt you. Not even in my sleep."

"It isn't true about that girl."

She has to stop this story while it's no more than a tightness at her temples, beat it back before it starts to throb and spread. Before everything between her and this boy unravels, comes to nothing.

"You only told me that to frighten me. Like some sort of test."

He stays silent a half second too long. "Yeah, that's what it was. A test."

"Did I pass?" One learns in an instant how to feign lightheartedness.

"Yeah. You didn't run."

He says it with that downturned smile. But with an edge, as if he wished she had.

"Goddammit, lady. I used to stare down at your lamp in twilight from up in the rocks. I'd wait for you to blow it out so I could come and hold you through the night outside your bedroom wall. Lady, I know how you fucking *breathe*. You got no idea how bad I want to stay."

"Then do."

She speaks the words as if she's in a trance. Saliva pours into her mouth.

"Oh, lady, lady. Goddamn you to hell."

He backs away and doesn't take his eyes off her until he's out the door. Until he turns and runs.

HE'S COMING BACK, HE has to. So much has changed so quickly she doesn't want to move even her hand or foot for fear she'll make it worse. He's run down to the privy, gone to have a look around outside, something. People don't just leave like that without telling you why.

But he does not come back, so her standing in her front room, waiting in a patch of too-bright morning sunlight is only foolish. She goes in the kitchen, turns on the sink faucet, stares at the good stream of water coming out, this gift he's given her. She flexes her splayed fingers under it, lets it pour through them, but it's not enough.

In the front room she runs her hand over the table, bends down and peers at its underside, at the cross brace where he nailed the planks—*I made this because I knew you'd come*. Sits on his bench, where he sat, imagines it still holds his warmth. Picks up his empty plate but cannot bring herself to wash it. Instead, seeks comfort in her loom. Her unfinished forest weaving lacks an inch or so of sky. She holds up first one yarn and then another.

Nothing works. Where is he?

She paces from window to window watching for him. When she goes outside it's worse, he could be anywhere. She keeps turning this way and that looking for him, takes forever to split such a tiny pile of kindling, overlooks half the day's harvest in the garden. What is the least she wants from him? If he lives with her for her whole life and never touches her, will it be enough? He can sleep in the loft and in a few nights, seasons, years, she might quit listening for him, quit hoping he'll climb down the stairs and come to her. They will live like brother and sister, mother and son, and it will be all right.

She runs a fingertip over the flaking leather on the book he brought her with the peaches. Wonders why he chose it, what it means. It was a test, he said. She passed it. There was no San Francisco girl. Strange it bothers her more thinking of him lying with this girl than that he might have killed her. Was this the thing he had to know?

She can, will, make a place for him.

Night. Sleepless, she gets up, sits on one of his benches and looks out the window. Hates the full moon for showing her a forest that does not contain him.

28

Endlessly Rocking

DANNY CLIMBS DOWN TO THE CREEK, TAKES OFF HIS WHITE GOOK
suit and washes it in the cold, flowing water, walks back up the hill and
spreads it on a privet hedge to dry. Naked, he stalks through his burnt-
out house. Even like it is, it's the most magnificent house he's ever
seen. He can lose himself in any of its details. The rosettes in the corners of the walnut window frames. The leaping deer carved into the
marble mantel in the parlor. The hundreds of tiny black and white
tiles that make up the single geometric design on the foyer floor.
Things he'd had to search for in his shelves of books to know what
they were and what needed to be done to them. If he took the whole
rest of his life bringing this one house back to how it was, then it'd be
a life well spent.

   He gathers all that's his, brings it and lays it on his mattress in neat
rows. Razor, nail clippers, hospital scissors, comb. The block sander he
used on the floors, the hammer he bought in Elkmont at the hardware

store, two fistfuls of nails. His old, broken-in boots, new boots, new mocs, new jeans, old jeans with both knees worn out, the rotting jungle camo he should throw away and can't. And the rucksack he learned how to fill with everything he owned.

He owns less now. No rifle, sidearm, tarp to shield him when it rains. No lots of things he used to own. Today's packing doesn't take long and he's sorry when it's done. Likes the order the rucksack forces on him. Place for everything, everything in its place.

He spends a good half hour calling for the dog, although he's sure she'll never show. His fault. He never did do right by her. Maybe he was testing her. Would she stay by him if he didn't feed her? Stay by him just out of love? Maybe he'll get dressed and head out with his rucksack, try to find her. Go to that little highway store, buy her some Slim Jims.

Fuck that, she's killed more meat in her short life than he ever will. Let her get her own damn meat, trot back with some for him.

He can't leave yet, his white clothes haven't dried. Or else he should have left a while ago, before the sun dropped down behind the trees.

Truth be told, he's not sure where he's going. Only that he can't stay here, so close to the Dead Lady and yet never close enough. He's either got to go down there and work it out to live with her, or live without her someplace far away.

He brings his damp clothes in, drapes them over a cane chair with a busted seat. Sits cross-legged on his mattress and stares at his rucksack. Wants only to go back to the cabin, mix his life up with the Dead Lady's in every way. He told her about San Francisco and she said to him, "Don't go," like it's God giving him a perfect sign.

Yeah, God, you made it so every goddamn thing I think is about her. I see a tree and wonder does she know its name. I feel a breeze and think how it's just come from sliding off her skin. I can't sleep nights for thinking about her.

He throws his head back, stares at the stain-splotched ceiling. *God, tell me—what the fuck am I supposed to do?*

Next thing, he's rocking, pitching violently on his moldy mattress, arms around his knees. *Can't do it, can't do it.* Back-and-forth, back-and-forth. He is *in control.*

He will not go down the mountain on the trail that overlooks the Old Man's cabin. Will not hide under the overhang and watch her. Will not smile at the girly way she splits her kindling with her arms stuck out like chicken wings. Will not see her little light wink out and know it's safe to stay beside her through the night. Will not feel her soft breath spreading through him till he wants to fuck her brains out for whole days and nights.

No, wants so much more than that.

Can't do it, can't do it. Rocking furiously to stop the tears.

He promised God he'd never touch her. Did his part, upheld his end. He warned her. Came right out and told her about San Francisco. Like talking to a goddamn wall.

"Oh, Danny, Danny, please don't go. Fuck me, love me. Make me have your babies." Because that's what this shit boils down to. Memaw said dreams don't come true.

Don't go.

He rocks now to Dead Lady words, a fast, hard rhythm he can't stop. His tears run down his naked chest onto his belly, where they burn and he can't quit rocking to wipe them away.

Don't go.

So long as he keeps rocking, all his present world will stay the same. If he stops, he'll have to do something. And that thing, whatever it is, will make his world spin out in one direction or another. The setting sun's turned everything around him red. He's thirsty and his vision's growing dim. His rocking's slowed. Sometimes he lurches to one side and has to right himself, regain his balance, start again.

Only, this time he doesn't. This time he falls over on his side and stays there. Closes his eyes, lets his whole world go black.

And cool.

And still.

Don't go.

29

Quilts

SHE EXPECTED HIM TO COME BACK ANY MOMENT, BUT THOSE MO-
ments passed. Now, with the sun so low once again that shadows cover
all the ground, she sits on her porch and gazes across the clearing at
the trees. She has lived these last two days outdoors on any pretext,
staring always into the thick forest looking for him. Because it is un-
thinkable he might not come.

He saved her that day in the snow, brought her inside and built a
fire; she thought it had been all her doing. The knowledge frightens
her, thrills her—that she needed him then for her very life and he was
there.

But now she knows better than to lie down in snow. Knows better,
even, than to give in to her loneliness. Yes, she can make a place for
him. But she has lived alone and she can do it still. Life alone, like
other life, is only a succession of events. You swing from one to an-

other to the next, like you're crossing a chasm on a vine bridge. These everyday occurrences suffice to carry you. Long as you keep moving. Long as you don't look down. Long as you don't contemplate alternatives. *How lovely it would be to have a lover; how glorious to have a child.* She is a foolish woman and deserves what she has gotten. He is a boy too young to grow a decent beard. What she has been contemplating is unnatural.

Yet she can't stop it, lacks even will enough to try, as if he's one last sickness and she's got no strength left to fight. Or as if he's God's gift and she deserves him. Because she didn't kill herself. Because she didn't die. Because she's forced by circumstances to give up what passes for everything. She goes inside to her loom and tries to weave what these two days have been. A rectangle of mournful grays, dark, lonely greens and dry clumps of weeds hurtful to touch. She works furiously, in a race to put this obscene longing behind her. She will not weave a thread for his white clothes in all that darkness.

She is so deep within her work she can't hear any sound outside her own sharp breathing. How else to explain how he gets all the way onto the porch, up to the open door, and she turns only when he blocks her light?

"I came back."

He does not smile.

She nods, needs suddenly to brace one hand against the wall. A thorn from the sharp weeds crosshatched through her weaving nicks the outside of her thumb, spreading a drop of blood in the gray wool. He sees it, sees everything. Wearing a backpack and carrying a huge bedroll on his shoulders, he has to turn sideways to get through the door. Once in, he drops the bedroll in the center of the room.

"I got as far as Elkmont and I bought these quilts, so I reckoned I was coming back. If I was you I'd get out while you still can, grab your little gun and run. Maybe wing me on the fly." He's grinning.

It's as if the floor has tilted and she's sliding off one end with nothing to hold on to.

The boy, Danny, rocks back on his heels. "Yeah, I broke into your house one day while you were gone. Walked all around, touched all your stuff. Held some of it a long time in my hands. It felt good, doing that. From the start I been watching over you just like you were my family."

Heat rises in her face. It seems suddenly important that she be afraid, that she keep her feet planted firmly, so she can maintain her balance.

But none of that is possible.

"Don't go."

His jaw muscles tighten. He bends down, unties the ropes that held the bedroll and unfurls it.

"The brown one's mine, the white's yours. I'll spread mine out up in the loft. Yours, too, if that's the way you want it."

She nods once, afraid to seem too eager. If he doesn't see it, then that's that.

He climbs to the loft with both the quilts and she's left standing there, hands crossed against her chest. Why should she care what he thinks of her? If that's even an issue—perhaps he only wants them to lie with their knees drawn up, like before.

In the kitchen she feeds wood into the stove, stokes its embers into flames, pays careful attention to all she is doing. Her hands shake when she measures out the rice. They will eat supper like normal people. All she's done is take him in. Who can say what will come of it?

"Faucet work all right?"

She starts, nods. He's come back downstairs, but she can't look at him. Instead she turns her back, takes two garden cucumbers off a shelf, slices them at the sink.

He drags a bench into the kitchen. She can hear it scrape against the floor, the creak it makes when he sits down behind her.

"You don't talk much."

She shakes her head.

"It's nice. Most of what folks say's not worth the hearing."

His odd speech, a mountain dialect, but tempered. She smiles then, lets herself turn toward him, catches him gazing at her as one might a racehorse, an animal one watches for one's own delight. She looks away. The cabin suddenly seems overcrowded with their movement, forcing them too close, too soon. She makes a small involuntary sound; he draws a quick breath like an answer, then climbs back to the loft. What is she doing with him here? Why can't she make it stop?

The rice has come to a slow boil the way she wants it. She slices tomatoes, cucumbers, conscious always of the sounds he makes above her, quiet and orderly, setting out his things. Her throat's dry and her face is hot, as if from fever.

Sitting across from each other at the table, they eat silently, can't meet each other's eyes. When they've finished, she washes their plates and forks. Then there is nothing left to do.

She comes back from the privy, runs a pan of water, sponges off in a corner of the porch, puts on her nightdress. When she passes him beside the stairs she cannot look at him. In the loft, he has spread the two quilts side by side, the plain brown one and then the white one with its fingernail-size flowers. No, this is a good thing, his being here. It will all be all right. She pulled that baby from the street and felt his small heart beat against her breast.

Downstairs, the front door closes and he shoots the bolts. In the loft, she lies on her white quilt in her white nightdress, arms folded over her chest, hears him cross the room, his bare feet on the first stair, then the next one.

Now whatever is going to happen will begin.

30

All of It Burns Him, Even Air

WHATEVER HE DOES, HE WILL NOT HURT HER.

Danny grabs a fistful of mint out of the garden, stuffs it in his mouth and chews. On the porch, with the bucket of cold water, he washes himself clean. Inside, he takes the lantern from the table. Stands still a moment to quiet his shaking.

"A right-broke horse won't lose its wildness, keeps it all for you." From a disintegrating paperback midway along his second shelf. That's how Danny wants his Katherine to love him, strong as his mama loved his daddy. The thought boils inside him as he climbs up to the loft.

She lies there in her white, flowered nightdress on his white, flow-ered quilt. In the dim light her eyes are enormous, their pupils large and black. Her gown comes all the way down to her ankles, where her feet poke out small and helpless looking. He needs to touch her. Somewhere. Now. Needs to begin the thing. Kneeling beside her, he captures her right ankle in the circle of his thumb and forefinger. Feels her tendons slide over her bones, like with her wrist bones that night in the storm. It's like he's looking at an X-ray, learning her clear through. He lets go of her ankle, traces with his index finger the thin bones that lead off from her toes.

He wants every part of her with equal intensity. Her foot is just the first part that he came to. It's strange to him, elegant, somehow. Different from anything he's always thought about as feet. He bends down, rests his cheek against it. She watches him and doesn't move or make a sound.

Danny lays her foot back on the comforter, looks in her huge eyes again. "I've never done this before, not really. I want us to do everything there is."

It's true, looked at a certain way. He couldn't get it up with that hippie girl in San Francisco. Should have done it earlier with some slant-eye gook girl who would not have mattered, except he thought Janelle was waiting. Over there it's all they ever talked about except the war. The perfect fuck. The perfect girl. Back home.

The Dead Lady, Katherine, lets out a tiny sigh and he can feel some caught-up thing inside her letting go. He takes the hem of her gown in both his hands, lifts it gradually and just looks at her, one part at a time. The offset bones beside her ankles. Soft flesh on the insides of her knees. That dark mystery between her legs that's no more and no less than all the rest. Her navel that's a small, dark hole.

He stops there. Wants to see her all at once.

"Take it off the rest of the way yourself. Your shift. Pull it off over your head." His words slur together like his mouth is full of mush. He will never hurt her.

She moves to do the thing he's asked. He looks away. When he turns back, he draws a hard breath through his teeth from just the sight of her. She lies with her arms above her head and the gown still twisted in them, like some woman in a painting. The tips of her small breasts are red as fire-pink blossoms, her dark hair's fanned over the quilt. All her separate parts call out to him, no one part louder than the rest. He aims to learn the ways of all of them, what each wants most.

Danny slides the gown off her arms without touching them, makes it a pillow for her head. He can do anything he wants with her and she will let him. *It's. All. Right.* The knowledge whips through him, muscular as a caught snake.

The sun has set and the first star has come out. Lone and bright, as if its being in the window, centered there, means something. He holds a match to the lantern he has brought. In its sudden glow she looks like a young girl, a girl his own age. He sits beside her, runs his hand slow-motion down the whole length of her body maybe an inch above it, watching for changes in her eyes, the rhythm of her breathing. Watching to see what he can know.

Sometimes he stays his hand a moment.

"Here?"

She nods.

"Here?"

"Yes."

"Here?"

"Please. Yes."

"Not yet."

When he does first touch her, except for when he held her ankle, it's the soft skin inside her forearm, nothing more. She closes her eyes, draws a sharp breath. It's what he wants to happen, how he's dreamed it. He touches her in other places, holds his right hand flat against them, cups them in his palm. He runs a finger slowly from her throat down to her navel and her body arches into it. He has dreamed this, too.

"Here?"

"Yes." Less like a word than like an exhalation.

He brought a tin cup of water, same as he brought the lantern.

"You should drink."

She shakes her head.

"Yes, drink now." It's happening too fast. He needs to slow things down.

He holds her head up, brings the cup up to her lips and tilts it. She takes large, thirsty gulps. Yeah, he knows what she needs even before she does. He drinks after her, puts the cup down empty. She rocks herself, her hips, against him. Gently, like maybe she's not aware of it. Like maybe it's something she can't help.

"Lie back now, that's a good girl."

He brushes her damp hair out of her eyes, loves it how she's like a child there on the quilt and he's her daddy. He can touch her now and does so. Does things to her he's only heard about, which is most things. Does new things he makes up on the spot.

"Don't do that, it hurts. I don't like it."

Loves how her words come all thick-sounding.

"Yes, you do. You just don't want to like it." He's heard talk that that's the way of it with some things at the first. "Or you don't want me to know you like it."

"That's not true."

"Want me to stop?"

"Yes. No."

"Which is it then?"

"Don't stop. No, please don't stop."

Her face is ugly and contorted and her hands are claws that dig into his shoulders. He loves her so hard right now he dares not think of it. Knows he must not, will not hurt her.

Inside, she's so hot it burns him, burns all through him. Makes it so everything he touches burns him, even air. Him dying from it, that will be all right.

No, not all right. It will be beautiful, more beautiful than he can ever say. So beautiful to die from how his Katherine burns him.

"Be still," he tells her.

"I am."

"Be still inside, too."

"I can't. Can't be still there anymore."

Her face twists up and her whole body arches hard and quick, like some animal hit in the road. Her eyes fly wide open and she stares at him like she might kill him to get all of him she wants. Wants him that bad. Wants Danny.

And he is made of glass that's going to shatter. Sees outside the window that bright star, knows it must fall because he can feel inside himself the arc it's going to make, how it will burn.

All stars must fall into place.

All.

Right.
Now.

THEN IT'S OVER. HIS head rests against her breast and he is in a strange and unknown world where he has everything he's ever wanted. He stays a long time there, afraid to move. Her body is this new world's hills and valleys and his breath's a breeze on her moist skin to cool her.

He runs a finger down her belly and she squirms beneath it.

"Want to." Her words come slurred inside a whisper.

Truly, his heart stops beating. He draws her close to him again. "Me too."

This time is different. As are the rest, each from the others. Different in the way all clouds are different. Or all people. Or all fingerprints. He knows that that's the way of it, no two will ever be the same.

At last, when Danny's bright star has become the morning star, he folds her in his arms and gazes at her face until she sleeps. Knows this is how he'll hold her all his days.

31

The Way It Is and Will Be

SHE LIES IN THE LOFT, WITH THE NOON SUN HIGH AND A FLY BUZZ-
ing at the window to get out. She has slept much too late. She has not
gone to the garden. She is sore and sticky and her mouth feels bruised
and swollen. The quilts, her gown, her body, the entire loft, maybe the
whole cabin, the surrounding forest, reek of their lovemaking. Irrelevant, all of it, this morning's word to live by. Irrelevant when weighed
against all that took place in last night's darkness, how she wants it all
again. Irrelevant against this morning's fact she did not wake—will
never again wake—alone.

He's downstairs doing something with the stove that makes its
iron eyes clank, a warlike sound if you're not the one making it. Frying
something. Fish. And she wants him so soon again. Wants him beyond shame. Even beyond hunger—the fish smells awfully good.
Wants to lie up here and think about the night before, relive it, revel
in it, wallow in it. Until he comes back and starts it all again.

In one night he's made her thoroughly a whore. She wants him, this boy, even though she can't remember what he looks like, can remember only that he looks like what he is, barely out of his teens. Beyond that it's bits and pieces. His scraggly beard that day in the courthouse park, not sun-bleached like his hair but red, the color of his pubic hair. His eyes, how their clear gray films over in desire. Thin lips, a mouth that tastes of mint. A body leaner than hers, stronger. That's all. Not someone she could pick out in a crowd.

Or want to.

But that doesn't matter, none of it. What he looks like is just one more irrelevance; she knows all of him she needs.

Because that's what it is. A need, like food or water. No, like air. She's never known a need so strong, her mommy's little good girl who never once did anything she shouldn't have, who made Phi Beta Kappa and learned how to draw so very fine. Oh, there are many explanations for why she squirms down in the quilts, wants him before she's even washed herself. But they all pale beside the strength of her desire itself. Last night. Some things. Things he did to her, or made her do, or that she did unbidden. Shameful things she wants to do again—her mind lingers on them, even as it wants to move away. In less than twelve hours he has changed her into someone she no longer knows. Dazed, disgusting, disquieting. Someone who begs, "Please, please, don't stop; don't ever stop," as tears run down her face.

Before last night she could not have imagined it. That she, that anyone, might find themselves so thoroughly, exquisitely alive.

Beyond that, what does she feel for him? She doesn't know, perhaps doesn't want to know. She was right that evening by the pond, there are great gifts in everything. For now that's enough. She rises, slips on her gown, smooths it over her bruised body imagining his hands, and descends barefoot from the loft.

He is standing at the stove, his back to her, wearing only the wrinkled linen pants that were the white thread in her weaving. His shoulder blades stick out like wings on a bird too young for feathers, bird far too young to fly. His youth, the pale skin of his back, repulse her: that she has done such things with someone still a boy and that this boy has mentored her. She stands quiet a moment, so she can know that seed of distaste nested deep in her desire, how one feeds the other, makes it grow.

He senses her and turns. "Morning."

"Afternoon."

"Whatever."

That deep voice that always catches her off guard. He gives a lazy smile and looks her up and down, seems older now despite his innocent white back, more assured than even yesterday. Older than she herself. The daddy.

She comes up behind him, circles her arms around his waist, pulls him against her.

"Watch it. The grease."

"Sorry." She backs away, her breath unsteady.

"It's almost ready." He turns to face her, nods toward the table in the front room. "Sit down. There."

He looks at her differently than yesterday. If he were to look at her that way on a street somewhere, a street with other people, she would die of shame for how it makes her want him.

He slides a perfectly fried fish onto her plate, adds to it sliced tomatoes. If she reaches out, touches his hand, his arm, it doesn't count. He has to be the one. This boy young enough to be her son.

He eats his fish and watches her eat hers. Watches her jaw grow slack from wanting him, until she has to gouge the tiny bones out from the sides of her mouth with her fingers.

"When did you get them?" Can't steady her voice.

"I set the lines last night. Checked them this morning before you got up, and there they were. You like yours?"

She nods. Wants him with fish bones dropping from her mouth. *Oh, God, please let him touch me.*

She lays her left hand on the table, flat, and doesn't look at it. He reaches out, traces along her finger bones.

"Want to." She can hardly mouth the words.

"Eat your fish. And wash your hands after."

His voice sounds harsh, and yet he smiles at her. His eyes are filled with light.

* * *

AND THIS IS HOW it is and will be, the sun so bright on everything it touches, the darkness a soft feather bed, and never anything to keep Danny and Katherine apart. Chores left undone, quick, guilty visits to the garden, kindling split in a race with the setting sun. Always knowing nothing matters but the two of them together.

How they devour it—there is no better word. She thinks of nothing else but him, the two of them together. Are they the only ones to ever live this way? Surely they must be. If they were the norm, societies, economies, whole nations would disintegrate. No one to teach the children, heal the sick, collect the garbage—they're all home in bed screwing their brains out.

She's changed, she feels it. How can anyone live constantly in such a heightened state and not be? She brought no mirror, thinking she would not live long enough to need it. One afternoon she tears herself away from him while he is sleeping, makes her way down to the pond to see her face reflected in its dark, still water. Sleepy, half-lidded eyes, a soft, complacent mouth—her very features cause her to desire him, that he has done these things to her and that it will continue. She runs her hands across her breasts and down her belly. Thinks how he sleeps always with one hand between her legs.

"I was afraid of sleep when I got back," he's told her. "I'd wake in the dark and not know where I was. Now when I wake up I always know—I'm here with you. You don't mind, do you?"

"No, it's all right."

"Yeah."

And so she wants him even in her dreams.

Who is he, this boy with a man's voice and old eyes, this boy she has let come into her life so completely? How much is there of him to know? It doesn't matter. He and she are so alike in all the ways that count. They two in all the world have found each other, recognized each other as members of the same lost tribe. And she has emigrated with him to some wild and undiscovered country. How lucky she is, luckier than anyone who's ever lived.

She runs back to the cabin, up the stairs, lies down beside him, presses her breasts against those sharp, white shoulder blades. Slides his hand between her legs, ashamed for doing so. Repulsion and desire. She is a goddess; she loves and is loved; compared to this, all the rest is irrelevant.

Fall

32
================

With People

THEY'RE SITTING NAKED IN THE LOFT, HIS BACK TO HER, HER LEGS straddling him. She is combing out the tangles in his long hair with her fingers.

"I need to go to town."

She has put off telling him, hates to say it now, when the afternoon sun slants through the open window where the maples and the hickories are just starting to turn. When the weather is just cool enough for her to nest into his warmth, stay quiet there.

He sighs, turns. "What for?"

"Food."

"I'll catch more fish."

"I want to leave a weaving at the gallery."

The muscles tighten in his back.

"If you go, I go." He grins, reaches around and pulls her to him. "Elsewise, somebody might steal you."

A thrill runs through her. That he would rescue her like some prince in a fairy tale. How silly. Yet he already has. She spreads her legs farther apart and slides in firm against him. Rocks gently there until he twists around and reaches for her.

AFTER BREAKFAST THE NEXT morning she rolls up the one weaving she's finished since he came, puts it in the cart, then kisses him in thirsty gulps. "Let's get it over with."

How used to their solitary life she's grown. To give it up for even a day disquiets her. On the trail they travel fast and rarely speak. Just before the big bend, the last place no one can see them, they stop—simultaneously, as if they had discussed it—cling hard to each other for a moment and then move apart.

She points toward the patch of laurel below them. "My car's down there, what's left of it. Somebody stripped it and then bashed it all to pieces."

He frowns. "You didn't need to be living here alone. No telling what some folks might do."

"For a while I was frightened they might come looking for me, but they never did."

He studies her a moment, slides his left hand into her right back pocket, kneads her buttocks until she plants her feet and doesn't want to move.

"Now. You put your right hand into my left back pocket. That way we'll keep each other close, even in a crowd. I'll always take care of you. You know that."

The way he looks at her makes her flush, makes her feel once more that he's the older, wiser one, this boy who's seen so much.

"We'll both push the cart one-handed."

She nods, and then they're on the dirt road headed for the highway. From here out for the whole day, even with his hand inside her pocket he will not be close enough. Already she knows this.

A truck whizzes past and she jumps back.

He pulls her to him, gives her butt a squeeze. "That truck won't hurt you. It knows you're with me."

She laughs, but it's strictly for his benefit. She is more frightened now, with him here, than when she walked this road alone. Familiar dimples in the asphalt become places she might stumble. ("Careful, watch out.") He has made her conscious of such things, of all the ways she needs him and has all along. Needs always his hand caressing her inside the dark of her back pocket, until she feels it everywhere, in all the places where she once felt only fear and pain. Needs him like that day she needed him out in the snow, to save her very life. Needs him to turn her body into some electric thing she can't control and doesn't want to. If this isn't love, she doesn't know what is.

Too soon Elkmont rushes to meet them. Smaller farms, closer houses, more cars on the road. Danny pulls her to him with his back-pocket hand and keeps her close. Now there are sidewalks, the courthouse clock tower above the trees.

The first person they meet is a grizzled old man walking toward them staring at the ground and muttering, "Purina feed, self-rising flour, salt." Over and over, his private mantra.

Danny grins, gives her butt a squeeze. "Geezer out shopping for his wife. Must be Saturday."

She should have known, feels remiss for not knowing. But why? Except here in Elkmont where the stores are open, what could Saturday possibly mean to her—to them—except one more irrelevance? One more piece of once-important information that no longer applies.

They wheel the cart into the market and she picks items off the shelves. Rice, beans, salt—staples. She's stored their garden vegetables in holes he dug deep in the ground, they two working together as one being.

In the post office there's a line. People fall in behind them and they take their hands out of each other's pockets. The air-conditioned air is icy on her fingers and she feels unconnected, as if some stranger's merest nudge might roll her far away from him like an unclaimed ball.

"Don't lose me." She mouths the words softer than a whisper.

He takes one of her freezing hands. "I won't."

She's got no mail, wasn't expecting any. Came only to check, because it's what one does with one's P.O. box.

After the hardware store, the bank, he steers their cart to a men's clothing store and picks out for them both sweaters of thick, dark Irish wool and warm canvas jackets with quilted linings.

He shakes out her jacket, holds it up to her. "Rain won't go through it, just the kind that pounds the shit out of you."

Her mother was the last, the only, person who took care of her. Before him.

"You'll need a pair of leather lace-up boots like mine. Can't be running around in the cold in those dumb fuzzy-kitty things you wore last year. It's dangerous." He grins. A little boy, a little bad boy. "Some mean man like me might take to watching you. You couldn't even run away."

She shivers with what must be desire.

Boots and shoes are at the rear of the store. He sits beside her on the bench, their hips, thighs touching, shows her how to wrap the laces. Puts his arm around her, chafes his hand along her upper arm as if to warm her.

"Go on, walk around in them. See what you think."

She gets up, takes a few reluctant steps.

"I like them." Reaches into her front pocket for her billfold.

His hand clamps hard around her wrist. "No. That's for me to do."

She nods. "Thank you." Should have insisted; surely she has more money than he does. Should have defied that tiny, undermining thrill of being cared for.

He puffs his chest out—oh, so proud—a little bantam rooster. Takes a roll of bills from his front pocket. "Stay here on the bench and put your summer shoes back on. I'll go up front and pay, come back and get you."

She nods, glad now she did not deprive him of this moment.

Danny saunters down a vacant aisle, disappears behind a rack of coats, and she is left alone. Already she misses his hand in her pocket, his warmth next to hers, stands up to go to him. Only, the aisle that took Danny away now holds a large man who is smiling, coming toward her with his hand extended.

"Kate! Kate Reid! I'd know you anywhere. Jeez, you look like a million bucks."

She stares, unsmiling.

"Mark Wickham, Kate. Great running into you like this."

His voice. So loud and strange. Voice of a tourist from some other country that she lived in for a while so long ago. He grabs her right hand, gives it three vigorous pumps.

Katherine continues to stare, does not remember him. He looks like all the men she knew back then. Tim, Tim's friends, other men she worked with. Disciplined haircuts, eager eyes that glitter coldly when they need to. Men who always look as if they're wearing suits, even when they're not. Mark Wickham's wearing jeans somebody pressed, a plaid shirt, a too-stylish leather jacket.

He is still talking. "'South's only lady agency head.' 'Stole Carolina Airlines out from under BBDO.' Said so in *Ad Age*. Heard you lit out for California. Hope you're back for good."

She looks only at his mouth as if she might see the strangeness of what's coming out of it, these words that seem about some other Katherine she knows only by hearsay. Steps back from him so he will go away.

He moves toward her, closing the gap. "You know, I always made a point to talk to you at parties. Thought of it as building equity, hoped somewhere down the line you'd hire me."

It's meant as a compliment. Smile. Look down at the floor, then back at him. Say something.

But she's left her script behind and doesn't know her lines. How to explain—her leaving, selling the agency, any of it? Help, please, somebody help. He's blocked her path and she can't get away. She jerks her head from side to side like a caught bird.

A hand presses the middle of her back. Slides down into her pocket.

"Mister, this lady here's with me. She doesn't want to talk to you. You got her mixed up with somebody else."

Mark Wickham opens his mouth as if to argue.

"Leave her the fuck alone."

Danny's words, how they burst out of him like gunshots, disturb her, thrill her.

"I—I . . . sorry, my mistake. Forgive me if I bothered you."

The advertising man, whom she now vaguely remembers, takes a few steps backward, pivots on his heel and hurries from the store.

Danny slides Katherine's hand into his back pocket, throws his packages in the cart.

"Dumbass city shit. Let's get the fuck out of here, go home."

"My weaving. We go right past the gallery."

When they get there they stop outside, look in the window. At the wall hangings, ceramic bowls, small sculptures made of wood and metal. He grasps her chin and turns her head to face him.

"I'll kill any man that bothers you. You know that."

His words disturb the air around her. She can't take them in. Of course he wouldn't, it's hyperbole. That soft, pudgy man, Mark Wickham, meant no harm. He has likely never known nor seen a man like Danny.

"He didn't mean anything. It's just—we were both in the same business. Knew each other by sight, that's all."

There are people walking past. He slides his hand back in her pocket, squeezes, with them both standing there on the sidewalk, and she rocks her hip against him in a way no one can see. *Please. Please.*

He pulls her hard against his body, his arm around her waist to stop her rocking. "What's that about? Your city boyfriend got you all turned on?" He isn't smiling.

"He's not my boyfriend. I want to go home." Her words come out all muzzy, like she's said them into cotton batting.

He brushes her hair off her damp forehead. "Hush, now. We'll be home soon."

She stares down the long highway. "No, we won't."

He studies her a long moment, then grabs her arm, jerks her into an alley by the gallery, slams the cart in after them.

"Climb up on that step there and undo your jeans."

She doesn't move.

"Go on, get up there and unbutton them." His voice is angry.

"They'll see us. People on the street."

"Course they will. But I'm in front of you and so's the cart. They'll see two people talking. The rest they'll never see because they can't imagine it. Come on, we haven't got all day."

His voice is angry, but his hand is warm as it slides down her belly. "Spread your legs."

The step's littered with cigarette butts, off to the side a condom. She does what he asks, can't look at him.

"Goddamn, lady. How long you been wanting it?"

"I . . . Since we left the forest. It's all I've thought about all day."

"My poor lady. Poor Katherine. You should have said something. Should have said, 'Danny, I need you to take care of me right now.' I would have found a way. 'Cause I'm the one takes care of you. The only one."

People pass by on the street but no one looks at them. She stares down at the cigarette butts, dead sprigs of wayward grass, gives herself over to the things his hand is doing.

"Don't you shut your eyes like that. You got to look at me and talk like normal if it's going to work."

"I can't. I don't know what to say."

"Say whatever comes into your head. Just do it." That angry voice again. "Do it, or I'll stop."

She opens her eyes so wide her lids feel propped with toothpicks, takes a halting breath.

"Once. Before here. I owned an. Advertising agency." Her words come out in shards. "Whole top floor. In a tall building. Don't stop, please don't. Why are you stopping?"

"Don't give me that shit about your goddamn glorious past. All that matters, the only thing that matters, is us. Right here. Right now. You're nothing but what you are here, now, with me."

"I'm sorry. Please don't stop. Please don't take your hand away."

"Okay, forget it."

He's right, they two live only in the present. The past, her past, is dead, something to be talked about only in a dead language. Which means not at all.

"Look out at the street and tell me everything you see. Do it. Right now, or I'll stop."

"Please, don't stop. Car. Green car." Her legs spread wide as a Paris whore's. "Black truck. Circling the square. Don't take your hand away. Please, more. Please."

It's as though she's split in two, her eyes, her mind attuned to what's outside of her on the street, while the whole rest of her, every part, cares for nothing save that gathering ecstasy between her legs. She wants it so badly, what he is offering her out here in front of everyone. Has never wanted anything so badly. Wants it beyond shame.

"Old man. Walking right past us. Looking straight at me. We could get arrested. I can't do this."

"Yes, you can. You're my good girl. You don't want me to stop now, do you?"

"No." The word so small she hardly hears it. "Woman. Blue sweater. Going in the grocery." Wants it even beyond fear.

Danny's mouth is slack, his eyes half closed; his breath comes in a ragged rhythm with her own. She stares into his face and sees there every nuance of the pleasure that she dares not show, as if they two truly have become one being. Out here where everyone can see. Looking into his face excites her more than anything his hand is doing. More than anything she can remember.

"Teenage girl. Licking an ice cream cone. On a bench across the street. Dressed in red, everything red. Strawberry ice cream. Sticky on her hands and face. Don't stop. Oh, please, don't stop. Don't leave me. Please, not now. Please, please never leave me. Please don't ever go."

She shudders in deep undulations, bites hard on her lower lip to keep her sounds shut in. Then it is finished. Danny jerks the cart back out onto the street.

"Think you can make it home now? Or will I have to stop somewhere and do you in the goddamn road?"

He says it as if the whole thing had been her idea, her fault, which in a way it was.

She buttons her jeans without looking at him. Out on the highway he slips his hand inside her pocket, keeps it there; she is forgiven. For what? For wanting him more than she could bear? It's not until they turn off at the little grocery and she is sick behind the tree that she remembers she still has her weaving rolled up in the cart.

Back home they climb up to the loft without their supper, make love fiercely, as if they'd been apart for months.

33
Running Away

WEATHER'S TURNING COLD. HE'S PULLED THE QUILTS DOWNSTAIRS by the hearth fire. They've been together since high summer. Ninety, a hundred days. Together in every way. They're in it for the long haul, that's for sure.

Nights, his hand between her legs, he loves how he can make her want him even in her sleep. Some nights it gets so bad, her wanting him that way, that he can't help himself, no matter how he tries. These times, he enters her so gently, comes in her so quietly she never wakes. Mornings, her just rousing from her dreams, he does it all to her again so she won't know what happened in the night.

"How come you never get your monthly?" he asks one afternoon, them lying by the fire.

She shakes her head. "It's part of whatever was wrong with me. The doctors said I never would again."

"Reckon we can't have a baby."

She frowns a little, shakes her head. Her face has gone all sad. Danny rocks her in his arms and a new peace falls on him. He's seen babies born, once saw a woman die from it even with Memaw there. Watched her turn from live to corpse before his eyes, Memaw's hands moving so fast trying to make things right. Whole house stank of blood.

"I don't want a baby," Danny whispers, his lips touching her ear. "I want only you."

HE NEVER SHOULD HAVE brought it up. Days now, all she does is roll those yarns she weaves with into balls, sort her dried weeds into piles, sing songs that sound like lullabies, only they're not. Nights sometimes she whimpers in her sleep. It scares him so bad that when she wakes he only does to her the things she asks him to.

Early mornings, she gets up before him and does her weavings, fingers working furiously in all those little strings. When she's finished one and takes it down, it's just a hairy mess to him. Still, that fancy gallery put some on their wall, so she must be on to something. Wanted to show him that day. He keeps close the memory of what they did instead there in the alley. Runs back through it, times when his soul needs quieting.

So who can tell him why what happens happens? This morning, when he gets up, she's standing staring at the wall, working on another goddamn weaving thing looped on those fucking nails. Got her back to him where he can't see the dawn light on her face, the big thing that gets him out of bed these days.

"Don't do that," he tells her.

"Do what?"

"Don't turn your face away like that."

"It's almost finished, I'll just be a minute." Fingers worming in among the skinny threads as if she hasn't heard. And all while the soft, pearly dawn light's turning to harsh morning sun.

"I said don't you turn your back on me."

"I'm almost through." Her fingers fly too fast to see. She still won't turn around.

"Goddammit, fuck this shit!"

He lurches toward her, pulls back his arm to hit her. Bitch sees it coming, jerks away. Danny's fist slams into the wall just inches from her face. How close he came, the sharp crack of it, how much it might have hurt her, scares him till he wants to puke. But it doesn't scare him half as bad as how she cringes into a much smaller Dead Lady with such wide-open, frightened eyes.

Dumb fucking whore. Made him do it. Wouldn't turn around. And now she acts so damn frightened and pitiful. Let her fuck her fucking weavings. That'll teach her. He, Danny, is out the door and gone.

Hasn't got his jacket, but who gives a shit? Just keep moving and you won't get cold's what Pawpaw used to say. Just keep moving and nothing can stick to you's what Danny says. Words to live by. Keep moving all your goddamn life.

He runs up the mountain out of sight. Doesn't turn back to look till he scuttles under his overhanging rock, where he watched her in the springtime, summertime, good times. Can't see her now. No one outside, door's shut tight. If she had run after him, called his name, he might have turned around, gone back. Made up with her. But she didn't. Or didn't run far enough, didn't holler loud enough for him to see or hear—a phony act with no meat in it.

Whatever. It's warm under his rock and he's comfortable out of the wind. Ought to have some jerky in his pockets, canteen full of water on his belt. Ought to have some reefer. Which he hasn't thought about in months. But he's good. Yeah, he knows how to watch and wait.

When the sun's slanting toward two o'clock she comes out, heads down to the woodshed. His heart quickens like it used to, like she's some kind of hard-to-bring-down prey. Oh, he could watch her all his days. How she moves now, rolls her hips. So different from when he first saw her. Yeah, now anyone with sense to look can see some man's been with her, turned her into a real Class A woman. Kind of man that satisfies her soul yet keeps her hungry for it night and day. Kind of man that's Danny.

If she'll just look up at the mountain like she gives a flying fuck, he'll climb back down and go to her right now. But no, bitch keeps her nose pointed straight ahead. Won't give an inch. Makes his insides squirm in some bad way. Like the song says, no direction home.

Yeah, him up here and her so far below not looking for him feels like right after he comes. Like he's spinning out into a void, an astronaut that's popped his tether. It's got so Danny hates to come. Hates even the incredible first part where it's like all the universe, even the dark behind the Milky Way, is balanced on the tip end of his dick, and he is part of everything that was or is or ever will be. Hates it because it's just God's shitty trick to make him do it in the first place. Make him do it so he'll get to where the universe packs up its atoms and goes home, leaves him flapping there in empty space. No comfort from the Dead Lady in those times. Might as well be a cold marble statue, even when she's warm and holding him. Stupid whore's got no idea.

The bad part wasn't bad at first. It's grown worse over time, till now he puts it off long as he can. In fact almost never comes, no matter how she begs him. In a weird way it's working pretty well. Him happy riding on the brink of things and her there squirming like a frenzied cat—oh-please-oh-please-oh-pleasepleaseplease. Oh, yeah, he doesn't want for more. And when she comes it's like he's coming, too. He wants to stop time, keep her there, a part of him forever. If Heaven's just one single moment God lets you live for all eternity, yeah, he'll take that one.

The air is cold and still and Danny leaves his refuge and climbs higher. How good his house looks up ahead surprises him all fresh again. Whole and perfect. Close up and inside, though, it's a different story. The leaks are worse, the rotting books stink, and something—a raccoon?—has nested in his mattress, clawed holes through the moldy ticking. What he gets for being gone so long.

Poor old neglected house. He goes after his bedroom floor with the sanding block he left behind till both arms ache. Feels so good he might just stay up here, let things go back to how they used to be. She won't come after him—even if she can still find the path, she'll be too scared to climb it.

Last time he picked up a piece of sandpaper, clamped it in the sanding block, it was June, July, and he was spending all his time with her and her not even knowing, all his days and nights running together. No more reading Gatsby's books by then. No, it was her bent over her little garden beds like she was petting baby chicks. Or whispering her breaths to him all through the night, his arms hugging the cabin's stones. Him so delirious just to be that close to her he didn't want for more, not even when she beckoned to him in his Long Dream. Now things he dared not even dream are real. Back in the city, before she took sick, she could've had anyone she wanted, her with her goddamn office in the sky. Now she wants only him. For always.

Weird how he got that day in town after chasing off that dumb Atlanta shit. Loved her so much he couldn't help himself. Dragged her off into an alley, made her come in front of God and everybody. When they got home, fucked her like he wasn't human. Did it and did it, shot off every time. Like the sun was never going to rise again.

HE GETS BACK TO the cabin a couple minutes before dark. She's at her loom and turns when he comes through the door, then doesn't turn away. Instead, she goes to stir the pot that's bubbling on the stove and when she passes close he sees her eyes are red.

"Don't ever do that again," she tells him. She does not say please.

And, oh, he won't do it again. He won't.

DANNY HUNKERS FAR BACK in his rock cave to keep out of the wind, pulls a pack of rolling papers from his pocket, peels one off, folds it and sprinkles reefer in its gutter. He licks one edge and rolls a perfect jay, lights it with a book match from the Elkmont Diner, "Home of the Bottomless Coffee Cup." A couple seeds crackle and spark as he draws a lungful of the pungent smoke. Who said you can't get no satisfaction?

Yeah, by now Danny's got the thing worked out. What it comes down to, most days he just needs to get away a little, go back to what's his. You can grow so used to having someone in your sight you get to thinking if they go away there's nothing left but empty. You'll do anything to keep them there.

Yeah, well, that's not the deal.

Deal is, you get the fuck out before they do. That way you get to say two things about it: how far and how long. You push them both up to the outer limits you can stand. Then and only then you go back home. If you left pissed off in the first place, then so much the better. Bitch'll know it's all her fault. You come back through that door, she'll love on you like you been gone for years. Just ask old Stanley Kowalski, he knew what to do. Danny'd never read a play. Not easy, but this one was worth his while. Sometimes you learn shit in weird places, even from plays.

The reefer helps. Instead of flailing unhinged out in empty space, he floats now, unafraid. That's what he does these days. Climbs up here soon as it gets light, changes into his old, ragged camo he keeps stashed under his rock. Doesn't read much now. Tokes up and waits for her to come outside, trip down the privy path, bring back some wood, poke around for that dried grass and stuff she threads into her weavings. Maybe a little side trip to the garden, dig up a beet or such. Two weeks ago he went to town, bought her a rocker at the Goodwill. No end to how she loves that thing. Sits in it every time she sits. A prime investment, is that rocker. Now she just loves old Danny's ass, all the home fires burning bright.

But, Lord, how he still craves to watch her from up here. The way she moves. Anymore, it's like she grew out of the goddamn ground, knows everywhere she walks and everything she sees or touches. She's like him when they sent him out to kill. Alive to everything around her. Watching her, that brings it all back. He wishes he could be like that again. Like he was over there. Or wishes he could be like her, be her. Not till she's gone back in and he's sure she's not coming out again does he climb up to his house and get to work.

Right now it's mostly patch-up stuff. Keep the rain and raccoons out. Steal some boards from someplace, nail them someplace else. He carted in a hammer and a saw from town, more sandpaper, a miter box. Lord, please let him live years enough to need a miter box for something in this house. Then he'd be down to finish work. No, he bought the miter box for something else. He's making her a loom.

And it's the best, most beautiful work he's ever done. A loom that's like a table, so she'll never need to turn away from him again. Nails all around the edges. Like what's on the wall except no wall. To go with it, a wooden chair the perfect height, and with a back for her to lean against. Cherry. Prettiest wood in the whole world. Glows like it's got a steady fire inside. Same as she does. Set it in the center of the room so he can walk all the way around it, see her face. Tore out the two dining room mantels to make them. Dining room's wrecked anyhow, rain always pouring in. If that mantel wood had sense, it'd crave to be a loom.

Today, same as always, Danny gets down on his knees before starting to work on it. He always means to pray to God, but ends up praying to the Old Man. Old Man who carpentered the Dead Lady's, Katherine's, cabin, their cabin now. And to Pawpaw. "Show me how to do it right, whichever part I got to do today. Help me do my very best. For her."

When the sun slinks down behind the tall pines and his high's thinned out and his mind is flashing once again on empty outer space, he scuttles down to his rock cave, tokes up one last time. Changes out of his old camo, heads for home.

She's waiting for him, missed him, and they climb up to the loft. Stoned, he can do everything, even come. And then she holds him. Afterwards, he stokes the hearth fire, lights the lamps, eats supper while she smiles at him across the table.

And it's a good day, all of it, clear through.

34

The Deer

SHARP LIGHT SILHOUETTES THE LEAFLESS TREES AGAINST THE SKY
and morning frost glistens. Crows caw at the garden's edge, their
sounds carrying in the clear air. By afternoon, working feverishly, she
and Danny have piled their table with the last summer vegetables and
filled the dugout underneath the porch with pumpkins, butternuts,
parsnips, potatoes. They make a good team. She picks, he carries; she
digs, he stores. They meet on the path from house to garden with
quick embraces, breathless smiles. In their shared, frenetic labor she
finds calm and reassurance. This is the true Danny, not the one who
would have struck her. A small core of resistance she has built up un-
awares crumbles—he is indeed as she has always thought him.

Each day comes slightly colder now. She takes a surprising, atavis-
tic joy that in the kitchen stand rows of mason jars, their contents
colored like the autumn leaves; that they have done this thing together, she and Danny. That they have made a home. On the morning

of the first hard freeze, the bright sun glitters. She hears him in the kitchen, dresses quickly, sees him out the door for town.

"Bring yarn. Colors you like."

She had expected some objection, not enough room in the cart. But he nods, smiles, is gone. The house is hers now. Strange how since they've been together she has come to hoard her time alone, to treasure it—another gift he's given her. She moves quickly through her daily chores, mindful always of the loom's pull. Danny's absence creates a peace for her to work inside, as if it's another room he's built onto the cabin. She never tires of him. He's like the forest: There is always more to know. They talk little, only of what's important at the time. She is coming to believe that people living in close physical proximity and with enough intensity of feeling will communicate without words as a matter of routine. Thus the unsaid doesn't matter, indeed may not exist.

They are so close in this way that sometimes she is brought up short by the strangeness of their pairing. On the face of it, they're not alike in any sense. Had they both lived in the city, they would not have known the same people, shopped in the same stores, driven the same roads. Had they passed each other on the street, they would not likely have looked into each other's faces. Had they stood close, on a downtown corner waiting for a light to change or in a grocery line, they almost certainly would not have spoken. Sometimes this realization chills her even now.

When he is gone she misses him, the essence of him—the feel of his skin, the smell of his hair, the sounds of his breathing—so much more than any conversation they might have. Their life together is itself one wordless, never-ending dialogue. He will come back today a different person, from the things he's done and seen without her. She will lie close to him and know those things, will feel no need to ask.

She loops a braid of dried pond grass through the loom's warp, lays a length of dry-grass-colored yarn above it. She does not see pictures of the city in her mind's eye anymore, only what is here around her—the huge, gnarled chestnut oak by the meadow, their winter wood stacked in the shed, Danny's face with moonlight on it in the darkness—as if none of her life that came before had ever been.

That man in Elkmont, she can't recall his name, only her shock that she had ever known him. If Danny hadn't come to rescue her, who's to say what she'd have done. Run, most likely. Hidden herself in a little copse of trees out near the edge of town. Where Danny would have found her.

Her weavings since that day are far better than anything she did before. They have a wildness in them, exhilarating and unsettling. A wildness beyond anything in that bought weaving she once hung so proudly on her office wall. Yet it's all done in his absence, the good work. She weaves very little when he's here. When he comes into the room her body grows more supple, moves more freely, turning her weaving into a performance, something done for him, not for the work itself. Too soon he reaches for her, pulls her down onto the hearth quilts, and her weaving is forgotten.

At these times she leaves bruises, scratches, without realizing it. Once, the day after, she came upon him gazing at a long welt she'd made on his belly. He ran his finger down it as if it were some precious treasure he wanted to keep always. She backed away in silence, so as not to let him know she'd seen.

Today he has many things to do and will be gone longer than usual. She will not let herself imagine how he might look, from behind and from a distance, walking out the dirt road toward the morning sun; or in town at the little grocery, stooping to heft one of the twenty-pound cloth bags of beans laid on a bottom shelf. As always, his being gone makes everything inside the cabin different. Flatter, perhaps. Pieces of bright-colored paper against a dark background. Often, like today, she walks through the house, stands in every shaft of sunlight so she can feel its heat without him, touches things he's touched—his razor, a soft cotton shirt—and tries to fathom how his absence changes them. Because it does. It changes everything.

The house settles and ticks in the cooling afternoon. When she goes to the hearth, throws on a log, the fire explodes in a shower of red sparks. She tosses on another just to see the show. Danny has been building all the hearth fires lately and she's missed this. Hard to accept her world as narrower in even one respect because of him.

By late afternoon she's weaving frantically to finish what she started in the morning, doesn't want to lose the flow. Sees this as her duty, so his return won't be an interruption—a secret bargain with herself that she has made. By the time the sun has set the lower sky on fire she's not accomplished everything she wanted, but she has reached a stopping place where she can know what's left to do. When he bursts through the door she's glad to see him, feel his wiry arms around her, glad they're together once again.

He carries beans and salt into the kitchen. And coffee, which he brought once before. She herself doesn't drink it, but likes when the house smells of it, because it is his. The rest of what he's brought is yarn. Skein after skein mashed in the bottom of the cart so he could carry more, yarn so soft and lovely she herself would not have thought to choose it. She squeezes a cream-colored ball that springs back lively as a young lamb in a meadow. He has brought a little white, more greens, browns, black—and the rest bright-colored as spring meadow flowers. She touches the skein she's holding to her cheek.

"You like that?"

She nods, smiles.

"Well, if you're thinking that's hot shit, you better step outside and get a look at my surprise."

He grabs her hand and drags her out the door. There before her lies a doe, her still head resting on the porch step. Her expression is calm, her eyes almost human. Katherine stares at the animal that breathed with her so long in all her fantasies, expects her to get up and run away, then realizes with a pang of sadness that this doe will never run again.

"Isn't she a beauty!" Pride's got him bouncing on the balls of his feet.

"She's—how did you—?" Can't think what to say.

"I bought a bow."

He squats beside the animal, runs his hand along her neck, as if she is alive and he is petting her.

"Wound's on her other side. They got such pretty eyes, does. I love looking at them. Love watching how they leap and run. They run so fast."

He says the words as if he's talking to himself. His legs tremble slightly from the strain of carrying the animal. When he pulls Katherine to him he transfers a wild, damp deer smell to her clothing; she inhales deeply, fascinated. Then he is hauling her by the hand to the shed, filling her arms with wood. Soon a bonfire blazes in the clearing, flinging its orange glow out through the humid night. Danny drags the deer into its circle, a ground fog of golden smoke curling around them. His movements have the economy of things done many times.

"Bring a pan."

When she returns with the kitchen dishpan, he slits the doe's throat. His work is quick and clean, for which Katherine is grateful. In the firelight nothing seems what it is. The blood's a thin syrup collecting in the bowl. Katherine holds her chilled fingers in its stream to warm them. Danny bends and fills his cupped hands with it, raises them to his mouth and drinks, then grins at her.

"Makes you run fast like the deer. I bet you won't drink it."

It's a dare; he's smiling. She dips her right hand in the bowl, fills her palm. Drunk fast, it's not repulsive. *Don't think about it. Any of it.* When she looks up he is no longer smiling. He dips his own hand in the bowl, touches a sticky finger to her forehead, paints a bloody cross that drips into her eyebrows. He undoes the buttons of her shirt, pushes her jeans down off her hips. His breath sounds like the hissing flames.

He bloodies his fingers in the bowl again, touches between her eyes. Traces a line straight down, over her nose, the cleft at the center of her lips, the hollow in her throat. Dips his finger yet again to trace between her breasts, past her small, round navel to end in the triangle of coarse black hair between her legs.

He steps back, looks at her. In the fire's flickering shadows she can't read his face.

"You are more beautiful than the deer. More beautiful than all the world."

His words come gravelly and slurred, and his eyes burn with small, reflected flames. A sudden terror flashes through her, bleaches everything around them white as bones, then disappears.

He bends down, grabs her flannel shirt up off the ground and thrusts it at her in a wad.

"Put your shirt back on, pull up your jeans. It's cold and I've got work to do."

Why does he sound so angry? Why did he start the thing if he did not intend to finish it? She buttons her shirt along the trail of the doe's drying blood, pulls her jeans over the last of it. He has turned back to the deer as if she, Katherine, had never been there.

The fire leaps higher. He strings the animal up on a low limb at the clearing's edge, where it sways like a hanged man in the eerie light. Danny's shirtless body shimmers, godlike, in a golden steam, as he works with his skinning knife.

When the deer's roasting heart sizzles in the flames, he slides it off its green spit, cuts a slice, turns back to Katherine and offers it to her on the flat of his knife blade. "It's a ritual, what a boy gets fed on his first hunt."

"I wasn't with you when you killed her."

"Yes, you were."

They share the heart between them, him gazing at her all the while. When they are done, he goes back to the swaying carcass, a scene surreal in the firelight.

Suddenly, what she has eaten rises in her throat. She whirls around and retches in the brush behind her. It feels almost comforting, this familiar thing that has not happened since she lived alone here and felt safe. She wipes her mouth and turns back to the fire, and to Danny.

Winter

35

Three Presents

THEY SPEND LONG HOURS UNDER THE HEARTH QUILTS NOW; IT'S gray outside.

"What day is it?" he asks.

"I don't know."

"I thought you made marks on the wall."

"I quit."

They have lost track of dates, recall days only by their small events, and not in sequence. Was it three days ago or four he caught the trout? Was it yesterday they walked out to see the frozen cattails by the pond? How many days ago was the full moon? Their order doesn't matter. They all run together, watercolors on absorbent paper, to produce the dreamlike whole that is their life now.

Winter isn't so much blowing in as falling on them in a stillness, like the last brown leaves. Some mornings she wakes late to woods that have been lightly brushed with snow. There's less reason to go outside. Some days Danny even forsakes his time up on the mountain. They are two against the cold. He's brought a book. They read aloud from it to each other in the gray afternoons. *The Last Days of Pompeii.* An odd choice, poorly written, boring, but he will not skip it—"It comes next on the shelf." After it there's *Catcher in the Rye.*

They know each other's ways by now.

"I never loved anyone," he tells her late one evening, the room luminous with snow-light.

He's turned away and she can't see his face, holds her breath for him to finish. He does not, there is no need.

Yet one morning when she goes out to the garden early, while he's still asleep, to dig the last of the Jerusalem artichokes before a bank of dark northerly clouds rolls in, she returns to find him pacing on the tiny porch, his hands jammed in his pockets.

He wheels around, blocking her way.

"Goddammit, you weren't anywhere in this whole fucking house." He grabs her shoulders, shakes her hard. "You can't just leave like that."

She steps back, stares in unbelief. "You were sleeping. I went to dig the artichokes."

He stands silent, doesn't move.

"It's cold. Let me in."

His mouth clamped tight, he opens the door.

When she goes in the kitchen to put the artichokes away, a window rattles. Suddenly their sturdy house seems frail.

LATER THAT AFTERNOON, AS if to make amends, he brings home a cut tree. To shake off the snow, he knocks its trunk hard on the porch step. Once, twice, three times, until she flings open the door.

"Tomorrow's Christmas." He's grinning like he's known it all along and kept it back for a surprise. Or for some unknown other reason.

"Are you sure?"

"Sure, I'm sure. Aren't you? It's cold enough."

He drags the tree inside, a gorgeous cedar that's a good three feet too tall, lops off its excess height, chops up the fragrant waste and throws it on the hearth fire. She rolls and ties small balls of brightest-colored yarns as decorations, shapes a larger one into an angel, gives it a pair of delicate green cedar wings. Believes she doesn't miss her mother's ornaments, or the trees she had with Tim: She and Danny are making traditions of their own to last them all their lives.

Their Christmas morning threatens rain. He presents her with a set of kitchen implements he's carved. Spoons, forks, spatulas, all of warm, red cherry wood. They are plain and perfect.

"They're beautiful," she tells him. "Like what the Old Man might have done." He smiles shyly, looks down at his hands.

When she brings out the poncho she has woven, hands it to him, he stares at it as if he's not sure what it is.

"It's the colors you like. I asked you once to get them."

His face crumples like a wad of paper. "Nobody ever—" He composes himself with visible effort, frowns. "What in hell did you go to all that trouble for? You never should have done it."

He turns away, but not so fast she doesn't see him pinching at the corners of his eyes. She stands quiet until he turns back to face her.

"What do I do now?"

"Put it on. The slit goes over your head. Depending on how you wear it, it's quite warm."

He drops it down over his head, wraps it around himself.

"Shouldn't have fucking done it. All that secret shit when I was gone."

"I wanted to."

He flings open the door, goes out, slams it behind him.

Katherine sits on the cold floor beside the tree, removes one of its yarn ornaments hung low and holds it in her hand, squeezes it rhythmically, in time with her beating heart. She knows this small house as she knows the lines in her own palm and as she knows this boy-man's body, inch by inch, completely. Yet lately she sometimes feels as though she's stepped into a mirror, where everything's its opposite, glittering and strange.

Something is bumping on the porch, scraping against its stones. The door bursts open and he stands there with what looks like a half-made table. Large, maybe five feet square, and with no slats across its frame.

"It's a loom." His voice is proud and quiet. "I made it for you."

He has changed so quickly it's put her off balance, as if the cabin has been tipped an inch or two. She glances toward her weaving wall. The nails are gone. They were there yesterday afternoon. He must have pried them out this morning while she slept. Without them, the room feels over-large and empty.

"I got 'em all, don't worry." He's fidgeting, the way he does when he's nervous, bouncing his weight from one foot to the other. "I'll hammer 'em in this afternoon. I made a chair for you to sit in, too. When you make your weavings. That way I can always see your face."

Tears well up from deep inside her and she shakes with soundless sobs.

Because she is surprised and touched.

Because he has taken away her wall that was essential, that enabled her to shut out everything except the patterns, colors, she was working with. He might just as well have knocked down every one of her imaginary room's imaginary walls, dispersed the peace it had enclosed. A silly, self-centered thing to cry over—he meant only to give a gift. But she can't stop.

Danny sits beside her on the floor, takes her in his arms and strokes her hair.

"Looks like nobody gave you presents neither."

She shakes her head, conscious of her silent lie, burrows against his chest. He wraps the poncho tight around the both of them. Together they stare out the window at the winter rain.

36

Memaw's Nightgown

THEY RECOGNIZE HIM AT THE HARDWARE STORE, BUT THEY DON'T know him. Not even his name. They rush to serve him anyway, the deep-voiced man with the wad of bills shoved in his pocket. Even so, he's a man careful to get exactly what he wants for his money.

"I just need half that fifty-pound bag of plaster."

"It'll keep. Cool, dry place." Adenoidal little shit. Adam's apple swooping like a sash weight.

"I only aim to carry twenty-five pounds out of here. Twenty-five pounds or nothing. I'll come back next week for the rest. I need an empty bucket with a lid. That there one."

"It's full of Sheetrock mud."

"Well, dig it out. Only way that bucket'll get empty. I'll pay you for it. Cash money in your hand. For everything. How much?"

"Eight dollars."

Danny peels off a five and three ones. "That's for twenty-five pounds of plaster, one bucket of Sheetrock mud, you digging out the Sheetrock mud, and you washing and drying out the bucket."

"Ten. You didn't say about the washing out and drying." Skinny shit whines like a mosquito.

Danny doesn't even roll his eyes, gives up two more bills. "Make sure you dry the inside good. I'll be back before an hour."

Time enough to put away three cups of coffee, two pieces of cherry pie at the Elkmont Diner. Time to stare into the window of the clothing store. Dress models with black electrical tape wound on their feet for shoes. One's got a red flannel nightgown on her just like Memaw used to wear. Little ruffles at her wrists. Nightgown for a fine and proper lady.

Lady like that Lady Chatterley. Oh, yeah.

"I'll take that red nightgown in the window yonder." Can't help the little smile that slides around his mouth. Nightgown to keep his own fine lady from the cold.

"We just put that one on sale for Valentine's."

The pinched-up lady store clerk gets a gown just like it from the back, folds it between tissue paper, slides it into a green bag. One more thing to carry.

"You staple that thing shut? I got a ways to go."

She wrinkles up between the eyes but still does what he says, her with her skinny hands, all brown spots and ropy veins. Someday their hands'll look like that, his and his Katherine's, their fingers intertwined. Like his mama's and his daddy's should have been.

He trudges back from town, taking the high trail up the mountain under a weak winter sun. The handle of the plaster-filled bucket cuts through his glove into his calloused palm. What is his house now, Gatsby's house, will be their house someday. House where he'll be King of the Mountain and she'll be his queen.

Back at the cabin, with the hearth fire built up to a roar, she takes a year unwrapping the damn package, long fingers worrying out each staple like she's got some further use in mind for the bag. When she's finally done and shakes the gown out from its tissue paper, she's so surprised she doesn't even smile. Just looks at him.

"You like it?"

She nods. "We need another blanket more."

"Goddammit! I'll buy you all the damn nightgowns I care to. And all the fucking blankets you could ever need." He likes how saying it makes him feel strong, tall, a man of substance. "Put it on. I been picturing you in it the whole afternoon."

She slips the gown on like a tent and takes her clothes off under it, one way to keep out the cold that creeps in two, three feet beyond the fire. Her hair lays dark and shiny against the red flannel. He grabs thick hanks of it in both his fists and pulls her down onto the quilts. The firelight flickers in her startled eyes. He jerks the red gown up and off her, wads it behind her head, can't hold off any longer.

Oh, how his fine lady always wants him.

He screams when he comes. Scream that trails off like a hawk's scream with a dying fall. Afterwards, he wraps himself so tight around her she can't ever go.

Yet he still falls and falls.

37

Lullaby

THEY LIE UNMOVING IN THE LATE AFTERNOON, HIS ARMS STILL coiled around her, the new red gown still bunched behind her head. Through the partly open window she can hear the winter birds settling themselves for the night, even their smallest sounds.

He breathes softly against her breast, cups his hand around it. "If you gave milk I'd suck your titties all day long."

She hates how he says "titties" like a nasty little boy. He is holding her too tight, his other arm biting into her side.

She squirms. "If I gave milk, there'd be a baby."

"You giving milk don't mean there's got to be a baby."

She can tell he wants her to ask why, but she won't do it. Instead watches the patch of sky outside the window darken to deep blue, ignores his hand playing between her legs.

"Tell you a story."

She doesn't want a story, wants them both to lie still now and listen, as the near, clear day sounds give way to the distant, deeper sounds of night.

But he won't be stopped, angles his head to look at her.

"Not long after I came to live at Memaw's, she took me with her to this one-room shack where a new little baby had just died. She came to bind the woman's tits with cotton cloth and give her herbs to make her milk stop coming. Inside, the place smelled like a cow barn. Like there was pails and pails of milk and cream all over. Only thicker, sweeter. Like my mama's milk I still remembered."

She is ashamed that his deliberately bad grammar irritates her. And she doesn't want to hear his story, not any story that includes a baby that has died. Readjusts her nightgown, tugs it down around her.

"All of it, all that sweet milk smell, came from this one woman lying in a corner on a rope bed. Her covered halfway with a blanket. And her titties hanging clear out of her gown they was swole up so big with milk."

He looks up at her, his eyes wide and innocent.

"While Memaw got out her cloth strips from her midwife bag, I went over to the woman, really close. I tried hard not to look down at her titties, tried to pretend I wasn't interested. Looked her square in the face instead.

"'Memaw brought me to drink up all your milk,' I told her.

"That woman smiled at me, such a sweet smile, and didn't say a word. Just lifted up her titty closest to me, squeezed its huge brown nipple to where I could see the milk bead on it, and held out her other hand to pull me in the bed. I reached out both hands toward her, licked my lips. A drop of milk fell off her nipple onto the dirty sheet, and I wanted it so bad I could have bent my head and sucked it up. I scrambled onto that bed quick as lightning, knowing the next drop, and all that milk forever from those two enormous titties, would be mine."

Katherine doesn't like his story, wishes he would stop it. Knows it's bound to come to a bad end.

"I spread my fingers wide to take that titty in my open mouth. But before I even touched it Memaw yanked me back and whacked my butt. Hard.

" 'That milk was for the baby,' she hissed in my ear. 'It wasn't meant for you.'

"I yelled bloody murder and she shoved me out onto the porch and slammed the door. I was so angry the whole world turned red. I wanted that milk more than I'd ever wanted anything in the good Lord's power to give me. That woman's baby'd gone just like my mama, so I knew God meant that baby's milk for me. Knew it sure as if He'd told me.

"I screamed and hollered for it till I spit out blood. Kept yelling to Memaw, 'Let me in.' But she never did. Just went about her work, I guess. Bound up that woman's titties, gave her the dry-up tea. I screamed in the vain hope I could stop her. Screamed to where I couldn't holler anymore 'cause no sound came. When Memaw finally got out on the porch, I was standing with my short pants down around my feet and flailing on my little peter like a banjo."

He laughs and shifts his head against Katherine's breast.

"Memaw beat the tar out of me right there and next day took me into town, bought me my first long pants. Said I'd got too big to suckle like a baby."

He props up on an elbow, looks at her. "Point is, the woman in that shack was full of milk without there being any baby. Like I said."

"Why are you doing that?"

"What?"

"Grinning that way, laughing."

He wriggles there beside her like a squirmy toddler, looks at her with his innocent eyes. "Because it's funny. Don't you think it's funny, me wanting that poor woman's big old titty so?"

"No, I think it's heartbreaking." All of it. An orphan, that's what he truly was. Is. A poor orphan boy that she has made a place for.

He frowns. His frown of pretending not to understand. Then he curls himself into her body's nooks and crannies, as close to her as he can get, stares up at her.

"Play like I'm your little baby. Hold my head and put your titty in my mouth. Just like that woman would have done back then."

His eyes beseech her. It's an easy thing to do, no matter that she doesn't want to. A gift given out of love. She tips his head forward, her fingers on the hard bones of his skull. He sighs so sweetly as she gently rubs his neck and scalp and with her other hand squeezes her breast, pinches its nipple hard, slides it along his closed lips until they open slightly and he takes it in his mouth. She is amazed she knows as if from instinct how to do it.

"I promise I won't bite you. Tiny babies got no teeth to bite."

The room, everything, is quiet all around them. His lips make tiny sucking sounds.

"Sing me a song," he asks then. "Sing me Memaw's lullaby while I suck on your tit."

His body wrapped around her shelters her from the cold. She shifts position, sings to him soft and low.

"Hushabye, don't you cry. Go to sleep my little baby.
When you wake, you will have all the pretty little horses.
Blacks and bays, dapples and grays, all the pretty little horses."

They lie there. His gray eyes glisten dark and wet in the twilight and his hand still plays between her legs as if he's unaware of it. She spasms then, without expecting to. Private and satisfying, deep inside herself. As if she has a secret.

"Sing it all again."

She does, then stops. Can't remember the next verse.

He looks up at her, takes her nipple from his mouth, rubs it along his slightly parted lips.

"You're everything." The words slide out against each other and against her breast, almost inaudible. "You're the whole world."

Later that night she wakes, untangles herself from his embrace, goes to the window. Moonlight silvers the bare trees, turning them stark and beautiful. She remembers the lost verse of Memaw's song.

"Bees and butterflies are picking out your eyes.
Oh, you poor, poor little baby."

Spring

38

Green Growing Things

THAT DAY AND NIGHT, THOUGH ONLY IN MID-FEBRUARY, MIGHT AS well have been the first few hours of spring. They've had nothing since but temperatures too warm for her new flannel nightgown and air heavy with the smell of leaf mold and the sounds of birds going about the most important business of their lives. Wild daffodils thrust up green spears around the porch.

A new lethargy that has to be spring fever has her wanting nothing more than to lie up in the loft to catch the breeze and rock him in her arms, thread her fingers through his baby-fine blond hair. It's where they are this afternoon. As if that first, hot, urgent rush has gone to something deeper, as if all clocks have slowed, even the sun. In its long warmth, her body has grown so exquisitely tender she can hardly bear it.

"Touch me light as feathers," she says to him. "Touch me soft as smoke."

It's all so peaceful then.

But once he's left her, gone up on the mountain, her fears escape the cages that she keeps them in when he is near, and they run free: He is a poison in her blood and she's the same for him; each weakens the other, saps the other's strength; they have infested themselves, infected themselves with each other as if with some disease, and somehow they will have to pay. Lying naked in the soft breeze from the window, she jams her fist against her open mouth to keep from crying out.

Get up. Get out. The sharp voice hisses in her head. She pulls on her jeans, their denim harsh against her thighs. Beneath the soft chambray shirt her skin feels sunburned, dry. Boots crush her insteps and she loosens their laces, descends the ladder with great delibera-tion, trudges through the house and then reluctantly outside. She car-ries her shovel upright, its blade near the ground, not slung over her shoulder in the usual way, for fear its weight will bruise her.

She has fallen behind in the garden, should have cleared the beds out days ago, brought new soil from underneath the trees. Her shovel bites into soft ground beneath the largest of the oaks, releasing famil-iar, earthy odors as intoxicating as perfumes. She plunges her hands in deep where she has dug, brings up both fists full of black dirt. A red worm hangs from her right thumb.

"Hello, little one."

She strokes its wriggling length, lets it twine around her index finger before depositing it in what will be this year's lettuce bed.

Lethargy slips from her shoulders with the shovel's rhythmic crunch into soft ground, and she works as though hypnotized, digging out two small beds, replacing the spent soil with new, black dirt, stop-ping only when her limbs begin to weaken and she knows she will be sore. Tomorrow she'll start planting seeds that spring's cold nights won't harm, seeds captured from last season's strongest plants. A crow caws in the shadows at the garden's edge and jays shriek out from nearby trees, the same sounds she heard her first day in the forest, a whole lifetime ago.

The dirt's rich smell has left her starved for something fresh and green, it's a sharp pang in her belly. Heading for home, she detours off the path to the low, spongy spot where last spring's fiddleheads raised up. Oh, please, let them be there, don't let her be too early. Already, in her mind, she sees the new ferns' slick white humps pushing through winter's crust. "April is the cruelest month"—save March, which forces fiddleheads from the dead ground. Already she imagines them, their sharp, green taste of early spring, runs toward the spot, can see them from this distance as a pale smear in the dark loam. She kneels in front of them and, with more gentleness than needed, brushes back dry, crumbling leaves. Then, with her garden knife, she slices the first fiddlehead clean and quick, an inch below the ground, wipes away the rich leaf-soil from the new shoot, slips it in her mouth. It tastes fresh as the start of life itself.

She chews greedily, swallows fast. How good it felt, that strong young plant between her teeth. How good it feels inside her, a swallowed blessing. She cuts another, then another, eats them quickly, then eats more. Later there'll be time to savor them; right now she crams them in her mouth, chews, swallows. Glorious to hold so much new life inside her. Glorious to contemplate a future of long, warm days and green, growing things that spring up everywhere she walks.

She eats until all the fiddleheads are gone, wipes her mouth with the back of her dirt-covered hand, pockets her knife. She has left none for tomorrow—and none for Danny, who eats nothing anyway but meat. Her mouth still tingling with the ferns' green taste, she gets up from the dirt, brushes off her hands and starts for home.

But something's wrong, her belly's knotting up with cramps. She wraps her arms around the sudden pain, bends over, throws up in the undergrowth.

Quick, kick dead leaves over it to hide it. That way it won't have happened.

She wipes her mouth with her palm. Won't look at the small pulse throbbing on the blue-veined inside of her wrist. Won't imagine things. She has not had enough fresh vegetables through winter, that's all. Her stomach is unused to so much roughage. Hereafter, she'll be careful; it won't happen again. In the unlikely event Danny asks after the fiddleheads, she'll say they never did come up. This lie creates a little lift inside her, as if from some small life that's all her own.

39

A Reversal

"Excuse me, sorry, can't help it."

She pushes away from the dinner table, overturns her bench in her haste to get outside, then dashes down the path, hands clapped over her mouth. Walks the few more steps to the outhouse, sits inside it, panting.

These last few days she can't bear the greasy smell of cooking meat. It's the same with many vegetables, even those from the garden. Not only is she throwing up her food again, her skin has grown so sensitive to even her own touch that she feels peeled. And she is so tired every day. It's all coming back, one horror at a time. Soon she will need to fight to hang on to the memory of her name.

And worse, oh, so much worse, already she no longer wants him. Not in that fierce, hot way she always has. Wants now only the rocking and the cradling, and once in a great while to love him slower, sweeter, deeper than she ever has.

And then for him to go away so she can sleep forever. She has not thought for a long time about the gun's dull metal. Her hands shake.

Meanwhile the light is fading. She needs to get back to the cabin before he thinks of coming after her. So much effort, getting up. More than anything, she yearns to curl into a tiny bundle in the corner where she saw the corn snake that first morning. *Hushabye, hushabye.*

Don't think crazy thoughts. Go wipe your mouth off at the creek and head for home.

"What the fuck's got into you?" He's sitting by the cold hearth, lashing reeds into a fish trap, jerking the leather tight.

"I had to go."

She turns away, goes in the kitchen to scrub the dinner plates before their meaty odor makes her sick again. Scrubs so fast it looks like anger. Done.

"I've got a headache. I'm going to bed."

"Shit. Work all day, come home to this." Mimics her: "'I've got a headache.'"

He flings a piece of rawhide on the table, gets up and grabs the fireplace poker, jabs repeatedly at a single red ember in the ashes.

Upstairs, she scrunches into a far corner of their quilts, wishes she could hide herself and hates the moon for shining.

Wishes she still lived alone. Wishes he would come and hold her. Even now.

40

In Too Deep

HE'S STANDING IN THE LOFT, BUTT NAKED, KICKING AT THE QUILTS she's balled up under like a possum. Bitch didn't used to hide from him like that.

"How come you lay around all day?"

"I don't. I go down to the garden. Times when you're away." Mumbles into the quilts, won't even poke her head out.

He squats beside her, sniffs a couple times, makes a huge, deliberate point of it. "You smell weird."

She, by God, sticks her head out now. Eyes all wide. "Weird how?"

He shrugs. "It's like, we used to taste, smell pretty much the same. Now you smell . . . I don't know . . . different. Down there. More like just you."

But that doesn't get it, doesn't come even close to this wild, animal scent so strong it scares him. Scent that keeps his nostrils flared out all the time craving like hell to smell it. Not a sweet scent like perfume or flowers. Something rank and strong. If she was lost from him he'd have to follow it and find her. No choice in the matter.

She sniffs lightly, like a prissy girl, wrinkles her nose. "More like me? That's crazy. How can I smell more like I do already?"

"I don't know, I don't know." She's starting to piss him off. "What I do know is the shithouse smells like puke."

He wants to shock her, make her cringe. Wants, needs her to explain it, explain it all away. But she won't. Just slips back under the covers. Inside his head, his heart, somewhere, he feels one of the rigid parts that keep him held together slide out of its slot.

She peeks out from the blankets. Frightened-possum eyes again.

"I threw up once yesterday. Must have eaten too much meat."

"Once? Stinks like you're running a goddamn puke factory."

She sits up in nervous little jerks, makes a point to keep her body covered with the quilt, something else she never used to do. Fakes a smile and shakes her head like he's some kind of baby. "I don't know what's got into you."

"Into *me*? Nothing's got into *me*. It's what's got into *you* we're talking about here."

Danny bites a ragged thumbnail, chews it smooth so it won't scratch her skin. Never used to bother with that shit. Never used to matter. Now there's weird times he curls up in her arms like she's his mama and that's all he wants to do. Just stay there, let her hold him through the night. Hold him through all the nights. Other times, she pulls him into her so deep he's scared he'll never make it out again. Some dude Jimbo turned him on to that wrote dirty—Henry Miller? Somebody Durrell?—wrote how he got sucked into some woman's snatch and found a grand piano. Danny and Jimbo laughed for months. Tromped through the jungle pounding make-believe piano keys.

But with her it's not like that. With her these days he has to leave the house right afterwards to keep from pasting her. That's how bad he needs to put a mark on her. Some little scar to keep him in her mind times when he's not around. Scar like a cattle brand that says she's his, won't ever leave him.

In any way. For any reason.

Because he knows now something's wrong. Whatever sickness he smelled on her that first day has never left her. Just gone underground to jump back up and take her now that he can't let her go.

He nudges the ball that's her inside the blankets, kicks it gently.

"Hey. I got to go up to the house."

"Will you be back for dinner?"

He loves how the words sound so normal, loves their muffled pleading. Waits, wants her to say them all again. Bitch won't do it. Stays so still he wants to shake her. Shake her till all her fucking teeth fall out.

"Well, now, I got to come back, don't I. Whether I want to or not. Can't work up there in the dark." Yanks his clothes on, pulls his boot laces too tight, slams the door on his way out.

All the way up the mountain he runs things over in his mind. Same as he does the nights he lies awake watching her sleep. Somewhere in everything that's going on with her, he feels the presence of some cold, dark little snake hole. Something he ought to recognize for what it is—and yet can't see at all.

YEAH, AND HE COMES back that night to sit across from her at dinner, watch her hand shake when she lifts her fork to eat her rice and beans, watch her clamp her mouth tight shut to keep what she just ate inside her. Watch her go to hell in a handbasket, puking under every bush, scuffing a few leaves over it like a sick cat. Yeah, he's seen that, too. Today. Oh, yeah, he spent time watching.

"What the hell is this shit?" He shoves his plate across the table. It tips onto the floor. "I brought you a rabbit. Why did I spend half a day sneaking up on bunnies before I could kill one? For you not to cook it? What did you do with the goddamn rabbit?"

"It's outside. On the porch." Pinchy little mouth. Lines around it, starting to show her age.

"What the hell does that mean?"

"I didn't want it." New, dull voice.

"Well, I do."

"We eat too much meat."

"Some of us don't eat nearly enough."

Jerks open the door—getting to be a habit—lets it slam behind him. Let her eat her goddamn beans and leaves. He pulls the shovel out from underneath the porch, digs a hole outside that she can see from the front window. Bitch needs to know what he's about, see how he has to feed himself all by himself in order to survive. He breaks dry branches into the hole, brings logs and kindling from the shed, rigs up a green-wood spit and roasts the rabbit on it. Sits in the shadows, keeping one eye on the window, watches her climb the stairs, watches her blow her lantern out. Just like old times, only not. Nope, not at all.

He eats the rabbit with the crickets and the owls for company, leaves its bones for whatever might want them. Goes indoors, starts up to the loft.

"Wash your hands in the sink. Please."

Yeah. Let her say please. Say it again. Say pretty please, you fucking whore.

"The meat smell on them turns my stomach. Please."

He does it, washes them a damn sight cleaner than the bitch deserves, then climbs up to the loft, takes off his clothes and pulls her to him so she'll never get away. Yeah, this is how they'll die someday. In each other's arms.

41

Snake Hole

BREAKFAST AGAIN. DAYS MARCH PAST LIKE STUPID ANTS, ONE BE-
hind another. She seems smaller lately, like she's always looking up at
him. Makes him want to gently brush her hair out of her face. Makes
him want to backhand her.

Because she isn't like she was. Because he's losing her.

"You want to go to town?"

"With you?"

"You see anyone else around we could be talking about?"

She sniffles, shakes her head. "Today?"

"I don't know, let me check my calendar. *Of course* today, why else
would I bring it up?"

"Yes, then. I feel well enough to go today."

She just looks at him. He thought at least she'd smile. It's trouble
bringing her along. He's only doing it to make her happy, quit balling

herself up under the damn quilts and trembling like a dying field mouse. Should've never brought it up.

"You got some weavings you should leave off at that gallery? We can stop on our way home."

She frowns, shakes her head. "I don't want to. They'll take up too much space in the cart. Too much time."

"Okay, whatever. Come on, get your shoes on then. We haven't got all day."

"I'll only be a minute."

Bitch hurries like she really wants to go.

MAYBE, JUST MAYBE, IT'LL be a good day after all. Dogwoods blooming on the trail, all that white floating through the woods like clouds. He stops the cart and points to one, so she'll quit looking at the goddamn ground.

"Look there, how pretty."

She looks up, trips on a tree root.

He grabs her, steadies her. Drops his hands. "You okay?"

She nods.

He glances up at the rocks where he used to hide and watch her. Too bad you can't turn back the clock. He thought up close she'd smile more. No such luck.

"You having a good time?"

She winces like he's poked her with a sharp stick. Nods. "It's a pretty day."

"That it is." He picks up a fallen branch, whacks at the undergrowth along the trail. "Yeah. Pretty day."

"Thank you for asking me to come along."

He buys her a silk shawl at the same place he got the nightgown. Doesn't ask her if she wants it, just says to the woman, "We'll take that."

"Thank you." She rubs the inside of her wrist against it, smiles. Dark, Dead Lady circles under her eyes like he hasn't seen since long ago. Memaw had dark circles, the year before she died.

He wraps her new shawl twice around her shoulders so the fringe hangs down in back. Like his mama used to wear hers so he wouldn't pull on it the times she held him in her arms.

At the post office, he stands behind her in the line, stares at the dangling fringe. His mama sometimes must have carried him around till the very end. How else could he remember to this day how she kept one hand on his back and one arm under him, her fingers curled around where he could see her nail polish like drops of blood? He never should've let her from his sight, should have stayed by her. Guarded her against her memories.

He grabs Katherine's upper arm, leans close to her ear. "What the fuck are we doing here?"

"I ought to check. I haven't checked in months."

"What for? Who'd write you? That dude from Atlanta?" Such a pussy thing to say, why can't he keep his damn mouth shut?

"No one. No one knows I'm here. It's just good sometimes to check."

Miss Flat Voice again. He hasn't even pissed her off. If she'd get pissed off she'd show some fire at least.

She tells the swishy little clerk her name and he disappears somewhere to check the general deliveries. Brings back an envelope, hands it to her. She stares at it like she's never seen one, turns it over.

Danny pokes her in her back ribs. "Hey, let me see. You got a letter from Atlanta Dude." Grabs for it, heart thumping way too fast.

She frowns, pulls it away and shakes her head. "No, it's some company. Carlisle-Colorado Mining and Development. I've never heard of them."

She steps out of the line, goes to the dusty window that looks out onto the street, tears the envelope open carefully along one of its short ends, reads silently, then looks at him and shakes her head.

"They want to buy the cabin. And all the land around it that I own."

Her words start something churning in him, some flywheel in his gut.

"Hey, maybe there's gold on it and we can dig it and get rich."

Him grinning like the whole thing's a big joke. Which it's got to be. "You're not going to sell it, are you?"

"No." Frowns. Looks back down at the typewritten sheet.

Got to get out of here, change the subject, get some kind of new reality. Got to keep that churning blade from slicing through his flesh.

"Hey, tell you what, let's get some burgers at the Rexall."

"You go. I don't want one. I'll wait in that little courthouse park."

Little park where he sat on a bench and watched her on that other scary day, day when he thought she'd gone away for good. Turned out okay then, going to turn out okay now. Got to.

"I can't go off and leave you. Your old buddy from Atlanta might show up and carry you away."

"He's not my buddy."

Won't she ever laugh? Anymore, her mouth's only a tight, thin line for keeping puke inside.

He pulls their cart one-handed, grabs her upper arm.

"Come on. I'll buy you anything you want. Egg salad sandwich, tuna fish. Buy you an ice cream sundae, soda, anything. 'Cause you're my girl." Like pushing a huge rock up a goddamn mountain, getting her to do stuff anymore.

He jerks the cart inside the drugstore, sits them down in a red vinyl booth, orders himself a double cheeseburger. She gets a vanilla soda, sucks the liquid through her straw, won't touch the ice cream. Finicky bitch. Danny dumps his coffee over it, finishes it off. No point letting ice cream go to waste, even vanilla. Through the drugstore's plate glass he can see the church, its stained-glass windows, where sometimes he used to hide. Wants to look at her, except her eyes are spooky and her jaw's all clenched. He stares down instead at the gold flecks in the Formica tabletop. Who'd want her piddling little land?

In line at the bank, he slips his hand in her back pocket, waits to feel her fingers' little warmth slide into his, but nothing doing. Won't look at him either. In the grocery store they walk down all the aisles. She puts shit in the cart he'd never think of. Early greens, late winter squash. Going home, he pulls up by the gallery and stops. Plays his nervous fingers on the cart handle.

"I said I don't have anything."

"Never thought you did. Just thought you might like looking in the window."

She nods, stares like she can't see past the glass.

"Thought you might like seeing that weird square-shaped teapot there, that black and red and green painting of who-the-fuck-knows-what."

She nods again.

He grins. "Thought you might like stepping over in that alleyway and standing on that concrete stoop and undoing your jeans."

She's staring at him like he's crazy.

"Come on. Just do it, for God's sake. That's why we're here. So we can have a good time like before."

Like an obedient child who knows to not ask questions, she backs into the alley, climbs up on the concrete step. He follows her, pulls the cart in behind them. The button's tight. She struggles with it.

"Here, let me at it."

He yanks hard at the waistband, pops the button off and slips his hand inside her jeans, kneads down along her soft, smooth belly toward the warmth between her legs. Oh, yeah, that's what he needs, what he's been wanting. All the rotten parts of his day slide away and he feels good, like he's the king of everything.

"Talk to me, babe. Talk to me like before. Tell me what's out there in the street. And I'll make you feel so good you won't want me to ever stop."

She starts in talking, Danny's good girl.

"There's a blue car and a green car, both driving around the square. There's a man in a straw boater hat."

Fuck. What's wrong? It's not coming out right. Coming out of her like some kind of scared-little-kid shit. Scared-little-kid up on a stage at school or something.

"A woman in a black dress is walking past the hardware store. I'm sorry, I can't . . ."

She claps both hands over her mouth, heaves into them. Stands there staring at the dripping puke. A clot of it's splashed on his boot.

"I'm sorry, I'm so sorry. Please believe I never meant to."

"Shit. Goddamn. Goddamn it all to fucking hell."

Danny yanks the shawl off her shoulders, wipes her hands and face, their shoes. Balls it up and throws it in the alley.

And sees down to the bottom of his small, round snake hole. All the way to that dark truth his mind would not give up to him till now.

Goddamn lying fucking bitch. Her shaking her head back and forth, like that'll rub it all away.

"Fix your jeans back."

He grabs her wrist and pulls her out onto the highway. One hand for her and one hand for the cart. Not a lot of difference anymore between them, is there? Both of them a drag.

But as they walk along, a strange peace falls on him. Lays soft on his shoulders. Because he hasn't lost her, isn't going to lose her. Because now he knows what's wrong and knows how to take care of things. Like Memaw did when she got asked to. Yeah, Memaw's Danny knows what's going on.

He knows what's going on—and he knows what to do.

42

Memaw's Tea

HE IS SO KIND SHE WANTS TO WEEP. THESE PAST FEW DAYS HE'S stayed by her almost constantly. Just once each morning he goes out, comes home with pockets full of mint leaves he brews into a tea and brings her every couple hours to drink.

"It's from Memaw. It'll make you well."

He says it with a kind of reverence every time, as if it were an incantation, then looks down shyly at his feet. He's even made a small, beautiful side table with gnarled dogwood legs to hold her cup. He sits on the floor at her feet, watching her drink. Reads to her about poor Holden Caulfield, who has his whole life ahead of him. Sometimes when she's too tired to finish, he holds the cup in both his hands and brings it to her lips.

It's too early for mint from the garden. This mint, the mint for Memaw's tea, grows wild on the far side of the pond. Its spearmint smell is sweet on his clothing, sweet on his skin and in his hair. Sweet in the walls and floorboards, for it is everywhere changing the character of the cabin, making it one with springtime just outside the door.

She is less fond of its wild, gamy taste that slides along the roof of her mouth and makes her queasy. And thus far it hasn't done much good. She's tried to tell him but he doesn't listen. And she doesn't press too hard, he means so well.

"Maybe I should only drink it in the morning. Or in the morning and at night," she suggests the second—third? fourth?—day.

"No!" It bursts out like a gunshot. "I got to do it just like Memaw did."

She nods and drops the subject.

There's so much of it to drink, and so often, they've marked the times according to the sun's position, made a game of it. First cup at dawn's light, second when the sun hits the low branches of the eastern pines, and so on until the last cup before bed. Six cups in all. He is so good with it, always. Reminds her when it's time, brews it himself and brings it, watches so intently as she sips, his faith in its efficacy as touching as a child's.

But it isn't working. True, the vomiting's some better, but now there are the headaches, and this willingness to spend all day in bed in a half stupor. Her stomach cramps each time she drinks it, yet she dutifully downs each cup, will not refuse him his illusion of control. If he'd leave the room, she'd throw it out a window. But he never leaves.

"Drink your tea. It's only for another week or so. Then you'll be well."

"Will I truly? Be well?" It comes out harsher than she intended.

"Memaw swore by it, said it worked every time."

It's all come back, just like before. Only faster, so much faster. She is ill, she is dying. At this rate she'll be dead before the leaves fall.

And he hopes to fight it off with tea. If all of Western medicine can't cure her, how can some granny woman's potion?

"Come on, now. Drink the goddamn stuff."

There's been eight days of it. His voice now is rarely kind.

"I don't want any more, it's no use. I'm hardly strong enough to sit up at the table. Everything I put into my mouth tastes bitter. Even Memaw's holy tea."

"Drink it anyway. It'll make you well."

"I don't believe you."

"It's not gradual like you think it's supposed to be. The healing happens all at once."

"Just, please, let me try a day without it, an experiment, to see if I feel any better."

She rises with the teacup in her shaking hand, heads for the sink, pictures the greenish liquid curling down the drain.

"No!" He jumps up as if he'd seen into her mind, slams both his hands flat on the table. "You quit one day, you got to start all over. You don't want that, do you?"

"No." The word comes out a small, defeated syllable.

She sets the cup back on its table, lowers herself into her rocking chair, squeezes her thin hands together at her waist.

At night he curls beside her on the quilts, kneads her belly under Memaw's red gown she's taken to wearing once again to ward off chills, kneads her belly to take away her cramping. Let him believe a few more days of Memaw's tea will cure her. There's no harm in it. She's not got strength to argue.

ON THE MORNING OF the eleventh day, all the little bird songs whirl around her head as she drags herself into a sitting position on the quilts. The bright sun on the floorboards looks like panes of brittle glass. She has to ask his help to climb down from the loft. His fingers are so strong around her wrist, like that first night—"Take me in." She knows by rote the stages of her illness, its peculiar Stations of the Cross. Wishes she could hasten them, wishes she could go ahead and die. Today is the first day that she has felt shame.

Shame for calling out to him to help her down the stairs. Shame for resting her head on her arm to get through breakfast. Shame that she has not started the tomatoes, peppers, hasn't planted squash seeds, doesn't know how many days it's been since she's been to the garden, doesn't care.

Shame most of all that she has to beg him to go with her to the privy because she fears losing her way. He takes her elbow as if he were helping an old lady cross a street. When they get there she shuts the door. Because she is ashamed. When finally she opens it and doesn't see him, cries, "Danny, Danny," and he doesn't come, she sits down on the step and heaves dry sobs into the quiet air, ashamed to need someone so desperately.

Then he is there, grinning like a Jack-in-the-box. "I just went behind some bushes, gave the weeds a shower."

The idea, image, both disgust her—and that he takes pride in it, as if it were some great manly accomplishment. He moves to take her elbow, but she pulls away. Doesn't want his hands to touch her. Doesn't want to need them, need him. To need him is defeat.

"I can do it."

"But I got to keep you safe."

"I'm safe enough." At the cross-path, she turns, hopes she is facing in the right direction. "I'm going to the garden."

He surveys the sun's slant through the trees. "You can't. You need to drink your tea."

"I won't drink it anymore."

He grabs her upper arm, turns her toward home. "You got to."

His eyes glitter like a reptile's. His fingers bite into her flesh as he propels her toward the cabin. He yanks the door open and drags her inside, pushes her down in her rocker, brews the tea and slams the cup onto the table. How can this be love? And yet it must be. He must be so afraid of losing her.

"Now drink it. I'm going to sit here till you do."

He spits the words out, plops down on the floor, watches until her cup is empty. Then he bangs the door behind him, leaving.

43

The Healing Cup

SHE SITS ROCKING SILENTLY. IT'S ALL HAPPENING JUST LIKE BEFORE, when Tim left. Soon Danny, too, will go. May have already gone.

Yet there's a quiet in her heart she doesn't understand, as if she were meant to sit and rock until she knows whatever it is she must do. Outside, woods sparrows and pine siskins chirp in the trees at the clearing's edge. Through the window she can see again those wild, green rooms that beckoned to her that first day. Beckoned her until he came and she quit looking at them—the beings she imagined lived inside them, watched her every move, had been neither animals nor trees nor spirits, only him. Someday she will step off the path and enter them, room after room, until she disappears. She'll soon be free to do it. Anything. Free to take down the gun.

Because, like Tim, Danny isn't coming back. Why should he?

He'll climb down the far side of Panther Mountain to whatever's there and stay there, the same way Tim boarded a plane and got off somewhere else. Already, after so few minutes, there are parts of Danny she's forgetting. The exact blond color of his hair, the way his deep speaking voice sounds high as a young boy's when he whispers. How long before she will forget the rest? All she remembers now of Tim is one gray suit, maybe a smile. And Michael? Does she remember anything at all?

She should get up, she's been sitting here so long. Maybe that's all she needs to do for now. But it's a laborious process straightening stiff joints, pushing herself upright from her chair only to walk tentatively along the edges of the room, bracing herself against the wall, touching things as if she's just arrived. She should go to the garden like she used to. Then to the pond, sit with the turtles on her sun-warmed rock, look down into the silt-black water at the fishes. Come back and pull the nails out of the loom he made, pound them back in the wall where they belong. Live here alone, take her comfort from the gun. He isn't coming back.

Through the kitchen door she sees a small pink flower curled beside the sink. A leaving from his tea herbs. Its fragile prettiness attracts her. The flower tops a slender, winding stem with small green leaves. She sniffs it, the light spearmint scent of this wild mint from the far side of the pond. She lays it delicately atop the flat plane of her palm and carries it across the room. Carefully, lest a small breeze whisk it away. Places it on the floor beside the storage bench flanking the fireplace, where she packed up her wildlife books when Danny came and she no longer used them. She's not sure what she's looking for. Something.

Weeds and Wildflowers of the Southern Mountains. She sits on the cold slate floor, leans against the sharp-edged wooden box. Weeds with pink flowers. Wildflowers that bloom in April. Types of mints. Here it is. *Pennyroyal.* Mentha pulegium. *A plant in the mint genus within the family* Lamiaceae. *Grows in moist, sunny soils, often near creeks or bogs.*

Among the cattails on the far side of the pond.

Useful as a mild tea against fainting or to settle the stomach. Fat chance. *Emmenagogue. Abortifacient.*

She reads the words again, moves her finger under them to make sure she has read them right.

Memaw swears by it. It heals you all at once. Abortifacient. Abort. Abortion. An herb to induce abortion.

What Memaw knew.

She drops the wildflower book back in the wooden storage bench, returns the mint sprig to its place beside the sink and stands there staring at it. She is cold, cold through and through. Did not know such a cold calm was possible.

Abortifacient.

What Memaw knew, what Danny knows. Might he know what she doesn't? Might the thing be true?

They tried, she and Tim, after that first baby. Tried with thermometers and calendars. Nothing. Like trying to relight cold, gray ashes. "You can't. Won't. Never again." What all her doctors said.

Don't hope.

Those same doctors who said more than a year ago she wouldn't live six months.

Everything is a gift. Everything.

Her heart pounds so hard she's sure she hears it. What if Danny's right, can see it, smell it, divine it with a ring tied to a string, boy if it sways, girl if it spins? What if he truly knows what Memaw knew?

"I don't want a baby. I want only you."

Whether the baby's real or not, the act's the same. And only one thing matters.

She runs into the front room to drag the bench across the floor where she can reach the gun on the high shelf. But before she pulls the heavy seat an inch, before she even stoops to grasp it, the door slams.

"How's my girl? It's time for tea."

He hasn't left her after all. How could she think it? Did she confuse thoughts with wishes? Has to slow her agitated breathing down so he won't see.

Even the odor of the brewing pennyroyal makes her belly cramp. *It heals you all at once.* The last cup of the day, tea and then bedtime. She has to do it this once more, there is no other way. Has to take this one last chance this isn't Memaw's "healing cup." That her tiny baby, if there is a tiny baby, will survive this one last ritual. Because their evening, hers and Danny's, must end like any other of their evenings. With him asleep beside her in their bed.

She drinks the foul tea, can hardly keep from gagging. Each swallow's a small, sidestepped death sentence, down to the last one, which she pours out on the floor. Because she can, because he isn't looking, will not look in that far corner. Because she should have poured out every cup from the first one on, not drunk it like a ninny who takes candy from a stranger. Because that's what he is. A stranger. No one she ever knew.

NEAR MORNING HE CRIES out in a dream and she awakens, hadn't meant to doze, not for a moment. She lays a warm and gentle hand on him to calm him, although inside she feels as strong and hard as iron. When he is quiet once again and breathing rhythmically, she makes her way downstairs without a sound. It's so close to the hour he usually wakes, she does not dare to drag the bench across the room. She picks it up instead, then silently puts it back down. Two inches, four inches, all she can manage at a time. The dark sky growing lighter all the while. It'll be full dawn before she can stand on the bench, reach up, take the gun. And the bullets, each one so heavy in her hand. Oh, please, she must not drop them, they might rattle. Might even explode.

One. Two. Three. Four. Five. Six. Each click of the cylinder deafens her. He's bound to hear, know what it means. But he does not, sleeps on. So now the bench, the bench he made. For her. Back to its place beside the table. Three inches, six inches. Again, again, again. At last she sits on it, waits. Tries not to think of him so long ago, a fierce angel there outside her garden. Or that night in the storm, that night she took him in. And in the morning begged him not to go. This changeling who would kill her child.

Groggy with sleep, he makes his way downstairs. Smiles at her, then sees the gun.

The look on his face, as if he must still be dreaming, squeezes her chest so tightly she can hardly breathe. But he is exactly where she wants him. Midway between her and the door.

"Get out."

"What th— I haven't got my boots on."

"I know what's in the tea. And what it does. Get out." Her voice so level, and so calm.

"Now look—babe? Wait just a minute. Put down the gun." He shakes his head as if to clear it, comes fully awake. "You lied to me, you goddamn bitch. You told me you couldn't. If you'd told the truth I could have done things, things I know from Memaw, so this shit would never happen. Stupid, lying whore."

His hands jerk as if he's a wind-up toy, toy soldier.

"I didn't lie. It doesn't matter. Just . . . please . . . go."

She is so cold inside she can look at him standing on her sun-warmed floor, look even at his vulnerable, sharp shoulder blades, his tangled hair—and not go to him.

"I don't want a baby. I want only you." Sheets of silent tears slide down his face and he is trembling. "I love you so much. I just love you so much I can't ever stop."

"Get out."

"Women die having babies. If you die I'll die, too. I can't live without you."

It was not supposed to be this hard. He was supposed to see the gun and run. Out the door, far away, and never come back. Run, Danny, run. Please. Now.

He doesn't move. "I smashed up your car so you would never leave me. I love you so much. Come on, babe, you're my good girl. Come here, give me the gun." He reaches out his hand, palm up like a serving tray, for her to lay it on.

She pulls the trigger hard and quick. The sound deafens her; the recoil wrenches her right arm.

You'd best aim low, the granny woman in the store had said. She didn't hit him, shot too high, shot only to frighten him. Why, then, is his right hand clapped tight onto his left shoulder? Why is blood ooz-ing out between his fingers?

She cocks the pistol once again, before she can think to go to him. "Get out! Get out! Get out!" Fires at the ceiling.

He backs away, wide-eyed and openmouthed. Turns, struggles one-handed with the door. Jerks it open, looks down at the thick, dark blood that drips onto the floor. Then runs unsteadily across the clearing and is gone.

Katherine stands with one hand splayed across her belly, the other wrapped around the gun.

44

A Good Woman's Love

HURTS. *HURTS.* BITCH SHOT HIM IN THE FUCKING SHOULDER. HE squeezes his eyes tight against the pain. All the way up the mountain. Sometimes crying, sometimes grinning like a silly fool.

Shot him. How bad she must love him to just take a gun and fucking shoot him. Golden girl "you-can't-go-below-the-waist" Janelle would never do a thing like that. Shit, no. But his Katherine, that one's a whole other story. Loves him so hard she fucking shoots him.

Goddamn. Got to laugh at that one.

Wild yarrow flowering white all through Gatsby's waist-high lawn grass. Danny yanks up an armful. Thank you, Jesus. God bless you, Memaw. Yarrow's good to stanch a wound. Might live after all.

The house, same as always. Only, Dog's come back. She bounds out to greet him, looks only a little puzzled when he draws back favoring his shoulder. There's love for you. Dog's come back.

"No, I ain't brung you nothing. You're on your own and so am I."

Get to the bed and lay there. Oh, sweet Jesus, how it hurts. Whole left side. Both sides of his mind—can't think of nothing else. Pokes his finger in the hole till he feels the bullet as a hard, mean lump. Listens with disinterest to his screams, shoves silver yarrow leaves into his mouth to stop them. Chews. Bitch's got no idea all the trouble she's brought.

Got to get it out of there. The bullet. Leave it and he'll surely die a mean, hard death from poison in his blood. Pincers, that's what's needed. Pinchers. Grab hold of the fucker. He lies back, stares at the ceiling, how it drops close, then backs away in rhythm with his heartbeats.

Pincers. Stops his mind on that and leaves it there awhile. Pair of springy twigs? Too soft, too slippery. Pincers. Look like scissors, scissors he carried off out of the hospital. Scissors don't pinch.

Pliers. Danny gets up, staggers around the room, rummages in each little pile of his possessions stuck in crevices and crannies till he finds the needle-nose pliers he bought for pulling rusted, headless nails out of the wall lath. Yeah, these ones will do just fine. Holds them in his lighter flame. Jams them in his wound.

Oh, JesusmotherfuckingChrist, goddamn. Spits out yarrow leaves. Digs around inside the hole with the pliers, can't stop screaming. Pokes at the bullet. Once, twice, scrapes against a bone. Oh, sweet Jesus. Finally gets hold of it and pulls like hell. Screams without ceasing till he's got the bullet in his hand. Slaps yarrow in the gushing wound. His work is done.

It's either good work or he'll die. Right now he doesn't give a shit. Right now just, please, dear Lord, let him pass out.

Pass out with her cool hand on his forehead, her long hair fanned across his cheek. His Katherine.

SOME MORNING. MAYBE THE next one, maybe several mornings past it, who the hell knows. Sky pulses in his eyes. Dog lies beside him. Something's carcass on the floor—she's eaten. Maybe he's got a fever, maybe not. Shoulder hurts, sweet Jesus, aches, but he can move it. Just a little. Lord love you, Memaw. He is still alive.

Takes lying there awhile to recognize the gnawing in his belly by its rightful name of hunger. Room whirls when he stands, hands flat on the damp wallpaper, steadying himself. Meat, that's what he needs. Moves to the middle of the room, stands still to gentle down its spinning. Meat. And see what's up with Katherine. Meat and Katherine, only shit that's real.

Checks the carcass on the floor. No meat there. Just feathers and bones. Picks up a handful of the feathers, holds them in a bar of sunlight so they'll shine. Seven turkey feathers gleaming gold, indigo, turquoise. Big and pretty as an eagle's. Ka-ther-ine. Every pretty thing he'll give to her.

Stuffs the feathers in his shirt. Staggers outside and drinks some water at the stream, splashes his face.

Heads toward the cabin.

It hurts worse climbing down than up. He grabs hold of little saplings, points of rocks. Swallows his screams. Making too much noise to sneak up on a rabbit or a squirrel. Want meat, you got to hike out to the store and buy some Slim Jims.

Ka-ther-ine.

It's slow going. He gets the shakes in shady spots. Gets them in the sunshine, too. Then sometimes they go away and he feels fine. Feels fine under his hanging rock. Always feels fine there. Meat can wait till he's seen Katherine. She's more real than meat. If he's Odysseus, she's his Penelope.

He eats some leaves, little ferns far back in his cave. The sun sinks into afternoon. Fire in his blood, fire in his wounded shoulder. Then comes a godsent rabbit, rabbit still as he is, just outside. Danny uses everything he's learned of quiet to sneak up on it, inches at a time. His stomach knots, spit rolls into his mouth. You only get one chance, one try. His good right arm shoots out. Grabs the rabbit by its neck.

One dead rabbit. Danny sits there holding it and drooling.

Ka-ther-ine.

He creeps farther down the mountain, rabbit's back legs hooked into his belt, turkey feathers tickling, scratching at his chest. Sun whirls around his head, sinks low. Can't go back up the mountain, grill the rabbit, till he sees her. First she shoots him, then she starves him. Can't beat a good woman's love.

Inches. All the farther he can go without making a sound. Every inch gets him closer. Then at last he's close enough, as close as he can get. Reach-out-and-touch-her close. Settles himself behind a rock, rabbit still tucked in at his waist, limp little rabbit paws so soft and scratchy. At last, when the setting sun's rays fall blood-red onto his hands and feet, Danny hears that sweetest of all sounds, that little bang the door makes when it's opened, when it hits the outside wall.

Door might as well have hit him in the gut. All his wind's knocked out. Just seeing her, being close enough to smell her hair. All his longing narrows down to that. Wrong to ask for more. Bad business.

Oh, here she comes! Just look at her, how beautiful she is. His Katherine.

She passes so close he can see the sun's red rays reflected in her eyes. See how she wears her shirt outside her jeans now, leans ever so slightly back, body already shifting for the baby. Wonders why he hadn't noticed it before.

Baby'll change her like he never could. Should have figured that out long ago, saved himself a lot of trouble. With him, she could always walk away, turn her back, take up her fucking weaving. Baby won't let her walk away. From it. From him. From anything.

His baby. Baby made out of their love. Just like he dreamed about with old Janelle. With Katherine, it's real.

He unbuttons two shirt buttons, slides the feathers out one at a time, stands up with great difficulty, right where she can see him if she'll only turn around. Fans out the feathers in the path for her to find them—one, two, three, four, five, six, seven. So pretty there. Then he scuttles back into the undergrowth. Waits with his heart up in his mouth. Where he can taste it. Suck on it. Chew it into little pieces.

Fucking whore! She sees the feathers in the fucking middle of the path, doesn't even look around. Knows seven feathers are no accident. Knows he's the one had to have left them. Knows he's close, so close she can call him with a whisper. Danny. Danny. Oh, how he listens for it, her calling his name. Thinks even that he hears it, like a whisper in the trees.

But that's all it is. Bitch doesn't want it, not any of it. Steps over his feathers and moves on. Runs. Slams her door and shoots the bolt.

Come back. Open your door. Call out my name and take me in. I need you, need to lie beside you, feel the hard knot of my baby in you. Hard knot with a little bird-size beating heart. He screams it with a voice that's silent as the rocks that hide him.

DANNY SITS IN HIS shallow cave, tries not to think about his shoulder. Skins the rabbit with his sin-cleansed knife, pulls away its soft fur from the glistening flesh. Fur so soft he'll keep it. Make a cover for his baby son. *Bring a little rabbit skin to wrap his baby bunting in.* Where'd that come from? Memaw? Someone, his mama, before that? What the hell's a bunting? He makes tiny cuts into the rabbit's fur. Scrapes the skin, gentle as a caress.

He's finished now. Puts the skin carefully aside. Holds up the rabbit by its ears and grins.

Bitch doesn't want him?

Maybe not right this fucking minute. But she will.

Oh, yes. She will.

45

Katherine's Bargain

It's a bargain she has struck. With whatever one strikes bargains with. If she locks the door and bolts the shutters and only goes out when she can't do otherwise, nothing bad will happen. Danny will not die from her bullet in his shoulder; he will go away before long to some other wilderness and she can have her baby and not be afraid.

Because there is a baby, she is certain now. And she is afraid.

If he does not go away, she has the gun.

It has all worked quite well so far. Except for the part where she rarely sleeps for hearing him in every little night breeze, every snapping twig, seeing him between the shutter slats in every moon shadow. And the part where she spends all her days with her heart pounding, starting at the slightest sound. The problem is the light's too dim to weave, to read; she has no distractions, only fear.

The problem is her food is running out.

Today, with her tiny knife, she makes one more. She has started gouging marks into her wall again, near the entrance to the kitchen. Fifteen, the number of days she has spent hiding in the cabin. She hasn't seen him, but she can feel his presence all around her, the way a gathering storm charges the air. Meanwhile, honeysuckle scents the breeze, spring's almost gone.

She folds the knife and puts it in her pocket, where it lives now. Sits in the rocking chair he brought her. Her heart hurts from missing him, as if she has an actual physical pain inside her rib cage, and it makes no sense. Makes no sense, either, that every night she rolls up two of their three quilts to simulate his body and lies there pressed against them, smothering her face in them to catch his scent; it's bitter, like the hulls of walnuts.

Her memories come then, not thoughts or images but pure sensations that spin and shake her. In dreams his face floats toward her as if he's traveling through fog. But who is it she misses, dreams of? Who does she remember? Not the man who smashed her car, not the man who bound her to him in ways no one should bind anyone and knew all the while what he was doing, not the man who tried to kill her child. No, it's the boy. The boy who stood that day beside the garden oak, so fierce and thin and frightened, he is the one she misses.

But which of these is real? The man? The boy? Neither? Both? It doesn't matter. It all comes down to the same thing. That's why she's shut herself in where he can't get at her. And will stay however long she has to, won't allow herself to think that far ahead.

She's gained strength as the days have passed, and her morning sickness is largely gone. Yet her confinement forces her to spend her hours drinking strong teas, eating thick soups, rocking and staring through a crack between closed shutters like a convalescent. Five days ago, she heated water on the stove and took a sponge bath. It felt like a celebration, a religious rite, her scrubbing away the ten days' worth of grime caked on her skin. She can't do it often; heating water wastes wood she has to bring in from the shed. The day before yesterday her body started once again to itch and stink. When she shifts position in the rocker, small puffs of foul air rise up from between the layers of her clothing. She sniffs—disgusted, fascinated—at the wildness she exudes.

Through the crack between the shutters, moisture from last night's rain still sparkles on the violets and young dandelion spears covering the ground. Saliva pools under her tongue. Later, she will dash outside and pick enough to fill the pewter mixing bowl, run back in and eat them raw. Only, the bowl is not on any of the dark shelves in the pie safe. Nor is it in either of the wooden storage bins that flank the fireplace. There's no place else to look but one. She climbs onto a bench and peers along the top shelf where she used to keep her gun. The bowl is not there either. It's nowhere.

She chafes her arms against a sudden chill. Did he somehow get in the house while she was sleeping? If that's what happened, why, of all things, did he take the pewter bowl? To make her see he's been here, been that close to her? She always thought she'd know this, sense it, with no sign from him. Will she wake one night to find him sitting cross-legged on the floor beside her, the full moon flinging blue-white light across his nakedness?

And if yes, what will she do?

Her last memory of the mixing bowl was two days ago. She was sitting just inside the open door, her gun beside her, picking clean some creasy greens she'd yanked up from the stream bank where the moss smells rank as a dirt basement. She had the bowl in her lap, would not have left it outside on the porch—outside is where he is. Nonetheless, she cracks the door, peers out.

And there it is. Last night's wild wind blew it back along the railing where she couldn't see it.

Or was it something else? The thought provokes a tightening in her throat, equal parts terror and desire. How long before she's rid of it, this wanting him no matter what? She must remember where she puts things. Some night he truly might break in and take something. She'll need to know.

She grabs the bowl, hurries in and bolts the door, settles herself once again in her rocker, in the half-light from the shuttered windows. It isn't pleasant in the house, it stinks. Once each day she empties the slop bucket, always at a different time so he can't anticipate it; something he taught her, something from the war—to excise him from her mind will take a lot of little cuts, not one big slash as she had hoped.

Yesterday she went outside in early morning, so today she'll go out in late afternoon. But it's always the same place, a sharp gouge of a ravine out past the privy, which is probably not wise. She's made a holster for the pistol from one leg of a pair of jeans already grown too small, ties it around her waist, nestles the gun inside it every time she leaves the cabin.

The sun is sliding low, but there's still time. She takes measured swallows from her teacup on the dogwood side table—the first peppermint leaves from the garden, delicate and with no pennyroyal aftertaste—tries to will herself calm.

The air outside is not as warm as she imagined. On the privy path she knows his presence as a prickling of her skin, a stillness among the trees. She runs with the bucket, nearly trips over a gnarled root, hurls the slops into the ditch and leaves with one hand clapped over her mouth.

Heading back, she veers from the path, skids down the slick bank where the stream rushes over rocks flung there like afterthoughts, and squats to rinse her bucket. He could be anywhere. She hastily sloshes water in the bucket, starts toward home. One more day he has not shown himself, did not sneak up from behind to cinch his arms around her when she couldn't see—sometimes fear can be confused with longing, regret with desire.

He tried to kill her child.

The path is all in shadow and the sun has nearly set. She used to long for sundown in this place, because that's when the sky looked capable of lifting her high up into itself, swallowing her into its afterglow; because on each side of where she walked the green rooms beckoned. Now she fears sundown because of Danny and she knows neither the sky nor the green rooms will save her.

Not looking at the ground, she almost doesn't see the seven turkey feathers, iridescent in the fading light, fanned out in the center of the path. She nearly steps on them, lets loose a startled "Oh."

He's left them. Put them there while she was gone. He came that close.

Danny! Her heart calls out to him so loud there is no damp, far, sun-starved cove that doesn't hear it. Yet her mouth makes no sound.

The feathers are beautiful and intricate. Their colors change like facets in a mirror ball when she steps over them, walks on.

She slides the gun out from its makeshift holster. It lies heavy in her hand. What if he's there when she gets back to the cabin, waiting for her? She's locked her door, but locks don't mean a thing to him. Clammy sweat crawls down between her breasts. She doesn't see him on the path. Inside the cabin she looks everywhere, even up the dark mouth of the hearth. He isn't there, he isn't anywhere. Relief masquerades as disappointment.

Or is it the other way around?

This night, even with the gun beside her, she falls into a broken sleep, unsure when she is dreaming and when she is not. Wakes wanting him, as she might wake from a sudden pain, and then remembers all she needs to, hates to, must. There's a cacophony out on the porch. Birds. Screaming. She reaches for the gun. Her mouth is filled with fear, the taste of metal. How has she come to be afraid of birds?

She jerks open the door. A pair of jays arc toward her, shrieking, dive-bombing her so she will back away. They're guarding something.

Then she sees.

Hanging from the porch rafters, trussed up by its feet and turning slowly, a membranous form glistens in the new light. A small, elongated baby with slick, pointed ears that stand out from its head.

That's what the jays have come for. They're flying at it, picking out its eyes. The birds have pecked the baby's eyes until they're bleeding. Just like in Memaw's lullaby.

Katherine screams and screams. Aims her gun and shoots. Once. Twice. First at the birds heading toward the baby through the air. Then at nothing but the dark trees.

46

The Gook

AGAIN, HE SITS ON HIS HEELS UNDER HIS ROCK OVERHANG. SHE'S GOT to come out sometime. Got to. If a blue jay shrieks four times in a row. If he sees an animal bigger than a squirrel. He wants her so bad he's trembling. Wants even just to look at her again.

You get used to things. How her skin smelled fragrant like the garden, even in winter. How, nights, he lay always with one hand coiled in her long, dark hair and the other warm between her legs. You get used to things, they're yours. Take them away, it's like gouging out pieces of your flesh.

Blue jay screams three times and flies away. Fuck that. How many bird screams, how many possums and raccoons rustling the bushes will it take to bring her out? Even with his bunged-up shoulder, he can run on four legs like a wolf. Quieter that way, safer. Less of him to see. Runs down to the clearing's edge, end of the trees. Bitch shot him in the fucking shoulder. Loves him so much she'll shoot him in the head next time. Didn't like his trussed-up rabbit-baby, though, not even with its little diaper.

Long after his feet go numb, the door opens. His heart pounds like a piston. He follows her down the privy path, just like that first evening. That's how far back he wishes he could go. Look there, she's still got the baby in her. Memaw taught him how to tell. That little paunch where she's tucked in her shirt to keep the bugs away. Weird how he can't take his eyes off it. Little shit got past all Memaw's tea. Kid's one tough little motherfucker, hard to kill. Like Danny.

So many tears you wonder where you've carried them, how you've borne their weight.

He follows close beside her all the way back to the cabin, his vision blurred, his sounds covered by a ruffling breeze. Watches her go inside and light a lamp. Watches her lamp move from window to window as she closes shutters, its glow nothing then but horizontal lines. The shutters tremble when she bolts them.

Cold now, dark. Night's a gook. Kill you when your back's turned. He climbs up to his overhang, sleeps curled into himself, fist jammed in his mouth to keep from crying out in dreams.

MORNING. SKY'S RED. GOOD day never starts with a red sky. *Red sky at morning, the sailors take warning.* Pawpaw's teaching, learned it in the Navy.

Got to get himself some reefer, reefer's good for tears. Won't dry them up, just makes it so you never give a shit. Sit and play with them. Wipe your hands in them. Use them to clean crud off your knife.

Reefer. The word pings off the insides of his skull as he climbs over rocks and scrubby saplings. Reefer, so he can watch her like that first day, come to her like that night in the storm. Reefer. Because stepping out where she can see him is like kicking in a plate glass window, walking through its rain of shards. Reefer that's in his orchard—and his mattress—in the house where he and Katherine will live someday.

The noon sun's a steel disc in a pale gray sky that quiets everything. Danny moves as usual, doesn't make a sound. Hasn't been home in some days. Worth coming in the front way, through the orchard. This time last year, just wanting to be near her, he ground one of its soft, ripe peaches against his open mouth, his teeth, till juice dripped off his chin and ran between his fingers.

Ka-ther-ine. How can she stay apart from him, untangle herself so thoroughly from him, after living how they did? Might as well just rip him clean in two. Memory seizes him so completely he almost misses the invasive scent, a flower sweetness mixed with sweat that calls up cinderblock juke joints set far back on highways out of town. He stops still. Only his eyes move.

There's sound comes with the smell. Boots crunching on dry leaves. Someone whistling some old song off some long-gone radio. Fucker even trills it. Aftershave, sweat, some corny song.

And blinding orange surveyor's tape knotted around a nearby hickory. That's when he sees the man. Skinny little gook in khakis skulking around outside Danny's hooch. Moves sideways like a crab, like maybe his knees aren't so good. Danny straightens, tucks in his shirt, pats the knife in his pocket. Approaches him without a sound. He's five feet away when the gook hears him, or maybe only senses him, and turns. Frowns.

Danny folds his arms across his chest, stares him down. "Excuse me, sir," looking him straight in the eye, "what might you be doing on my property?"

Gook's shorter than he seemed. They're all short, gooks.

"I think there must be some mistake, sir." Glares at Danny, gives back what he gets. "This house and all the land around it is the property of Carlisle-Colorado Mining and Development, the company that hired me to survey it."

Danny's turn to glare. Important not to miss a beat. "You'd think they'd let the neighbors know. I've rented right beside them, kept care of this place up here going on two years now. Cared for it like it was my own."

Gook's face brightens. "You live in the cabin, then." He nods in the direction Danny came. "You must know how to get in touch with the lady that owns the place. That Mrs. Reid. Mr. Carlisle wants to talk with her."

"What for?"

"Wants to buy her out. Good price, too." He stops, considers, then goes on. "Mr. Carlisle means to turn this whole area, right up to the government wilderness, into some kind of big year-round showplace. Golf course, tennis courts, horse stables, even a man-made lake with a real sand beach." Gook says these last words with wonder, like they'd won some kind of prize. "Lake's what he wants the cabin for."

"Wants the cabin for a lake?" That's crazy.

"Wants the land." Gook's getting wound up now. "Lowest point around, creeks running through it. Dam them up, you got a proper lake. And houses, people living everywhere around it when it's done. People living in big houses all around here, that's what Mr. Carlisle wants."

The gook's words buzz in Danny's head, hard to translate.

"She won't sell. Tell you that right now." The knife weighs heavy in his pocket. "No, she loves that place. She'd never leave it."

"Oh, he'll make her a good deal. She won't be one bit sorry."

"She won't sell. Wouldn't sell to me, won't sell to you neither."

Gook's got an axe stuck in a stump maybe thirty feet away. Second nature, scoping out the likely weapons.

"What's your name, son?"

Son. How long since anybody called him that? "Danny MacLean. What's yours?"

"Lonnie Washburn."

"Well. Where you hail from, Lonnie, Mr. Washburn?"

"I come from Wynne, other side of Elkmont."

"Wynne, huh? You've come a ways. You the only man out on this job?"

"Am today. We're mostly done. I'm just up here confirming where the house sits on the property."

"What's Mr. Carlisle plan to do with it, the house I mean?" Danny waves his good arm at it. Gook hasn't noticed the gimp one. Must not see too good.

"They say this here's going to be the clubhouse. Say he's going to build it back just like it was. Velvet curtains, crystal chandeliers. Rent it out so folks can have their parties."

"Reckon he'll keep the orchard?"

"Orchard? Couldn't say."

"He'd be smart to keep it. It's beautiful in springtime. Summertime and early fall, it gives good fruit."

Gook nods.

"Last year I did some work on it, some of the trees. My wife Katie and me, we picked the fruit. She canned a lot of it. Wish you could meet my Katie. Got that long, black hair down to the middle of her back. We got a baby coming in the fall." Danny grins big and wide.

Gook smiles. "Well, that's great, son."

Danny wishes the gook hadn't said that, about it being great about the baby. Wishes he hadn't called him son again. It's given him a sadness, a kind of wistfulness he badly wants to get shed of.

"You seen the orchard yet?" he says.

"Walked around it. Never really gave a look."

"Let me take you. Show you what we've done."

"I don't want to put you out, son."

"No trouble. Only take a minute."

"Okay, I'll have a look. Got a couple apple trees myself back in Wynne."

"This way, Mr. Washburn. Down that path right there, I'm right behind you. There's thick blackberries growing alongside it. We picked gallons of them last year, me and my Katie. Best berries I ever ate."

The knife still fits his hand like it was made for it. Trees rustle with the same papery sound as palm fronds in the wind. Danny doesn't need to think about it, grabs the gook's chin and jerks his head up, cuts a deep, clean slice across his throat. Holds him like a lover while he spasms. Gray hair, blue eyes, pink skin.

Shit. What has he done?

Oh, sweet Christ Jesus.

His own blood runs cold all through him. He lays the old man gently down and pulls him by his ankles to the orchard. Pain in Danny's shoulder turning everything he sees to silver as he drags him to a gully by the peach trees. Kicks dirt over him, over his face, his head. Maybe enough to keep the buzzards off him, maybe not. Must have hiked up here, no way to bring a truck. Maybe no one'll find him.

But now everything's all changed. Just like San Francisco, no matter how you look at it. A mistake. A jolt of memory. Could happen anywhere.

With anyone.

With her.

Inside the house, Danny's reefer's still stuffed in his mattress where he left it, with some papers not too damp. He rolls a joint slowly, tries to think of nothing else. Flicks open his lighter, stares into its fire. The joint flames, its seeds crackle and spark. He takes a long drag, holds the smoke and feels a singing in his blood.

Together forever.

She shot twice at the rabbit. That leaves two bullets in the gun.

Summer

47

His Baby, Too

KATHERINE DIGS DOWN TO THE BOTTOM OF THE BURLAP RICE SACK, works her fingers into its ragged seam, comes up with eleven dirty and chewed-looking grains. All the beans are gone. She slides her hand along the grim edges of all the pie-safe shelves. Nothing. The weather is hot and dry, even for early June; what few vegetables she managed to plant this year are withering for lack of rain. There's nothing else to do but walk to town. Otherwise she'll have no food. Nor will her baby.

It's begun to move, the merest flutter, as if she'd swallowed live a small tropical fish. Just like that other baby. But this baby will move inside her every day and every night, until it moves in the wide world all on its own. Because she wills it so. Because she will go to town for it, get food for it, for her. Because she will pay attention. Because she will not be afraid.

She goes into the front room, sits in the rocker, strokes her belly lightly through her jeans.

"Dear little fish, my little fish, I promise you'll grow up with sing-ing grass and forest animals. And always have enough to eat."

She does not deserve this child, its innocence. Her fears for it arise from circumstances she created through her weaknesses, circum-stances that already have endangered it. Yet these same weaknesses led to her child's creation. What was the right of it? What was the wrong? She can't unravel the one from the other. Would it make any differ-ence if she could?

Today she would love nothing better than to lie all morning on her warm rock at the pond's edge, her shirt hiked up to show her belly. Would her baby feel its warmth, see its rays as the same deep, pulsing red she sees when she looks through closed eyes at the noon sun? But Danny is out there somewhere watching, so her lying with her baby at the pond's edge will not come to pass.

She gets up from the rocker, puts on a shirt too thick to hint at any shape inside it, too thick to let in any sun, jams the gun in her jeans pocket, loops a second shirt around her waist to cover it. Prays her baby cannot sense her fear.

"We'll go now and hurry, little fish, stop only for groceries, some-thing at the hardware store." She smiles in spite of everything. "And larger pants so you will have more room to breathe."

She can't pinpoint exactly when she started talking to the child out loud, or keeping one hand always on the little tummy bulge it lives beneath, stroking it gently. Nor can she name the day she started sing-ing softly to it in the house. The only lullaby she knows all the way through is Memaw's and she won't sing that. Sings instead the old songs about looking over four-leaf clovers, taking slow boats to China, waking to mockingbirds' trills. And sometimes medleys of advertising jingles so closely akin to nursery rhymes: "Plop, plop. Fizz, fizz. Oh, what a relief it is." "You'll wonder where the yellow went, when you brush your teeth with Pepsodent," "Use new White Rain shampoo tonight, and tomorrow your hair will be sunshine bright." Sometimes she makes up songs about what's handy. Birds and squirrels, the gar-den and the trees. She does not sing love songs.

And she does not sing this morning when she ventures out onto the trail, where the cart's clatter can't quite mask the wind rustling the trees, the rhythmic chirps of shade-loving crickets, the trills of distant birds.

Or other sounds that might be Danny's.

She hears him even in the smallest whisper of dead leaves, sees him in every shadow and on every ridge. Her heart rises in her throat and she holds on to her breath. Fear feels like so many things she does not want to remember. She tries desperately to divert her thoughts from it, welcomes the highway, with its drivers who see everything that happens on its roadsides. Every house she passes is a blessing, someplace she can run to, people who might take her in.

When they come into the town—lately she thinks of herself always as a "they"—Katherine wraps the gun in her twill shirt jacket and lays it in the cart. On the street she looks into the faces of everyone they pass. The blue-eyed, birdlike little man with razor stubble, the plump, gray-haired woman with the cabbage roses on her yellow dress, the sullen teenage girl who stares down at the ground. She searches there for memories of him that have twisted their mouths, afterimages that linger in their eyes. Finds nothing. She walks quickly, shies away from vacant buildings, alcoves, trash alleys, all the places he might hide. A car backfiring, a burning cigarette tossed on the sidewalk, a sudden bark of laughter, all cause her heart to hammer in her chest.

The cashier at the little grocery smiles at her. "Haven't seen you around lately."

No mention of Danny, but that is to be expected. In stores he tends to disappear. Indeed, for the people in the town, Danny has already disappeared as if he never once existed. No one asks about him, not even the postal clerk. Yet Katherine senses he is near. No matter how quickly she turns, it's as if he's just moved out of sight and is still watching.

In the hardware store she buys a hunting knife like his. The man with the Adam's apple runs his thumb down the blade edge. "It's plenty sharp."

"Yes, I can see that."

She eyes the indentation along its length.

The clerk slides his finger through it. "Blood gutter."

She should be thinking of a hunter with his deer. Or of her baby's cord this knife will cut. Instead she thinks of Danny, buys a box of bullets for the gun. Wedges them down near the bottom of the cart, good ballast for the hike back to the cabin. She doesn't load the gun, is not sure it's allowed out in the open. Anyway, it's got two bullets still, in case she needs them.

Heading back, she feels safe on the open road. Knows now he will come to her, if he is going to, in some private place, not here. Here, she is free to walk a normal pace. Free to look around at what delighted her in other circumstances.

"Fish, swaddled in your amniotic bubble, if I take a deep breath and hold it can you smell the honeysuckle? The bank on this side of the road is covered with it. And bees. And look—but of course you can't look, no, not yet—there's the red barn. We're almost to the turn-off."

Only in the past few days has she allowed herself to think of the child alive, out in the world and growing. Every day she lets herself imagine just a little more without a penalty. Hard not to cry.

"And here's the Wickles Store. We're almost home."

But she has lied to her baby, they are not almost home. In fact, if measured by the likelihood of danger, their journey has hardly begun. When she leaves the highway she takes the gun out of the cart and shoves it in her pocket. The little asphalt road seems safe enough but she knows otherwise. She pushes the cart down its middle, as far away as possible from the concealing brush on either side. Honeysuckle, young red blackberries—lovely things made fearsome now. When the road narrows, goes to gravel, then to dirt, she starts at every sound, half expects him to jump out from behind her mangled car before she jerks the cart onto the trail. Sometimes her hand lets go the cart handle, moves to her pocket just to touch the gun.

It's hot, midafternoon. The woods are hushed; even the leaves don't move. She does not talk to her baby now, nor stop to wipe the sweat out of her eyes. Just plods on, fast as she can, in silence.

As if silence made a difference. Danny is the Prince of Silence. He could be six inches from her elbow and she wouldn't know it. Rocks, trees, are you hiding him?

Afternoon thunder grumbles in the distance. Danny hides from thunder—yet she knows at the same time that this safety's an illusion. If he were truly gone, she would feel his absence as she would feel air in an empty room. Around the next bend she will see the cabin. Soon they will be home and safe. She bought seeds today, from what sad, dog-eared packets remained. Eggplant and other vegetables nobody wanted. If he's gone . . . If—when—he's gone, she'll plant them. Pictures tiny, chubby hands splayed around a ripe tomato, small fingers digging deep into a basket filled with beans.

"Hello, Katherine."

He steps onto the trail, perhaps ten feet in front of her, and blocks her way. She knows it now—he was ten feet away from her in town, ten feet on the highway, ten feet on the trail. Ten feet ever since she left the house this morning. Ten feet every moment of her every day. Her heart, her breath, everything stops. Except for her right arm, which shakes obviously and uncontrollably as she reaches for the gun.

"Go away from here. Leave us alone." Her words have hardly any sound. The gun shakes violently in her hands.

"I came to see my baby."

"You've seen all there is to see." The space between them is choked with her forbidden memories. "Please go."

"I came to feel it move." He takes a step toward her.

His voice is calm, steady, as if this were an ordinary conversation. He takes another step.

"I'll shoot you."

"No, you won't."

He smiles, reaches out his hand in which she is supposed to lay the gun.

She looks only at his face. The head's a messy target, the gun shop grandmother had said. Her entire body trembles. She sights down the gun's short barrel, pulls the trigger. Hears only the click of an empty chamber. Oh, dear God.

He smiles. "See? You can't shoot me. I'm U. S. of A.–certified magic." He takes another step toward her, oblivious to the growling thunder.

Again she pulls the trigger. Another click. Where are the bullets? Surely there are two left in the cylinder, she's seen them. She pulls the trigger once again.

Click.

Three clicks. All empty chambers. One more empty, then the bullets. That's how it will be. Worst-case scenario.

She pulls the trigger one more time. Once more the chamber clicks, its sound muffled by his hand.

His arms are around her now, fingers prying the gun away.

All this time her greatest terror was what would happen if he touched her. But she feels only the struggle, and that she must prevail. Under their scuffle, she hears again the rumble of the distant storm.

The gun barrel is a cold ring pressed against her temple. His other hand is spread over her belly.

He gazes at her, his smile filled with sadness.

"You could just have let me feel my baby move. You didn't need to try and shoot me." That familiar voice low in her ear. The wind rustling the trees. All of it so terrifying. And so peaceful.

Then in an instant everything is changed. His voice, his sad smile, vanish and there is only fury in their place.

"I'll kill you. Don't think I won't."

Their baby gives a small shudder beneath the hard warmth of his palm. He snatches his hand away. Shoves the gun's cold mouth against her belly where his warm fingers had been.

"No. Please, no."

She's somewhere in the treetops looking down. At herself. At him. At the gun pointed at her baby.

"I'll kill you. The same way you killed Jimbo."

"Danny, no! I'm Katherine!"

He stands quite still. Every emotion moves across his face, as if he were the keeper of them all for all the world.

Another thunderclap. Closer. Danny raises his arm then, points the gun up toward the sky.

"Katherine, look there."

She whimpers, turns her face up to the gathering clouds, looks back and he is gone.

48

A Good Day, All of It, Clear Through

DOG BOUNDS OUT TO GREET HIM SOON AS HE NEARS THE HOUSE. Jumps, wags her tail. He squats and puts his arms around her neck, buries his head in her warm fur.

"I didn't bring you anything."

He wipes his eyes. She licks the salt tears off his hand.

"I'm sorry."

Kicks at her, not very hard.

"Now git. You need to go away." She doesn't move.

In Gatsby's library, the room where he, Danny, has lived, he starts pulling books off their shelves, stacking them into pillars at the corners of his mattress. Books he has read, six shelves of them, not near as many as he wanted to. Books he had meant to read. Books he had thought to read with her. Books about places he has never gone and people he has never met. *For Whom the Bell Tolls, Tender Is the Night,*

Anthony Adverse, Daisy Miller, On the Beach, Animal Farm. So many more—*As I Lay Dying, Peyton Place, The Odyssey, Fahrenheit 451. The Big Sleep.* And *Gatsby.* Stacks so high they waver when he takes his hand away. When they played *Three Musketeers,* Jimbo always played D'Artagnan; since they were only two, Danny could be any of the other three he wanted. He always told Jimbo his Musketeer was stronger than D'Artagnan; Jimbo always went along. Danny shifts the larger books to the bottom for stability. Dog follows after him, her nails scratching the walnut floor. The floor he's finished sanding. Thunder rumbles. Danny's body jerks.

"Go on. Get on away."

Janelle's hair was gold, but Katherine's was almost black; he loved to look at it against the whiteness of the quilt with its tiny blue flowers. Danny shoves the dog toward the door. She backs up and looks at him.

"Shit. This'll get you."

He pulls out his Zippo, flips it open, dials up a foot-high flame. Grins at her through it. She backs out the door and stares.

"Yeah, you'll be gone like a flash."

He squats beside a dusty panel of the faded velvet curtains that hide the west windows with their missing panes. Holds his flame against the fabric. Till it starts to smoke, till the smoke breeds small licks of orange fire. Danny used to ride on Pawpaw's shoulders when they went out hunting, like a boy riding a bear.

The dog watches, puzzled, wary, as the curtain starts to burn. Backs away another foot or so.

Danny hears the thunder, but it's nothing to him now. Lights the second curtain, watches the flames climb, satisfied only when they engulf the window moldings. Wood floors, roof timbers, beams, lath, lots of shit in this old limestone house to burn. Collapse the whole damn thing this time. No clubhouse, no parties on Gatsby's lawn. Nothing for Carlisle-Colorado Mining and Development, all of it for Katherine. He should have bought an orchid for her. White orchid with tiny pearl-tipped pins.

Danny lies down on his mattress, the gun by his right hand. Dog comes running, jumps onto the bed beside him.

He shoves her hard, but she won't budge. Except to lick his hand. Glances from him to the burning curtains and then back, as if asking what the two of them should do.

"Aw, shit. Get the fuck out. Go find some other dude to hunt with, other dude who'll let you lick his hand."

The far wall has begun to flame, bright patches crawling toward the ceiling, flames licking at the shelves still stacked with books.

"All right, get up. This is your last chance." Danny shoves the dog off the bed. "Get the fuck out! Now!"

Sends a bullet singing inches from her ear.

Dog yelps, hightails it out the door.

Danny lies back down. Thunder getting close. Sixteen kills, every one he got sent out on. He was a good soldier, no matter what they said. Eight years old and he could hit a squirrel square in its eye.

He got to see his Katherine, touch her. Got to feel their baby move. Homecoming Day he ran the ball, so far they all stood up and cheered. Yeah, today's turned out a good day. All of it. Clear through.

He jams the gun's barrel in his mouth. Gatsby loved his Katherine more than he loved life itself.

It's.

All.

Right.

49

The Heart of the Forest

SHE SITS MOTIONLESS IN THE ROCKING CHAIR HE BROUGHT HER, IN the heat and distant thunder. Unsure what to hope for, trying to smother the little bud of panic that keeps wanting to bloom inside her.

He held the gun on her so he could feel their baby move. His baby, too. And then he would have killed them both. What demons has he given shelter to? And for how long? And why did she know so little of them, she who had loved him?

She gazes straight ahead, at the corner he so long embraced outside the cabin, his arms and legs hugging its cold stones. Gazes out the same window where that first morning snow clung to more trees than she had ever seen all in one place. She tries to think of nothing, listens for what will happen next.

It isn't long in coming. A faint, innocent popgun sound from the far side of Panther Mountain sets her trembling. She sits straight, poised. Was that the end of it, of him? There were two bullets in the gun. Where is the other? Is he still alive and is it meant for her? She rocks now, her shallow breathing in time to the chair's rapid movement. Danny. Danny. Danny.

With the second shot her rocking stops. He is dead. She knows it now, as surely as if she had been there. Feels it as if her mind, her heart, had suddenly been numbed. Outside herself it manifests as emptiness, as if suddenly the wilderness holds too much open space, too many vistas. She sits quietly with this new knowledge, so that she might grow accustomed to existing in that openness. Accepts that he is dead but she is still alive and once more free to move about, that she no longer needs to watch for him, fear him. Understands that she will no longer feel his eyes on her, no longer hear his even breathing in the night, and that perhaps never again will she be watched by anyone in the consuming way he watched her, perhaps not watched by anyone at all—that she might become invisible, white smoke in a white sky. Right now, if there were not a baby, only she would know that she exists. If there were not a baby, this gift he's given her, she would have no one other than herself to love.

But white smoke, in truth, does not long remain invisible. What billows from the other side of Panther Mountain in playful whorls soon drifts to form a brown gauze curtain with a deceptive hearth-fire fragrance. She is glad for her distance from it, will not let herself picture him at the smoke's origin, his pyre. Imagines instead him hiking back that day from Elkmont carrying the rocking chair she sits in now, how perhaps he smiled and held it upright by its rockers, on his shoulders where it swayed above his head like a sedan chair on an elephant; or perhaps he held it by its arms, inverted, its back making a turtle's shell. Pictures again the first time she saw him, standing in the shade of the huge chestnut oak, while the oblivious tomato plants exuded their astringent perfume; that deep voice—"Unbraid your hair"; and that night in the storm, in the electric air, his hand hurtfully circling her wrist—"Take me in"—and how she knew a need that strong would put an end to loneliness. They come crashing in, these memories, after the long, parched time she's forced herself to live without them.

She barely notices the coming of the promised storm, its violent lightning, sheets of rain no more than an extension of her grief. Why did she so desire him, desire him far beyond all reason? Had he shown up on her front porch in the city, demanding to be taken in, she would have called the police. Had she met him as an equal, sat at his table at an Ad Association dinner, say, they would likely not have felt the smallest spark of primitive attraction. She should have feared him, should have feared the depth of her desire that bordered on insanity. She wanted him the way a starving animal wants food; had he not met her halfway with his own desire, she would have torn him into pieces.

She should have stopped it, never let it start. She could not do it.

Near late afternoon, when the rain has passed and the sun's low edge touches the tallest trees and she has no tears left for crying, a dog that must have been his dog trots onto the porch, a dog she's never seen but only heard about. She opens the door for it. The animal comes in, stands still and looks around. It's a middling-to-large female, with a deer-colored coat that's full of burrs and smells of smoke. Her gaze at first seems wary. She looks Katherine up and down, then cautiously approaches the rocker. When she gets close enough, Katherine grabs a handful of her fur, holds on until the dog sits beside her on her haunches, then eventually lowers her head, rests it in Katherine's lap beside the baby.

They three sit like that for what seems a long time. Then the dog gets up, goes to the door and stands there, as though she wants to be let out. Katherine opens the door, follows the dog outside. The animal circles the garden, stops beneath the oak that shaded Danny that first day, lies on the ground and peers into the wilderness beyond. Katherine follows the dog's gaze, stares long. Stares until, as if in a trompe l'oeil painting, the jumbled mass of trees and undergrowth that's the beginning of the forest arranges itself into those beckoning green chambers she has yearned toward for so long. Rooms opening one into another, endlessly. Rooms that must reach to the forest's heart.

Katherine circles the garden and moves toward them, as if pulled by some invisible cord. Looks once over her shoulder, but the dog has not followed. She wades alone through a thick tangle of fleabane daisies at the meadow's edge, their feathery blooms filled with soft-spoken bees that do not make a move to sting her; then she walks into the wilderness, that dark, high-ceilinged green, where sun sifts in aslant, as through cathedral clerestories. That she might lose her way, should perhaps turn back, does not deter her. She walks on, creating her own path, as if she has a destination.

The air, fragrant with moss and damp bark, grows cooler. Katherine turns slowly in a full circle. She's not gone far, she's certain of it, but can no longer see the garden, surely a trick of the peculiar light. A small wet-weather stream gurgles noisily near her feet. She continues alongside it, follows it deeper into the wilderness, whispers names of trees she passes, trees whose shapes, leaves, bark textures she memorized her first days in the cabin: red oak, white oak, chestnut oak, chinquapin, red maple, sweet gum, locust, beech, poplar, white pine, cedar, dogwood, serviceberry, a single princess tree.

There's little light now, though the sun's still high. Her whole world's turned a deep, watery green. The stream has widened between banks of laurel and rhododendron through which she must make her way. Her hand, when she places it against one of the chestnut oaks, comes away with the bark's haunting fragrance. She cups it over her mouth and nose, breathes in, as she has done so many times before. And then walks on, deeper into the forest maze, until there's hardly any light at all. The birds she hears in this place sing liquid, complex, unfamiliar songs. They flit high in the trees, do not descend, do not reveal themselves. Threads of mist glide past and dark leaves glisten with condensation that slides in soundless drops onto the mossy ground.

For some time now her heart has felt less burdened. She skirts a thick expanse of ferns, enters another of the trees' green chambers. She is not lost: The clearing, her cabin, and the garden are behind her to the west, as is Panther Mountain. Or are they to the south—or north, or east? She can see nothing now but trees, smell nothing but leaf mold, its odor old as the red earth she walks on: "Take me in."

A light breeze fluffs the small hairs on her arms as it might ruffle a bird's downy breast feathers, then moves away. But the sound it made remains. Grows. Into long, low notes that call to mind the meadow's singing grass. Yet unlike the grass's one low note, these notes are held in harmony, as if by many voices.

She advances with slow, measured steps toward the sound, which is beautiful. Then she stops. For it now comes from all around her, from rocks, leaves, trees, from fallen branches, jagged boulders, whitened bones, small flowers beneath her feet. From other living and dead things she cannot see, their individual notes distinct, each one, in tone and pitch. Yet joined, an exaltation.

She lays her hands on the thick trunk of a sweet gum—to feel its vibrations, to know the sounds are real. The same way as that first night she pressed her palm flat against her cabin's stones to feel the deer's moist breathing that was Danny's.

When she takes her hand away the tree's soothing hum lingers inside her. No, not the tree's; when she tries to move away, the sound stays with her, in her. It is her sound, she knows this now, a sound that kins her to the rocks and trees: low, resonant, distinct. Katherine stands motionless and listens. Until her sound seems all there is, as if it has absorbed her, her corporeal self, and made her one with air. And with a second harmony—high, insistent, sweet, and like her own song emanating from inside her. The vibration of her unborn child.

Katherine stands listening for a long time and with her full attention, then walks on inside these harmonies, inside the knowledge that she and her child are the same substance, and that their substance is the same substance as water, wind, the wild grass in the meadow, the boulders that jut out over the trail into the forest; the same substance as the bear, the owl, the mockingbird, the vole, and Danny.

Her baby squirms inside her, its movements like the rainbow trout's concentric circles on the quiet pond. Minutes, hours, there is no difference as she journeys deeper into wilderness—so wilderness can take her and her child, that singing air they have become, into itself, enfold them. She walks on, prepared for darkness, magnificence, and terror at the forest's heart, prepared for sacrifice. But when the trees thin, accepts light instead. Accepts even that the music fades and she has come out where she started.

At the garden.

Epilogue

A Brief History of Bartram's Mountains, from an Interview on a Late Summer Afternoon

THE WOMAN, VIRGINIA "PUG" WINSHIP, HOLDS THE CELL PHONE awkwardly against her left ear. It's an upgrade, smaller than the one she's used to. Stancil got it for her so she could take Facebook pictures of their grandchildren.

The phone is ringing on the other end of the line. She leans back in her easy chair, so she can see both the lake and the mountains out the sliding glass deck doors, a view that generally calms her. She never would have volunteered for this position if she'd known it involved interviews.

"Hello? Hello? Who's calling?"

She snaps to attention, sits upright in her chair. "This is Virginia

Winship calling for Mr. Frank Carlisle, Sr." Her actual name sounds strange to her, she has been Pug for so long.

"You got him. What can I do for you?"

Already, she's caught off her guard, had counted on having to go through at least one, maybe several functionaries before getting him, rather like warm-up exercises before the main event. But here he is, right out the gate. His voice is gruff, a trifle phlegmy. An old man's voice. An old man she may well have caused to get up from a comfortable lounger like hers and walk across a room with perhaps every step a goad to his arthritis pain, all to answer her unwanted call.

"I chair the History Committee in Bartram's Mountains, a community Carlisle-Colorado developed in north Georgia in the early 1970s." She hurries her words, afraid he will hang up on her.

"We're doing a series of reports on what was here before. The first three covered prehistoric times and how our mountains formed; the Cherokees, who lived here until the Trail of Tears; and the farmers who came after and eked out their meager living on our rocky soil"— she has loved this phrase, perhaps too well, from the instant she wrote it—"until Carlisle-Colorado bought their farms and they could move to town or buy land somewhere else. Now I'm working on the fourth report, about the valley that became Lake Whippoorwill. Courthouse records show you purchased it several years after you assembled all the rest of what's now Bartram's Mountains."

She pauses, should not have said so much at once, wanted to get it over with.

"I was curious why it took so long." She takes a breath, had expected he would jump in by now with an answer. "My husband and I live on the lake, and so I guess I have a special interest."

"Ah, yes, Lake Whippoorwill."

She hopes this long-delayed response means that he's ready for his turn now. Perhaps it will all go okay. Amazing how tense one's shoulders get before one even notices.

"You know that Carlisle-Colorado built a dozen or so places pretty much like Bartram's Mountains," Frank Carlisle continues. "Golf course, clubhouse, tennis center, riding stables, lake with a sand beach, the whole shebang. Can't do it now. Land's too dear and too hard to find. I'm eighty-eight years old, and I'd still do it if I could."

"Oh, my." He's eleven years older than even she herself, who for some years has felt so very ancient.

"Bartram's Mountains was the first, the good old days. Those mountains were so pretty I thought people ought to live on them, enjoy them. But there had to be a lake, you know. So we could sell enough high-priced lots to turn a good profit. No lake, no Bartram's Mountains. Simple economics."

Virginia nods, forgetting for a moment that he cannot see her. Simple economics. A cold truth she has never thought about in relation to her beloved Bartram's Mountains but that she can understand.

"Getting the valley, so we could reroute the two creeks and fill it, was crucial. That valley was owned back then by a weaver woman name of Katherine Reid. Just her, no husband. I saw some of her weavings once. Looked downright peculiar. Wild. Like they might come to life and swallow you."

Virginia knows about the weavings. She copied the name off the deed and searched for her in Google, felt like a sneak doing it. One more new thing she can't get used to, like the phone. Katherine— Virginia has come to think of her by her first name—had a show once at some important New York City gallery, she tells Frank Carlisle. "I tried to contact them but they'd gone out of business. A dead end."

He chuckles deep down in his throat. "Yeah, you won't find her. She never did want to be found. We sent letter after letter saying we wanted to buy her land. That we'd pay top dollar for it, too. Never heard a peep."

A series of creaks on his end of the line calls to mind somebody settling back in an old wooden office chair.

"Not one peep. Finally figured there was nothing for it but to go back there myself, see if she might be living on that land. I did, and sure enough she was."

"Katherine Reid lived here?"

Virginia can't say why this is a shock. Perhaps because she always thought of Bartram's Mountains as carved out of virgin wilderness, even though deep down she knew better. Even before writing the report about the farms.

"Sure did. Her little cottage is the rock pile at the bottom of Lake Whippoorwill. Lived back there like some hillbilly. Her, her little girl, and their scruffy old dog. No plumbing, no electricity. No nothing but a fenced-in garden, all a-tangle with green growing things like that was how they fed themselves. Hard to imagine in this day and age why anyone would choose to live that way."

Outside, the slant of the sun has changed, turning the blue-green mountains to late-afternoon tobacco gold.

"What happened when you saw her?"

"Well, she wouldn't sell to us. Held us off for sixteen months. Knew she had us over a barrel." His voice has climbed into an upper register.

"But you got the lake land in the end."

"I reckon we just wore her down. She finally said she'd think about a land swap. Like for like. A piece of land she'd have to hike to get to and that never would be built around, far as the eye could see. For a while things just went back and forth, until it finally came down to two parcels, one in Colorado, one in North Carolina. Even then she kept on stalling. I came to think she meant to hold us off till she was dead and buried."

Virginia scribbles furiously in her notebook. This will be by far the most interesting History Committee report she's ever delivered.

"I'd never seen the like of it," Frank Carlisle continues. "She wanted in her contract that Carlisle-Colorado had to build her an identical stone cabin to replace the one she would be vacating. Same with all the outbuildings, even the privy. Same materials and every-thing. We tried to work with her as best we could, but she wouldn't budge. Finally, Wilt Bradberry started framing in the Holstons' house, halfway down Panther Mountain where she saw it every day. That's when it hit her things were never going to be the same."

"Which land parcel did she choose?" Virginia's excitement rises. If Katherine's in North Carolina, maybe she can track her down and talk with her. Meet her in Asheville for a good, long lunch.

"Where is she? Oh, I can't tell you that," Frank Carlisle answers gravely. "She had it put right in her purchase contract the location of her residence can never be disclosed."

"Why would she do that?"

"Just wanted to be left alone, I guess. Although she probably sent the little girl to school, at least when she got older. Wouldn't consider any place more than a two-mile hike out to a highway on a school bus route."

Virginia strives to hide her disappointment. "What was she like, the time you met her?" His answer will be all she ever knows of her.

Frank Carlisle goes a long time without speaking, as if he's gotten lost inside his thoughts.

"To this day I can still see them standing on their porch," he says at last. "Perfectly still, like they had some Indian, Native American, in them. Like they'd maybe come back from some distant time. Even the dog. I have to say Katherine Reid was a handsome woman. Something almost otherworldly happened when she turned her gaze on you. You felt you'd never been looked at or listened to so thoroughly in all your life, as if she was staring straight into your soul. Her little daughter— couldn't have been much older than four—seemed already some the same. Brought me a dish of blueberries and a glass of spring water, without my asking."

Mr. Carlisle pauses, then adds, in a voice that sounds quite far away, "Even now I see them in my mind's eye: her, her toddler, and their dog, standing there together on that porch, like in a photograph."

After a second or two, he breaks his own spell. "Tell me," he says, his words clipped and crisp. "Has the snakeroot started running down the mountains yet?"

"Beg pardon?"

"Snakeroot. White flowers. Bloom all over the mountains after the first cool late summer nights. They're poison, you know. They'd kill a horse or cow that eats them; deer never will come near them. But they're still one of the prettiest sights I've ever seen. Blossoms flow down the mountainsides like water."

"Oh, yes. They'll cover the ridge behind our house about a month from now. I'd never heard their name."

"Most things about most mountains never change," Frank Carlisle says then. "Year after year they hold on to what's theirs and keep their mysteries."

Virginia feels something mildly unsettling starting up inside her. Like a thought that's slow to form, only more so. She had meant to ask about that other thing, the thing that she found yesterday going through back issues of the *Dunne County Advocate*. How the men who cleared away the ruined mansion atop Panther Mountain had turned up the remains of two skeletons. One was a surveyor who went missing three years earlier; the other could not be identified.

Now, however, she can see no point in bringing up this grisly incident, thanks Frank Carlisle for his time and they say their goodbyes. Outside, the mountains are turning to deep purple. Soon the sun will set.

She lays her annoying little phone down on the chair arm and realizes she is crying, soundlessly, tears sliding down her cheeks. She's not quite sure why. Something to do with that poor woman, Katherine, having to leave her land so she, Virginia, and all the rest of Bartram's Mountains could live on it, play golf and tennis on it, swim, hike, ride horses on it, all of which they all could just as easily do someplace else.

But why cry over that? What's done is done. Perhaps she's only crying because of how Frank Carlisle remembered the white flowers after all those years, how he recalled their rightful name. Snakeroot. A name she herself had never thought to learn.

She gets up, crosses the room, and puts her hand flat on one of the glass doors just over where she can see Panther Mountain, now nearly black beneath the sunset's afterglow. She wishes she could touch the real mountain this way, cover it with her whole hand. This mountain that has been here since eons before even the Cherokee Indians. The trees on Panther Mountain will die one by one and be replaced by other trees that may still be growing after Bartram's Mountains—its clubhouse, golf course, tennis courts, roads, all its houses—have turned to mold and dust. When even the lake has filled with silt and disappeared. But Panther Mountain will not die. Nor will the other mountains. They will be here for her grandchildren and her grandchildren's grandchildren, and their grandchildren's grandchildren in turn. It makes her dizzy just to think about it.

For an instant, her hand covering the mountain, warming the cold glass, Virginia knows what Katherine Reid knew, in the way one might experience a brief electric shock: That a mountain, or a wilderness, is very like a child, your child, whom you must cherish throughout all your life. Not because it's right and good to do so, but because you are compelled to, in some unspoken partnership with life on earth.

But that's silly. It's just her hand pressing a pane of glass.

Or is it?

cAuthor's Note

In Wilderness, set in 1966, 1967, and 1968, presents two illnesses un-recognized at the time—post-traumatic stress disorder (PTSD) and environmental illness (EI), also known as multiple chemical sensitivity (MCS)—and, in story, posits possible effects of this lack of recogni-tion in two instances.

The late 1960s were the years when developers throughout the mountain and coastal South began assembling huge tracts of land for "resort/retirement communities." Before that time, vast marsh and mountain acreage throughout the southern states remained wild and virtually untouched.

I placed Katherine and Danny in such a mountain wilderness. Both are unique fictional characters who seek extreme solutions to their disabilities. They are not meant to stand for any specific indi-viduals or for any group or category of persons.

—DIANE THOMAS,
   Santa Fe, New Mexico, April 2013

Acknowledgments

I worked on this book, off and on, for thirty years and owe much to many:

To my agent, Deborah Schneider, who found my manuscript in her slush pile and took it on with the fervor of a cause; and to the inimitable Kate Miciak, who championed the book at Random House and is that rare editor every writer dreams of, who seems to understand your manuscript even more deeply than you do yourself;

To Susan Turner for her beautiful and sensitive visual interpretation of the story; to Priyanka Krishnan and Julia Maguire for seeing to it that the book's course ran smoothly; and to Kara Cesare, Denise Cronin, Rachel Kind, Jennifer Hershey, Allyson Pearl, and Susanna Porter, all early Random House supporters of *In Wilderness;*

To the many friends and fellow writers who offered critique and encouragement along the way, including Destiny Allison, Christena Bledsoe, Hannah Burling, Linda Clopton, Jessica Connor, Thomas

H. Cook, Alexandra Diaz, Hillary Fields, James and Carole Garland, Nancy Lehrhaupt, Marilyn Staats, Jim Taylor, Donna Warner, Fred Willard, Patricia Williams, Justin Witt, Lisa Witter, and Joyce and Gene Wright;

To early manuscript readers who offered encouragement and praise, including Susan Gardner, Devon Ross, Nina Harrison, Bill Fajman, and Melody Sumner-Carnahan;

To my sister, Betsy Jones; my writer stepson, Chris Osher; and finally, bearing in mind that the point of greatest emphasis is always last, to my dear husband, Bill Osher, himself a writer, for his insightful comments, encouragement, praise, and steadfast devotion throughout all these years.

I thank you all.

About the Author

DIANE THOMAS holds an MFA from Columbia University
and is the author of the novel *The Year the Music Changed.*
A longtime resident of Atlanta and the Georgia mountains and part-time resident of the Florida panhandle, she
now alternates between Atlanta and New Mexico.

About the Type

This book was set in Caslon, a typeface first designed in 1722 by William Caslon (1692–1766). Its widespread use by most English printers in the early eighteenth century soon supplanted the Dutch typefaces that had formerly prevailed. The roman is considered a "workhorse" typeface due to its pleasant, open appearance, while the italic is exceedingly decorative.